TROPICAL PASSION KILLER

Gabriel Lee

Copyright © 2020 K.McBride

All rights reserved

The characters and events portrayed in this book are fictitious. Any similarity to real persons, living or dead, is coincidental and not intended by the author.

No part of this book may be reproduced, or stored in a retrieval system, or transmitted in any form or by any means, electronic, mechanical, photocopying, recording, or otherwise, without express written permission of the publisher.

ISBN-13: 9798667645528
ISBN-10:

Cover design by: Art Painter
Library of Congress Control Number: 2018675309
Printed in the United States of America

I dedicate this book to my wife Marie, my sister in law Maureen and son in law Lee with whose constant encouragement I completed my first novel.

I also dedicate it to the Thin Blue Line of dedicated officers around the World.

CONTENTS

Title Page	1
Copyright	2
Dedication	3
Introduction	7
Chapter 1	9
Chapter 2	17
Chapter 3	28
Chapter 4	37
Chapter 5	44
Chapter 6	52
Chapter 7	58
Chapter 8	63
Chapter 9	68
Chapter 10	73
Chapter 11	79
Chapter 12	87
Chapter 13	94
Chapter 14	101
Chapter15	110
Chapter 16	115
Chapter 17	129

Chapter 18	132
Chapter 19	137
Chapter 20	145
Chapter 21	152
Chapter 22.	155
Chapter 23	161
Chapter 24	168
Chapter 25	173
Chapter 26	176
Chapter 27	184
Chapter 28	190
Chapter 29	205
Chapter 30	218
Chapter 31	224
Chapter 32	237
Chapter 33	245
Chapter 34	251
Chapter 35	258
Chapter 36	265
Chapter 37	268
Chapter 38	278
Afterword	283
About The Author	285

INTRODUCTION

Two young men from the North of England; Newcastle upon Tyne and Alderley Edge in Cheshire met and became good friends while studying at Newcastle University.

They are both from wealthy families and at the end of their studies planned to travel to the Americas for a holiday exploring their respective interests. Filipe wanted to see and experience Latin America, The Inca Trail, Aztec culture, the lands of his decendants. Josh on the other hand wanted to experience life as an Native American Indian working with a tribe on the reservation. Their plan - to enjoy themselves together on the beaches and in the cities before separating and enjoying their own experiences.

The holiday was going so well until they took the canal boat in Panama City, which initiated a series of events that leads to major crime enquires in five countries. Murder, drug trafficking and corruption.
The investigation begins in Newcastle upon Tyne.
Acting Detective Inspector Steve Bond of the Newcastle Major Crime Team is assigned the case by the boss Colin Tinkler.

No one said it would be easy!

CHAPTER 1

Monday 16th May 2016

The room was gently lit from the moonlight cascading through the drapes covering the windows, there was a vibrant warmth with a slight breeze from the overhead fan. It was silent, protected from the noise of the Caribbean party at the nearby bar by the double-glazed windows.

She opened her eyes and lifted her head from the pillow. Looking down her body she could see his hand caressing her left breast. His hair was dark, shining, she couldn't see his face but he was making her feel so completely lost in her own body, excited. It felt good, her head fell back onto the pillow and she closed her eyes, it was getting warmer her body becoming so sensitive.

He smiled as he briefly looked towards the bedside drawers where she had placed his mobile to record them being together.

Her arms were above her head and as the first waves of orgasm started to intesify she lost all sense of her surroundings, her body began to shake and eventually she gave in to the warmth of her feelings.

She reached down and gently stroked the soft dark hair of her lover then slowly enticed him upwards, he was smiling at the recording as he rolled onto his back.

Seeing the passion he had stirred in this beautiful woman it made him look forward to more, much more for them both. Moving down, her face always away from the recording, she kissed his body and took hold of the strong erection in her left hand. She began to slowly caress him, he was alive, she could feel him fall back onto the pillow.

He felt so good, he thought this was his dream time, excited and yet still in control, she was good, very good.

Reaching inside her bag at the side of the bed she pulled out a 20cm vibrator, he could hear the buzz as it was placed between his legs, the gentle vibrations were intensifying in him.

She removed the slim blade from the pouch of the vibrator, 10cm of highly sharpened steel. Slowly she moved across his body and turned, careful not to be seen, his eyes were transfixed onto her slender back now bent over his body. Moving upward towards his face, she now straddled his chest her strong legs over his arms which were gently pinned against the bed.

Striking hard, remembering what she'd been told, the sharpened blade penetrated through the chest cavity straight into his heart with ease then fully into his body. No blood escaped from the precision entry wound. His body tried to heave, she pressed back and down on to his face, he couldn't scream, his body convulsing in sudden pain and shock. After seconds the convulsing stopped. Moving her body sideways and away from his face she placed her hand over his mouth to stop any final shouts.

He was staring at the ceiling fan slowly turning then at her face looking down into his emptying, dark brown eyes. He was silent, his mouth moving slightly but making no sound, what was happening to him, he was certain he was dying.

It looked as if he was saying "Why". She slowly and carefully pulled the blade out of his chest to prevent blood escaping from the wound and took hold of his now limp penis. After cleanly slicing through it at the base, she placed it onto his chest. His eyes moved slowly as he looked down his body.

She picked up the mobile and rewound the video and looking down into the now near empty, dying eyes of her victim, played the recording. "I will be your last memory." The mobile was slipped back into her bag.

Moving around the bed, he stared upwards as she loosened the bottom sheet together with the carefully prepared black plastic covering underneath it. He was now aware that his body was about to be wrapped into the envelope she was creating for him. Firstly his legs were placed inside then his arms were tucked neatly under his body. She paused, and using medicated wipes, cleaned his blood from her naked body. She was thorough he thought, as she placed the wipes on top of his chest.

His eyes were fading. Bending over she kissed his forehead, "Gracias, you should not have fucked with Colombians." If he could see her, he'd have seen the tears in her eyes.

She meticulously cleaned the blade with a wipe and put it back into the vibrator pouch, placing it gently next to his limp penis which was still releasing blood onto his chest.

Time to seal his body.

The sheet and plastic were pulled in tightly over and around his body at the sides then finally from the top covering his head. He resisted slightly at that point, then nothing. Retrieving a large roll of strong black tape from the holdall in the wardrobe the envelope was sealed around the neck, chest, waist, thighs and ankles. In her mind, as she stood back and looked at the body shaped package, she agreed it was as she'd been shown.

The tears were still rolling down her face.

The newly filled body bag was pulled by the feet from the bed onto the floor with a thud. Taking a large towel from the bathroom she wrapped it around her body and then opened the windows slightly. The warm breeze entered the room at the same time as the salsa beat and the laughing crowd. After taking several deep breaths from the fresh air, it was time to finish off her work.

Remaking the bed with the fresh linen that had been left inside the wardrobe, she rolled around on it, including the pillows and threw back the top sheet. The long, straight, dark brown wig she'd been wearing was put into the holdall before returning to the bathroom. Not waiting for the water to run hot in the shower, she stood for a short while with her face into the falling water crying without sound.

Using the toiletries provided by the hotel she washed herself thoroughly removing any trace of her dead lover. The hotel room would be cleaned thoroughly and probably used again the following night.

Makeup free, she put on a new wig and dressed in fresh clothes from the holdall.

It was time to make the call. "Coleccion, ahora". (*collection now*).

The collection arrived within ten minutes. Two non-descript men in white coats, caps covering their heads pushing a large white cotton sack laundry trolley. They didn't draw any attention from the partying holiday makers. Sheets had already been put in the trolley to disguise the shape of the body bag which was dropped on top then folded to fit easily into the sack. The holdall which contained her previously worn clothes, sheets and pillow cases were placed on top of the body bag which was then wheeled out from the ground floor room into the garden of the hotel and along the path to the waiting van. No words were exchanged. She examined the room one last time looking for any forensic evidence that may have been overlooked. Job done, she thought.

The music was playing and the bar was still occupied with a few holiday makers dressed in Hawaiian shirts, shorts and flip flops, drinking their all-inclusive Margaritas and Mojitos and dancing to the loud beat and rhythm of the Salsa and Merengue. No one noticed the collection.

Once they'd left, she put on a wide, floppy brimmed straw hat, walked through the garden, and as the room had been pre-paid through an agency, took a waiting taxi into town.

She went to the Mosquito night club, the largest club on the island and after acknowledging one of the doormen she was escorted to the VIP lounge. He was a tall man, handsome but menacing. His black hair in a ponytail hanging over his dark suit which covered a muscular yet slim body. She had a table reserved for one and they didn't speak. As she sat down a waiter arrived with a large glass of something exotic which he placed on a gold coaster then left immediately without making eye contact.

Uninterrupted by the small crowd of invited guests in the room, she slowly sipped her cool, refreshing glass of rum which had the undenying taste and smell of fresh mint and lime. The others were all too interested in their own groups to take any notice of the single lady with the Mojito.

As the night drew to a close and the guests and patrons were leaving the club, the doorman returned. He handed her a brown padded envelope. Looking inside she saw a DVD in a plastic covering.

"Todas?" she asked (*is that everything*).

"Si" he replied, nodding, then walked away.

The CCTV recording from the club was the only record of her having met the now dead man and it had to be destroyed.

A few hours later the hotel room was stripped bare and thoroughly cleaned, the toiletries removed and replaced by the unknowing cleaner.

About the same time that morning, she walked into a shop in the back street of Porlamar and paid cash for a cheap, new mobile phone and sim card. She looked like any of the locals, tanned, slim but curvy with dark hair, and wearing a tight light blue T shirt and jeans.

She walked towards the marina and sat on a white plastic seat outside a cafe on Calle Marina which was overlooking the harbour. Keeping her distance from the other customers, she inserted the sim card into the phone and disposed of the packaging in a street bin on an adjacent lamp post.

"Café con leche" was enough to get rid of the waiter. She entered a number.

"Si"

"Completa" she said (*complete*)

"El sabia?" (*he knew*)

"Si"

"Bien" (*good*)

"Siguiente" (*next*)

"Si"

The call was ended. She sat and watched as a large blue speed boat with an open deck was leaving the harbour. Two men were visible on the deck as the boat was guided through a group of small open fishing boats and headed out to sea. Her coffee arrived, complete with a wrapped biscuit and a sachet of sugar.

The Caribbean was flat calm, like a mirror, the sunlight bouncing to the horizon. When the boat reached the safety buoys, it turned away from the fishermen and headed out to the deeper sea before accelerating, leaving a white trail in its wake as it disappeared towards the horizon. She finished her coffee, leaving the biscuit and sugar and walked off into the town centre. As she walked, she removed the sim from the mobile phone and disposed of in a large waste bin that was overflowing with cardboard, the phone was then placed under the wheel of a bus at a temporary stop and she waited until it departed to ensure the phone was destroyed, before picking up the pieces and dropping them into a drain. She stopped a local taxi "Aeropuerto".

On her journey to the airport she knew her life had changed forever.

After a twenty-minute journey across the Caribbean, the boat engine was put into neutral and gently rolled on the flat sea. Two men were at the controls of the boat, both were in T shirts and dark thigh length swim shorts. They studied the horizon and there was nothing visible that caused concern either to the eye or with technology. A sun shade was erected over the back deck of the boat for further protection. They went below deck and dragged up the lifeless black body bag into a position next to an opening just above the deck which was usually used for bringing large Marlin and Tuna on board. Having tightly wrapped a heavy steel cable around the bag, a concrete sun shade base was placed on what would have been the chest of Filipe and the cable passed through the securing steel handles. One more check towards the horizon and still nothing to be seen, they pushed the bag and weight towards the opening, the legs hanging over the sea, one more push, "Adios gringo". There was a big splash from the concrete weight and both watched as the bag and weight sank rapidly into the depths of the clear sea.

Both men sat under the shade for another hour drinking Polar ice-cold beer. There was no other sea traffic in the area and what went down to the bottom of the sea had stayed there. After taking down the shade, one of the men started the engine and they slowly returned to the harbour.

It was now 13:16 as she looked out of the window of her room at the Hilton Hotel. It was on the tenth floor and overlooked the mountains in the distance that surrounded Caracas. She'd made time for a bath, requested room service and was sat at the desk in front of the mirror when she took Filipe's phone from her bag and attached a power lead to it. After a few seconds it jumped into life revealing several emails, texts and WhatsApp messages. She started with the photos, Filipe was always with Josh, in Mexico, on the beach, in Panama, on a boat in the canal. Then WhatsApp messages, another photo of Josh, he was standing with a beautiful smiling girl with shoulder length blonde hair in what appeared to be an airport terminal. The message read, "Good company on flight!"

She replied to Josh, "Looks good. Wher'e you staying."

She found the contact for Mother, which was again on WhatsApp and attached *the* video recording. There was nothing which showed her face, no distinguishing marks, only a woman, the Latino's all look the same. The vicious murder of a loved son. It was what she was told to do, what she had to do.

A few moments later and thousands of miles away in a large detached house on the outskirts of Newcastle upon Tyne a mobile phone activated. In the spacious living room, Angelina Lopez was watching television when she received a video recording from her son on WhatsApp. "Having fun." She shouted for her husband "Manuel, nos ha enviado un video." (*he has sent a video*).

Filipe was on a career break travelling the Americas. He wanted to visit the land of his family, to explore the wildlife and beauty of Central and South America and to learn more of the history and culture.

She was so happy and excited that he'd eventually got in touch. Manuel immediately stopped making the coffee and walked into the large airy room to sit beside his wife on the brown leather four-seater sofa to view the video together.

Angelina started the recording. It was't what they expected, Filipe was having sex with a young woman. Angelina looked shocked her mouth opened. Manuel grabbed the recording, "What the fuck?"

He walked away and continued watching with a wry smile and nodding "um, si, si, whoa, no no no, no mi hijo, mi hijo, no no!" He fell to the floor. Angelina ran to her husband and they both sat crying on the tiled kitchen floor.

"MI HIJO" *(my son)* he shouted again and again "Por Que" *(why?)*

The video had been edited. There were no other messages.

CHAPTER 2

Tuesday 17th May

Steve Bond was a seasoned officer, now in his mid-thirties at the rank of Sergeant. He'd passed the examinations necessary to get to this stage in his career and although it had been thought the promotion board would have been a walk in the park for an officer of his experience, he was resisting the many requests to go further up the ladder.

His base, the Newcastle Major Crime Squad was the most enjoyable work he'd done. He is one of two Sergeants in the squad and although there is no rank structure when they worked together, he was Acting Detective Inspector in name only when the role was required, but without the title due to the financial restrictions and loss of numbers in the force.

The squad worked against serious crime and the eventual arrest and conviction of major criminals, using the organised methods of investigation. They'd worked on several prolonged high-profile enquiries and they all enjoyed getting the result together, as a team. Steve was a team player, he enjoyed the squad but didn't suffer fools gladly and senior officers had identified him as "one to get the job done".

He was born and raised in the City of Newcastle upon Tyne, otherwise known as "The Town", and although he still hadn't married, did have female friends he socialised with. An attractive man with masculine strong features and at just over 1.85m tall he cut a rugged and sporty figure with green eyes and short dark hair. He believed in the ethos of "work hard, play hard" and was known by colleagues as "James" or "Jimmy".

He was reading the occurrence log for the previous night at his desk in the long narrow squad room, which was in a building on the West Road in the City.

Sitting in his office at the end of the squad room was Colin Tinkler, the Detective Superintendent in the City, his back towards the window which overlooked the west arterial road and the hospital. He was well educated and now in his late forties. A tall, slim, good looking man with an envied rapport with his officers. He'd done it and got the "T" shirt. He'd chosen the promotion route, however he kept in touch with all his officers and enjoyed being close to any action, even if it was just decision making.

It was a typical non descript office, devoid of any human touch other than a few photograhs adorning the walls, showing courses attended and conviction celebrations on the Quayside. There were four chairs and three green filing cabinets that were full of case files, authority papers and the officers' personal records and reviews. The walls were a lime green colour, contrasting the darker green cabinets.

It is 08:42

"James"

"Yes Boss" as he walked along the green linoleum floor to the boss's office.

"Shut the door, take a pew. You ok?"

"Yes Boss, what's up?"

"Whats app actually. A WhatsApp message needs investigating."

"Yes Boss, no problem" taking a seat opposite the boss.

"The Lopez family live in Gosforth, they moved from Mexico over 20 years ago. Manuel has a business and is a lecturer at the University, Angelina, his wife was working at the Hospital as a consultant before retiring. They have a son or should I say had a son Filipe, who is, was 25. Last night, they received a WhatsApp message from their son's phone with an attached recording of Filipe being murdered. Allegedly. It shows Filipe having sex with a young lady before she stabbed him through his heart, then cleanly sliced his dick off. Professional, no doubt. Ok?"

"Yes Boss."

"The recording has been examined and there's no facial appearances by the woman in question or identifying marks. She does look like a Latino lady by the colour of her skin." Tinkler paused a while to let it sink in.

He continued, "There have been no other messages. So far?"

"Yes Boss."

"It obviously looks like Filipe has been murdered, but I don't know where, not in the Town though, when, why or by whom. We don't have a body. We don't have a motive. We don't have a weapon but know clearly what was used, a commando type killing knife. All we have is a WhatsApp recording."

"Yes Boss."

"I'm not putting resources on this until we have a couple more of the W's sorted. I want you to liaise with the family, get as much information as you can about them, their history, Filipe and his travel plans. I've arranged for a copy of the video to be made available to you and you only, for your eyes only, get it?"

"Aye Boss" Steve said raising his eyebrows.

"Go and chat to them, they're a decent family, use your usual charm. Keep me in touch."

"OK, boss."

Steve walked to the IT forensics office on the top floor, a sanitised white place with more large screen televisions than Curry's, (a high street retailer). After being allowed through the double locked doors into the secure room he met Walter, the senior technician. He was wearing a white coat and the name badge to prove it! Why he had to wear a badge was a mystery, everyone knew Walter.

He was in his mid-forties, long wavy hair to the shoulders. He liked ladies, booze, hard rock music and of course Newcastle United football club, known locally as The Toon. He was a great lad to socialise with and very good at what he did. Not your typical techy.

"Hi Jimmy. I've got the recording ready for you. I've obviously seen it but no one else has. Do you want to look at it here?"

"Might as well Walter, in the private viewing room?"

The large screen lit up and Walter played the recording.

Steve and Walter watched intently and never spoke during the entire recording.

Steve shook his head," Nasty, very nasty. It looks very well planned and professional. Definitely a hit I'd say. He must have upset her or someone quite a bit. Can you do anything about the clarity?"

"I'm trying but I doubt it, it's dark you know."

"No good Walter, what about background stuff, anything there?"

"There's a bottle of water on top of some drawers at the end of the bed, but I doubt you would see that with what was going on."

"Alright, how many times did you watch before you saw the bottle?"

"Never mind," Walter said, "it's not good but I'm trying to enhance the image. The more you watch the more you see."

"Let me know asap what you get."

"Did you have to say that? No. See you later Jimmy."

Steve stood in front of a large detached, ivy clad Victorian house. It was surrounded by large metal fencing and hidden by a thick hedge which was peeping through it. A large weeping willow and an apple tree sat in the garden. In front of double garage doors was a red Mercedes S650 sports car. The door to the house was wooden with a single wide opening and ornate black metal fixings.

He rang the bell and could hear footsteps approaching from inside, a wooden floor he thought.

The door was opened by a man with Hispanic skin reddened around the eyes from tears and tiredness. He had dark greying hair which wasn't brushed, at 1.75m tall and slightly overweight, he was wearing a dark brown woollen jumper and khaki slacks.

Steve showed his Police ID card and introduced himself, "Mr Lopez I'm detective Steve Bond from Newcastle Major Crime Squad. Can I come in please?"

"Yes, come in officer" with a hint of a Spanish accent. "We were told to expect you, please, this way, we are in the drawing room."

He walked across the wide hallway into the drawing room at the rear of the ground floor overlooking the expertly manicured rear gardens. Mrs. Lopez was looking out of the open French doors.

"Angelina, this is officer Steve Bond."

She turned slowly and Steve saw an attractive woman with dark wavy hair. About 1.70m tall, athletic, same skin colour as her husband and looking very tired. He guessed she would be about 50.

She didn't speak but walked to a large soft chair and sat down slowly.

"I totally understand that this is not easy for you both, but I do need to ask some questions."

Manuel nodded "Yes Officer."

"When was the last time you spoke to Filipe or received a text, email?"

"It was on Sunday 8th May. A phone call, we both spoke to him, Angelina more than me."

"Did he say where he was, or what his plans were?"

"He was very happy. He was in Panama."

"Did he say where in Panama?"

"I don't remember the name but at the end of the canal. He had travelled the canal on a boat from the Pacific."

"Was he travelling with anyone?"

"He was with Josh but they were going to split up. Josh was going to the US and then New Zealand to meet his family when they finished Central America."

"Was Josh with Filipe at the end of the canal?"

"He didn't mention Josh to me, did he speak about Josh to

you Angelina?"

Angelina shook her head.

"Do you have contact details for Josh?"

"They're in a book in the desk."

"Did Filipe say what his plans were, where he was going?"

"He did say he was leaving the town the following day, it wasn't the best of towns and he was heading to Colombia and Venezuela, some beach resorts."

"Anyone specific?"

"No, he just said he was having a fantastic experience, loving the Americas, the food, drink, everything, people huh. The last thing he said was that he loved us both, hasta luego."

"Is Josh from up here?"

"No. Cheshire they were friends at Newcastle University."

"Could I have the contact details for Josh please? I'm sorry, but can I have a look in Filipe's room? I'll have to speak to you again so if you can remember anything that might help, if Filipe had any places he wanted to visit or had been to before."

Manuel took the contacts book from the desk in the hallway and wrote down the details for Josh, handing them to Steve. He took Steve upstairs and into the room used by Filipe, leaving him alone while he returned to Angelina.

Filipe's room was large, a suite almost, with a black leather sofa and two chairs, a large screen TV and a desk with an "Apple" computer. A door led into a large bedroom with a king-size bed which was made and had not been slept in, with floor to ceiling wardrobes the length of the wall. There was another large screen TV on the wall facing the bed. Another door led into the modern en-suite.

Steve used his mobile phone, "Walter it's Steve, eh, yeah Jimmy. I need you to come to the Lopez house now and collect some computer equipment. How long? Ok quick as you can. Any joy on the bottle? I know, I know you did say. Cheers."

He began a systematic search of the drawers. The desk was clean and everything in its place. Top right drawer revealed an atlas, traveller's guide to Mexico and a note book. "Good start let's have a look."

Opening the book Steve looked at an itinerary.
Newcastle to Barcelona - flight
Barcelona to Mexico City - flight
Acapulco
Yucatan
Belize City - flight to San Jose?
San Jose - flight to Panama City?
Canal trip
Cartagena
Aruba
Caracas
Angel Falls
Lima
Machu pichu
Rio
Buenos Aires
NZ

He kept looking through the drawers, contact books, reference books. He heard the door bell and a short time later Walter walked into the room.

"Have you got plenty of bags?" He got the look from Walter, "Sorry I asked."

"I need a couple to take these books."

He packed up the books then spoke to Mr Lopez for twenty minutes obtaining the family history. He left to head for the office with Walter staying behind to do what Walter does.

On his return to the squad office, Steve went to the Detective Superintendent's office, there was a grey door sign which was always on open under the title and open it was. Steve gave a polite knock and walked in.

"You free Boss?"

"Yes, come in and shut the door, coffee?" Steve nodded.

The boss shouted through to the squad room for the coffees.

"Yes Boss" was the loud reply.

"What have you got?"

"Briefly, the Lopez family came here in 1988 from Mexico. They'd met in University in Mexico City. Angelina Lopez was studying Medicine and he was in electronics. They were into political debates, that's how they met. After graduating she started working in the NHS in Newcastle and he initially took a further engineering degree in Newcastle. He later started his electronic business and lectured at the Uni. They say they have no criminal records or no known dealings with any criminal families in México or the Americas. They have family in Spain and USA but none in Latin America. Again, no known criminal connections, no problems anywhere that they know of. Filipe was born in the Town in 1992. No other siblings, he went to the RGS (*Royal Grammar School*) and then on to University here, he didn't want to leave the Town, loved the place apparently. He was going to join his father's business when he returned from this trip. He had local friends both male and female but nothing serious, loved having fun in the "Town" and enjoyed all sports, mostly watching The Toon."

"So far so good. Go on."

"He'd planned this trip but didn't have any booked flights other than the initial flights from the Town to Barcelona and then on to Mexico City. He had a lad called Josh Newton travelling with him, who was a friend from University."

"Right, stop there. Who is Josh, where is he, he could be involved, in danger or dead?"

"I have a contact number but I wanted to go through you, which way you want to pursue the enquiry. I have a mobile and a home number where his parents live. I could get Walter to do a trace to see if the mobile is still active?"

"Have the Lopez's been in touch with the parents of Josh?"

"No, and I've told them not to."

There's a knock on the door and Andy brings in two mugs of coffee.

Andy is the other sergeant in the team, a fit guy, he runs marathons and fell runs. Quite solitary but has a brain that retains everything and can often link evidence together without the use of a computer. He does like a pint of real ale or Guinness when out with the group though but won't get involved in the partying. He's married but no kids.

"Sit down Andy. We've got a new job on. James will get you up to speed. You're running the office, keep it tight, just our crew. There may well be some travel involved, we've a limited budget but if there's any problems see me. I want daily briefs and any significant issues I want to know immediately ok? James is the lead. Get Sarah to do the research end of things, Billy, Alan and Lauren for the enquiry team at the minute. Everyone here in an hour for a brief ok."

Andy gets up to leave "Yes boss on it now."

"James, I want one of Walter's team on the phone enquiries now, paper work can be done by Andy later. Give him everything you've got. When was the last time the Lopez's know Filipe was with Josh?"

"Apparently Filipe didn't keep in regular contact with his parents but the last occasion was in Panama City, there was a photo of them both at a quayside with a canal cruiser in the background. He'd planned to take a cruise along the canal."

"As a matter of urgency, we need background checks on Josh and his family, we need the correct info before we approach the Newton's. Off you go, I'm off to HQ to try and get some funding. Keep in touch."

An hour later, Steve started to brief the team with all the information they have to date. All of them have experience of dealing with different enquiries and all trust and work well with each other. An excellent team of contrasting characters, he thought.

Andy'd already set up the data programme and intelligence data for the Operation. Sarah knows how to trawl for anything and had already completed the family research into the Newton's. Nothing to show after criminal checks on all the family who live in Alderley Edge in Chehire. Sarah isn't a police officer and at 32 lives life to the full. Gym, restaurants, holidays with the girls, likes the guys but still single.

Billy and Alan on the other hand are Police Officers and joined the squad the same day and have been inseparable since. They're from south of the river and travel in together. If anyone is going to cause a problem, it'll be one of these guys. Great workers but they prefer knocking down doors and lifting collars to sifting through documents and CCTV recordings. Give them a job and it'll get done! They've been given the arduous task of examining the books from Filipe's room!

Lauren is to accompany Steve to Cheshire to visit the Newton's. She's the same age as Steve and has been through a bitter divorce. She did keep the house in Whickham though and is happily single. Her ex was a copper and left her for another cop in the national training school down south and although she is still wary of close relationships, enjoys being with the lads. Attractive, slim with blue eyes and natural shoulder length fair hair, she has the Midas touch when extracting information, especially from guys.

The squad headed off to the IT forensics viewing room, sitting in front of the large screen with note pad and pen ready, they watch the recording four times!

Steve felt the mobile phone in his pocket vibrate and left for afew minutes to take the call.

"That was the boss, he's got funding so the job is on but we have to keep it tight. We need the phone records done urgently. Sarah can you chase it up with Walter's team and get Filipe's and Josh's done, the last one to Filipe's may well have been our murderous lady. Also, everything on Josh, is he still active and where is he?"

"Lauren pick your bag up we're off to Cheshire in the next twenty minutes. Lads just work through the books, anything at all give it to Sarah. Everything into the info pot and keep Andy in the loop.

Andy you keep in touch with me and the boss, any issues straight to him."

"Oh Sarah, Filipe was supposed to be in a port at the Atlantic end of the canal cruise on Sunday 7th May. Also bank checks for payments for hotels or spending in the port, boat, whatever, you know what to do."

"Will do Jimmy. Enjoy your trip." Sarah gave Steve a wink.

CHAPTER 3

Sunday 8th May

It was a bright sunny day in Panama City, it was only 06:30 but was already 24 degrees. The taxi stopped at The Flamenco Marina adjacent to the small, three-deck canal cruise ship 'Reina del Canal'. The crew were busy preparing to accept passengers on board and had just lowered the blue and white striped canvas upper deck shades.

The sun was shining at its glorious best and the sky a vibrant blue when Josh and Filipe got out of the taxi and stretching after the quick journey from the city. Josh paid the short, smiling driver with a US $10 note. They retrieved their rucksacks from the boot and asked the driver to take a photo of them using Filipe's mobile phone. Great place for a holiday pic, in front of the canal cruiser with the large marina behind them.

Filipe, although twenty-four, was as excited as he'd been as a boy waiting for Papa Noel on Christmas morning. He'd dressed for the day wearing a floppy, white, wide brimmed cricket bucket sun hat and wrap around Oakley's, teamed up with a close fitting grey Adidas T shirt, blue shorts and walking shoes, his camera hanging loosely over his shoulder. Freshly showered, he felt good.

Josh was 15cms taller than Filipe, a good rugby back row size. His blonde hair, which had not been groomed, was sticking out from under his well-worn and tattered NY baseball cap. He was wearing 'aviator' sunglasses a green T shirt which showed off his muscular upper body and brown knee length shorts. All finished off with well used scraped and damaged, yet sturdy, comfortable walking shoes.

They walked together up the entrance ramp to board the boat and showed the crew their tickets. There was no allocated seating for the 8-hour journey so they placed their rucksacks in the storage area adjacent to the ramp. The lower deck was was home to the restaurant and bar area where the breakfast and buffet lunch would be served, they could see a colourful selection of fruits and the smell of cooked food and coffee was circulating around the deck. They decided to make their way to the upper deck instead and took up a seating position with an uninterrupted view over the bow.

A short time later a brown coloured tourist coach with dark tinted windows stopped adjacent to the entrance ramp of the boat. The excited passengers were walking the twenty metres from the coach to the boat and donning an array of sun hats as they began to form a long queue at the ramp. The driver of the coach walked to the head of the group with the matching brown livery clipboard and after greeting the boat's crew, handed them the required boarding passes.

The cruise was going to be full and Filipe was pleased that he had planned to get to the boat early to get the best vantage point.

It seemed to take an age for the boat to be ready to sail but all was going according to plan and timed for their canal lock appointment.

As the last of the passengers were walking up the ramp, the crew were releasing the ropes from the mooring and the boat slipped away on smooth waters to start the cruise. The safety announcements were made in Spanish, English and German and then breakfast was served. They took it in turn to get some food whilst the other kept the seats and their prized vantage point.

Filipe had his breakfast first and when Josh returned with extra coffee and mixed fruit he was followed by two young Latino women who took seats behind them both. Filipe was intrigued by them as they sat eating oranges and bananas. Both women were typical of the locals he thought, attractive with black hair, wearing T shirts, jeans and converse shoes and of course the obligatory large shades. Not tourists, neither had a camera.

"You guys American?"

Josh turned around and smiled at the women, "English, actually he's half Mexican."

The women were smiling and it was easy to start a conversation.

"Hi, I'm Josh."

"Hola mi nombre es Filipe."

The women laughed "Hola, Susanna y Maria" Susanna said from under her wide brimmed white sun hat, Maria was quite the opposite wearing a dark blue baseball cap with her pony tail through the gap at the back of it.

"Josh you speak Spanish?"

"Poco." *(little)*

"OK we speak English" said Susanna in an American accent.

"That makes it easy" Josh laughed.

"You guys on holiday and touring?"

"Is it that obvious! What are you two doing, holiday? You live in Panama?"

Maria laughed "No, we are also on a short holiday, just a week. We pick up a cruise ship in Colon and go to Aruba for a few days. Where are you going?"

Filipe looked directly at Maria "I've always wanted to go to Aruba". Then gave her a smile.

The four continued talking as the boat followed a large container ship into the first lock. Filipe excused himself from the conversation and started taking photographs of the locks in operation. The girls went below deck and returned with chilled fresh orange juice for them all.

The four of them stayed together for the entire journey through the canal, Filipe stopping to take photographs of the two bridges, the Miraflores locks, wild scenery and a variety of wildlife and birds. After a warm lunch together with a couple of ice-cold bottled Balboa beers, they enjoyed sitting in the shade as the ship sailed across Lake Gatun.

"Where are you guys staying tonight?" Maria asked.

"We haven't booked anywhere yet" Josh replied.

"We're staying in the Radisson, maybe we could meet up later?"

"Yeah, that would be good, do you know anywhere to

meet?"

"Arecifes, great food and cocktails, good music too, it looks good on the web."

"Should we call you?"

"No, just be there for eight. Ok? Just get a taxi they will know it."

Filipe stopped one of the passing crew and asked him to take a group photo as they were crossing the lake. He stood to the right with his left arm around Susanna's waist, Maria had her arm around the shoulder of Susanna and Josh stood on the left with his right arm around the shoulder of Maria.

As they were leaving the ship, they gave each other kisses on each cheek and a small embrace, all agreeing to meet at eight. Susanna and Maria boarded the same coach that dropped them off at Flamenco Marina which would take them to their hotel. The guys gathered their rucksacks from storage and took a waiting taxi towards the nearby city.

On the advice of the taxi driver, Filipe made a call from his mobile and booked a twin room for one night in the Hotel Andros.

The room was on the fourth floor, it was clean with two large beds and a powerful shower. However, there was little security and no safe but it did have a good lock on the door with no signs of damage which was reassuring. They left their rucksacks on the floor, the iPad and camera were next to passports and bank cards on the bed. They'd decided to take cash and needed to find a safe place for their valuables. Filipe removed the bottom drawer from a dressing table and placed the iPad, camera, bank cards and passports in a bag with a hook and attached it in the void space and then slid the drawer back into place.

Both men were looking forward to having female company for the first time on this adventure, they were a little more than hopeful of having a good night.

After a shave and shower Filipe used the only deodorant they had with them! As he brushed his hair he smiled at himself in the mirror. He had high hopes, he liked both of the girls but Susanna was the one for him. She was slightly smaller than him, soft bronzed skin a small nose and deep dark brown eyes. She reminded him of his mother. He put on the only clean shirt he had which was red brown and cream checks with a collar, lightweight trousers to keep the busy mosquitoes away and his walking shoes.

Josh showered, washed his hair and just left it to bounce into shape. He too used the deodorant (need to smell nice for the ladies, he thought) then put on a clean T shirt bearing The Gym motive, long green lightweight trousers and his walking shoes which he wiped with the used towel.

He was happy with Filipe's choice as Maria was taller and had more of a rounded shape than Susanna, more his type. Her hair was naturally wavy and fell to the top of her shoulders. She was a good-looking woman, and he enjoyed her company, a pleasure to be with he thought.

Colon was not the best of cities and was dated. It seemed a good idea to get a taxi, so they used the card the driver had given them earlier to call for one. Too many dark roads and hiding places, a robber's paradise. The guys were using American dollars in small denominations, neither wore jewellery or watches and they had decided to leave their mobiles in the room, best be safe than sorry. This is what they'd done throughout their Latin American adventure, don't attract attention, or trouble for that matter. Dollars were welcome everywhere and with a good exchange rate.

It only took fifteen minutes and the taxi stopped at 'Arecifes' restaurant. It was overlooking the harbour and adjacent to the Radisson Hotel, brightly lit outside with eight tables and chairs on the veranda and the sound of the local music was coming from inside the building. The driver arranged to complete the return later, he said the bar would call for him when they were ready to leave. $5 was more than enough to keep him smiling.

As they entered the restaurant, they could see Susanna and

Maria in a booth to the rear of the room, they all smiled in acknowledgement and kissed cheeks in the formal way. After sitting down, they were quickly attended to by the staff who took the order of four beers. They ordered several plates of food; grilled tuna, plantain chips, mixed seafood, tropical salad, toasted bananas. The music was playing, the beers and sangria flowed, it was a good night.

Josh and Filipe told of their travels and life back in England, Susanna and Maria of their upbringing in Colombia. They'd been friends since they attended the same University, their parents had businesses in transport and hotels and they now worked for their families in travel, hotels and logistics. During the conversations it became apparent that none of them were in a relationship.

They were dancing and by now Filipe was with Susanna and Josh with Maria, they were attempting a salsa, the girls were experts and took great delight and fun in teaching Josh and Filipe. The other customers, locals and some cruise passengers were watching the four dance with some joining in while others were taking photographs, a very friendly and happy place.

Susanna whispered to Filipe to take her back to her hotel. A brief discussion took place between the four of them and Maria decided to go with Josh. The girls were due to sail at 08:30 so they quickly made plans and made call for the taxi.

It was approaching 23:45 when they left the restaurant in the taxi. Susanna and Filipe got out first at the Radisson leaving Josh to pay the driver later. There were only a few guests still at the foyer bar as they walked through the lobby, but no one took any notice of the young couple.

Just on midnight the taxi stopped outside Hotel Andros, Josh gave the driver $10 and they both smiled and gave each other a wink. The hotel was deserted as they made their way to the room.

At 07:00 the next morning Josh and Maria returned to the Radisson, they walked into the breakfast room and joined Susanna and Filipe. There were courteous smiles between them and nothing was said about any late-night activities. After a quick breakfast of fruit and coffee, the women returned to their room to finish packing for the next part of their journey while Filipe and Josh took a seat outside the hotel overlooking a small park to enjoy the early morning sun. As usual Filipe was taking photographs of all the activity, the birds in the park and the nearby ornate buildings. He told Josh of the night he had enjoyed with Susanna. It was the best experience of his life, never to be forgotten and one he eagerly wanted to have again.

Josh didn't elaborate on his night but did say it was very enjoyable.

After a short time other guests began leaving the hotel with their luggage, some boarding the coach or sitting in the sun, others taking photographs. Susanna and Maria walked through the revolving doors followed by a male member of the hotel staff pulling a trolley with four large cases. The driver took the cases and placed them in the belly of the coach. Maria gave the hotel porter some cash in a clenched fist which was acknowledged with a quick glance into his palm then a smile. He nodded, said "gracias" and walked away.

The girls walked towards the guys and Filipe took a few photos of Susanna and Maria at the side of the coach. Another member of the tourist group was taking photographs of the birds in the park and Filipe asked him to take some some of all four of them with his camera. As the group were being called onto the coach, the two couples held each other briefly, kissing on the cheeks and then slowly walked away backwards from each other.

The guys watched as the women took their seats on the coach, they all waved as the coach was driven away and Josh and Filipe walked the short distance to 'Arecifes' for a full review of the previous day.

After ordering breakfast of burritos and coffee, they sat outside on the terrace with a view of the liner and harbour and chatted. Not one of the four had exchanged mobile numbers or contact details, it had been a 'one-nighter'.

Filipe wanted to get to Aruba as quickly as possible, which was in his plan, but after meeting Susanna even more so and Josh had made plans to go to the US and Hawaii before New Zealand to meet up with his family before his sister's wedding. They spoke to Leonardo, the owner of the place, who gave them advice on how best to travel and he offered to help make the arrangements. After twenty minutes, they shook hands with him and left the bar with their new travel plans made.

They returned to the Hotel Andros, collected their bags, valuables and documents from behind the bottom drawer, and after paying $40 cash for the one-night stay they walked back out into the sun lit street. The same taxi was outside and the driver was smiling, waiting for his next cash bonus. His smile widened when they put their bags in the boot and told him they wanted to go to Panama City airport.

The cruise ship 'Alisios', awaited its new passengers. An impressive sight she was large, gleaming and luxurious. A Panamax ship, just narrow enough to fit through the Panama Canal. At 92,000 tons she could accommodate about 2000 passengers and was halfway through a cruise that originated in Fort Lauderdale in Florida, USA. She had sailed through the canal to Panama City and returned to berth in Colon and was now headed for Cartagena, Aruba then back to Fort Lauderdale.

Dockhands and some of the crew were busy replenishing the stores from the parked trailers others were dressed immaculately and greeting passengers who were new or had ventured ashore. The area was a hive of activity.

Maria and Susanna got off the coach with the other cruise passengers and their luggage was removed from the coach by the driver. They both examined the four cases and removed their details from the pocket on the side of two of the cases which now showed those of another passenger. They watched as the driver and porters loaded the cases onto the luggage trolleys of the cruise ship.

As they boarded they were greeted by the smiling crew and then taken by a porter to their cabin which was to be their home for the three-day cruise. It was extensive, two large beds, soft leather lounge furniture, a table with four chairs. One door opened into the large bathroom and shower area with a double-glazed door opening onto the balcony which had sun loungers, chairs and privacy screens. They tipped the porter and as he left the room both jumped onto the beds and burst into laughter. They ventured onto the balcony from where they could see Aricifes. There was a knock on the door and a porter brought in two black cases. They tipped the handsome young man and flopped back onto the bed. Job done. Now to enjoy a paid for cruise.

CHAPTER 4

Tuesday 17th May

It was late evening when Steve and Lauren stopped outside a large modern detached house in Alderley Edge. The property was surrounded by a two and a half metre high cream painted wall and had a highly polished wooden gate across the entrance to the driveway. It was a pleasant evening as they got out of the car and walked to the electronic panel at the side of the gate. Lauren pressed the call button and they waited.

"Hello."

"Is that Mr Newton?"

"No. He isn't here. Can I help you?"

"Is it possible to speak to Mrs Newton?"

"No. Not here. Who are you two?"

"We are police officers and would like to speak to Mr and Mrs Newton urgently."

"Show your ID to the camera." They both looked up at the small CCTV camera on top of the gate post and showed their ID cards.

"Wait there."

After a short time the smaller pedestrian access gate buzzed and opened revealing a dark skinned muscular man in the entrance. He was wearing a blue shirt with matching coloured trousers, the shirt had a JOB Security badge stitched onto the left breast pocket. They looked at each other. "Can I have a closer look at the ID cards?" Steve and Lauren handed them over and after a quick examination, the man handed them back before making a note in a small book.

"The Newtons are not at home and won't be for a good few weeks, this house is still 24/7 protected though."

Steve smiled, "As we can see, and very thoroughly too. Can you tell me how to get in touch with them? It is urgent."

"The office has contact details for them both but they can't give you the details direct, understand?"

"Yes. What's the office number?"

"It's probably easier if you go to the office, it's in the middle of town opposite Waitrose above the Oxfam shop, here's a card, I'll tell them you're coming."

Steve looked at the card, JOB Security - Bespoke Security Services.

They got into the car and headed off towards town.

Lauren rang Andy back at the office, "Hi Andy any updates from Sarah yet?"

"Nothing yet, all the applications have been done and sent off and I've asked for urgent priority, probably get the banking details first but still waiting. Nothing found by the lads in the paperwork either. Keep in touch."

They rang the bell at the security office and the door opened automatically. As they entered and went upstairs they were met by a similar uniformed security guard, the name on the badge read "Jessica". After introductions Jessica O'Brien, owner of Job Security, directed them into the office adjacent to a control room with several monitors and three operatives.

Steve told them why they were there.

"I'm sorry if this is frustrating she said, but our customers want privacy and security and we pride ourselves in this service. Unless this is an extremely important matter to them, I cannot contact them now."

"I can assure you that this is important to them, Steve replied. Do you know the family?"

"Yes, I do. I have known the family a long time."

"You know Josh?"

"OK, what's wrong, is Josh in trouble."

"He may be in danger."

"Josh can handle himself, very well in fact. He's in Panama or somewhere isn't he?"

"Where are his parents?"

"They're on a cruise, they'll be somewhere near Thailand and heading towards Australia. The three of them are meeting up in New Zealand for Polly's wedding in a few weeks. Polly is

Josh's sister."

"Do you know Josh's friend Filipe?" Lauren asked.

"Not well, I've met him a couple of times when he's visited the area, in the gym, in a couple of bars. I'm on WhatsApp with Josh, the last one was from next to a canal ship with Filipe."

"Can you get away from here for a while?"

"As I'm the boss here I suppose I can. Give me twenty minutes to get one of the crew back into the office and I'll get changed."

After arranging to meet at the nearby Alderley Edge Hotel, Steve decided to call the boss.

He explained that the Newtons were on a cruise between Thailand and Australia headed for New Zealand, it was middle of the night at their present location but he'd met a friend who was in touch with Josh and there'd been no contact since Panama.

They discussed the next move and decided that Jessica should contact Josh and be asked to provide as much information on both him and Newton family as she could. If possible the Boss would contact the Newtons in around two hours.

At the the Alderley Edge Hotel Lauren ordered coffees and they waited for Jessica at a table in the garden. She arrived wearing a bright orange tight fitting top with short length jeans and her dark hair was tied back. A complete change from the woman who had been wearing the uniform only ten minutes earlier. She walked straight and looked strong, Steve thought to himself. How impressed he was with the change in the woman he had only just met. Lauren ordered her a coffee, Americano.

The three of them were alone and it felt easy to talk. Steve asked Jessica what she knew about Josh and then told her that Filipe had been murdered.

He explained to her how important it was to contact Josh so he could be eliminated from the enquiry and for them to gather any information or any evidence from their time together in Central America that might assist in their investigation and of course to ensure that he was still alive.

Jessica had known Josh since he was 16 after they met at the local judo club. They'd been competing at different levels as he was seven years younger than her and they'd both trained at different clubs before that. Polly was also a member at the club but was two years older than Josh, she also played hockey at a high level while Josh played with the local rugby union club. Polly had moved to New Zealand and continued to play hockey there, but Jessica hadn't seen her since she'd left Alderley Edge.

Jessica would occasionally meet with Josh when their paths crossed when he came back from University, at judo or socially in Edge and Manchester. He was well liked with a great personality, he had good friends but not a girlfriend that she was aware of. He was going to work in his father's manufacturing business.

Time to contact Josh.

They decided that Jessica should call and ask for permission to give out his mobile number.

She dialled and waited for the call, it went straight to "leave a message".

"Shit, sorry" Steve said. Can you send him a message in the way you normally would and ask him to get in contact with you? Would he reply?"

"I don't see why not."

"We're heading back to Newcastle now. We need the numbers for his parents so if you can you send me them while we're on our way please. As soon as you have them."

Jessica handed the contact numbers to Lauren, "I will use my initiative on this. They know me."

"I'll send a couple of lads down tomorrow to do a search of Josh's room, Steve said, for his travel arrangements, documents, passport details, OK. I'll let you know as soon as I've been in touch with his parents."

They walked to the car park together and shook hands. Steve and Lauren watched as Jessica slipped in to her grey metallic Porche 911 Carrera S cabriolet. She glanced at Steve with a smile then waved to them both and drove slowly through the car park.

As Steve started to drive away, Lauren commented "I think she likes you". He smiled at her and said "Who wouldn't". To which Lauren replied, "Who wouldn't what?" They both had a childish laugh then Lauren made a call on the car speaker.

"Hi Andy, it's Steve, no joy down here. Can you prep Billy and Alan to drive to Alderley Edge first thing or tonight if possible and stop over. Whatever suits? They need to do a full search of Josh's room and documents. We couldn't contact Josh, he might not have been near his phone who knows? We've left a message. I know it's getting on but keep Sarah going. The parents are on a cruise near Thailand, Lauren will send a text with their contact numbers."

"Sarah's had word back from the bank Steve. Filipe's account. A withdrawal of two thousand dollars was made at a bank in Panama City on Monday the 8th of May. A day after he left Panama City and travelled to Colon!"

"Has she managed to find anything on Josh's accounts?"

"Yes, he paid for his flights from here to Barcelona and Mexico on his credit card but nothing else back yet."

"Thank her mate. Is the boss about?"

"Still in his office Steve, do you want to speak to him?"

"Tell him. Ask him, to call me as soon as he can. We should be back by eleven for a debrief. Cheers Andy."

After a few miles the phone rang, "Hi James, what've you got?"

"Not a lot Boss. We couldn't get in touch with Josh or his parents but you might be able to get a call through now. We've sent a text to Josh's mobile to get in touch with a friend of his, Jessica, she owns the company that's looking after the family home. JOB Security. We'll be back at eleven."

"I'll get it done. See you back here."

The 'Super', attempted to ring the numbers given but couldn't get a reply. He called Headquarters communications and requested they identify the cruise ship with the Newton's on board and get in touch with the ship's purser and ring him back.

It was 22:32 when the communications room rang back. "I will put you through to the purser Sir."

"Hello, Detective Superintendent Tinkler from Northumbria Police, who am I speaking to please?"

"I am the Purser on the 'Norwegian Star' Sir. How can I help?"

"It is a matter of urgency that I speak with Mr Newton and possibly his wife."

"Can I inform them of the nature of your call?"

"No but they could possibly need a comfortable chair."

"Oh, of course Sir, will you wait?"

"Yes. It's urgent."

He waited for 10 minutes.

"Hello?"

"Is that Mr Newton?"

"Yes, who's speaking please?"

"I'm Superintendent Tinkler from Northumbria Police. We need to get in touch with Josh and I was wondering if you've had any contact from him recently. There's been some trouble with Filipe and we just want to make sure Josh is OK."

"Josh left Filipe about a week ago, maybe more. He's on his own now somewhere in the States. Is Filipe ok?"

"Filipe has been involved in an incident in South America, we are making enquiries at this moment. How long is it since you heard from Josh?"

"About five, six days ago. He was on his own, he'd left Filipe in Panama and was heading for Los Angeles to do some stuff before we meet up with him in New Zealand a couple of weeks from now. Is Josh in any trouble?"

"No. We just think he may be able to help us with our enquiries about Filipe. Does he have any other contact numbers?"

"No just the one you'll have and the email, which I'm sure you'll have too."

"OK it sounds that he is safe and well. Can you tell him to contact me if he gets in touch?"

"Of course, I hope you get Filipe sorted out."

He ended the call and shouted, "Sarah, anything back on Josh's phone yet or any emails?"

"Still waiting Boss."

Steve and Lauren returned to the office and had a very short debrief. In reality, they'd not gained anymore information and decided to finish the shift, returning for a 08:00 start, hoping tomorrow would be a more productive day.

CHAPTER 5

Wednesday 18th May

It was 07:40 when Steve walked into the squad room, the Boss was in his office, Sarah was at her desk, the kettle was on and there was the smell of fresh toast. Andy came in, he had ridden in on his bike and had been for a shower. Billy and Alan walked in together and the noise volume went up a few notches, shortly followed by Lauren who was carrying a large take away coffee and a croissant. Billy and Alan headed straight for the toaster and loaded two extra thick slices each with loads of butter and strawberry jam. Sarah took Steve a coffee to his desk.

They all started to take seats around the briefing table. In reality it was four tables pushed together and could sit 16 in a squeeze. There were twelve grey cushioned plastic bucket seats in place, Andy had prepared a briefing power point.

Steve received a phone call, checking the screen it was Jessica from JOB security. He walked away from the table. "Hi Jessica, You Ok?"

"Yes, I'm fine, didn't sleep much though. I've had no reply from Josh so I contacted some of his mates in the area. I've had a text back from Marty saying Josh had left Panama was on his way to the states. Las Vegas and then to Hawaii. That was on 8th May. "

"That was ten days ago"

"Maybe he has lost his phone and his contact list."

"He could still get a new phone and call someone he knew, or your business number maybe. If you don't mind can you try some more of his mates, don't tell them the reason why though. I'm in a meeting I'll call you back?"

The boss took his seat at the head table with his coffee and toast, Andy started the power point briefing.

"What we know so far. Filipe and Josh travelled to the Americas together from the town via barcelona on Tuesday 19th

April. They are both 25, healthy, wealthy and loved life. This was a trip that had been planned together when they were at University in Newcastle. We know they visited Mexico, Belize and Panama. They are using currency, US dollars and take cash from banks rather than using their cards. Some cash was taken from Filipe's bank in Panama City on Monday 8th May. It's believed that they took a canal cruise through to a town called Colon on the Atlantic side of the canal on or about that date. Filipe spoke to his mother on that Sunday saying he was in Colon but would not be stopping as it wasn't a pleasant town. Neither of the lads contact their parents regularly unless they wanted something as Mr. Lopez says, they're big lads now. There has been no contact from either of them since."

Steve, "Sorry Andy, but I have just taken a call saying that Josh was in contact with a friend in Alderley Edge on the 9th May, saying he had left Panama and was on his way to the USA."

Andy" Great I'll input that. Going on, they were due to split up in Central America, Panama probably now. It was thought that Filipe was to continue around South America, Colombia, Venezuela, Peru and Josh was going to the states and New Zealand."

"On Monday 16th, the Lopez family received the WhatsApp video recording we have all seen of Filipe being murdered. Somewhere, by the female. And that's what we know."

"Actions, Walter and his team are tracing both phones and email tracking. Sarah is waiting for the bank returning their records. Billy and Alan, I want you to get down to Cheshire and do a search of Josh's documents for plans and get a statement off the last contact person with him, liaise with Steve for that info. Boss anything?"

"I've spoken to the parents of Josh who are on a cruise near Thailand. They have not heard from him since he left Filipe on his own and was heading for the USA. You cannot assume anything but it may well be that Josh knows nothing of what happened to Filipe. But we do need to trace him and the movements of Filipe before that video. At the moment we are waiting for something, anything to get this started. I've got funding for this so green light on let's push ahead. Hopefully the banks and phones will come back today. Ok let's get to work, keep Andy in touch."

Walter strolls in, "Sorry I'm late but we've had some results come through"

Boss, "Sit down and give us the good news?"

Walter takes a seat," We have identified the water bottle as Polar water which is distributed in Venezuela, might narrow your location search down but a big country. The initial record of use of the phone used by Filipe has just come back which links in. It was used fairly regularly until Monday, when it was used to send a message to Josh's phone and the WhatsApp message to his parents. It has not been used since. The last messages were originated in Caracas, prior to that it is sited in Porlamar, on the island of Margarita when it was used several times. We are waiting for any information back from WhatsApp which we should get today."

Boss, "Great stuff Walter, thank the lads for me but keep them at it. Give the printed details to Sarah. Sarah full checks on all numbers used, hotels, transport, restaurants, known persons, the works. Andy liaise with the police liaison officer in Venezuela as much info as you can give him, any unidentified bodies, similar MO's . Lads, you two get down to Cheshire pronto as much effort into tracing Josh through his contacts and any documents in the home. Lauren, contact Panama police liaison with as much info as you can give them, is there any CCTV on the canal cruiser, hotels. Get cracking. Jimmy my office now".

The table quickly cleared. Billy and Alan picked up their overnight bags and document holders and headed towards the car park. Sarah and Lauren sat at their computer desks; Sarah was downloading the phone results from an email from the IT department. Lauren was checking the police almanac, it was only 4am in Caracas and 3am in Panama. Andy was updating the information board. Walter went to the toast machine.

Steve followed the boss into his office. The Boss shouted "Two coffees". Walter put the kettle on.

"What are you thinking Jimmy?"

"I think Filipe was murdered before the phone was used in Caracas, so possibly in Margarita. That would mean that it was probably the murderer who contacted Josh"

"Right. Why would they want to contact Josh if he was in another part of the world?"

"No idea, unless something happened before they split up in Panama"

The Boss was thoughtful. "Whatever it is, Josh is either in danger or dead for some reason or another. They have upset somebody, really upset serious people. It is a fucking dangerous place over there. Were they into drugs?"

"Cannot find any trace, or anyone with any knowledge that they were into drugs. They did have a canny bit of cash access though?"

"I've got some funds, like I say. Fancy a trip to Latin America? I can only afford one to go. I will get you met by the liaison officers for some local knowledge. We need to work fast on this to establish facts before we can pass it on to the relevant Country".

Steve, "I'll get in touch with Jessica in Cheshire and ask her to keep trying Josh and his mates for any contact and I will have a look at maps to see where Margarita is?"

"I want you to start in Panama City. We know they were on the cruiser together. I'm hopeful that Sarah will have the hotel and transport details sorted today. Get home and get packing, don't forget the sun cream, you won't need beach shorts. I'll get HQ to sort out the flights and some currency. Get out and back with your gear don't forget your passport."

Walter walked in and gave the boss his coffee and kept the other one for himself as he walked out of the office with Jimmy. Steve headed for the car park.

Just over an hour later Steve was getting out of the shower and drying himself down when his mobile rang. It was the boss.

"Jimmy, got you a flight from Manchester with Virgin to Atlanta then on to Panama. It's an open ticket. Go to HQ they have printed your tickets and got some dollars and other stuff for you, the flight is early tomorrow so they have booked a hotel at the airport for you. OK. You alright? We are contacting the liaison officers now"

"Yes boss, what about communication?"

"Fuck, I forgot about that. I'll get someone to sort that out at HQ"

"Boss remember my name is Steve when the contacts are made"

"Fuck off Jimmy, get the job done and maybe some free sun. But. Do not do anything daft or stupid. These people are obviously, very nasty"

"Aye boss, no worries"

Steve finished drying off and got dressed.

His second-floor apartment in Gosforth to the North of Newcastle was immaculately clean. Highly polished wooden floors. In the living room there was a three-seater black leather sofa and two single bucket chairs. A large screen TV was placed in the centre of the wall. A small glass coffee table was in front of the sofa where there was a framed photograph of Steve in army uniform with a group of four others smiling and lounging against a troop carrier in desert colours. Two more photos of Steve on the wall, one in dress uniform, whites, at attention and the other in a large group of Commando regiment in desert fatigues. He walked into the square minimal bedroom. A King-sized bed which was made but had been slept in looking at the creases in the pillows. A working desk with a cleaned surface and closed laptop the only item on the desk. One wall had full length fitted wardrobes. He picked up his black medium sized case from inside one of the wardrobes. He didn't know what to pack as he looked at his neatly arranged clothing, racks of shirts, each in a colour order. Dress shirts, casual smart, polos. He took a mixed selection and folded and rolled them neatly. His underwear and socks were neatly folded and sorted in colour inside the drawers of the wardrobe. Again, he took a mixed selection. The shoes he selected were placed in the bottom of the case. The toiletries bag was always packed but he included some mosquito spray and suntan cream, then he packed two pairs of beach shorts. Just in case. Packing completed he collected his passport from the desk drawer and walked to the doorway. He put a lightweight jacket on and stashed his sunglasses in their pouch in the inside breast pocket, mobile phone in his right pocket, checked his passport and put it in the breast pocket with his sunglasses. He picked up the car and apartment keys, set the property alarm and left the building.

At HQ he picked up a secured tablet, a mobile phone authorised for overseas use, travel tickets, US dollars and a business credit card in the name of Northern Ventures.

Steve then drove off to Manchester. He decided he would meet up with Billy and Alan and one of them would drive his car back.

He phoned Jessica, "Hi Jessica its Steve."

"Hello Jimmy." She laughed.

"I gather you have been talking to Billy and Alan"

"They don't shut up. Funny people. They are away talking to Marty who got the text from Josh"

"Is there any more joy from anyone?"

"Unfortunately, not. I have contacted everyone I can think of. Do you think it's bad?"

"It doesn't look good. Ehm, what are you doing tonight? I'm flying out to Panama tomorrow morning from Manchester so I have some time to kill tonight if you're free"

"What time you flying tomorrow?"

"Just after 10"

"OK, I'll make some plans to get free tonight, text me the hotel and I will pick you up about 8."

Later that afternoon Steve walked into the Radisson hotel at the airport. He took his case, document holder and tablet carrier out of the car and made his way to the hotel room. He contacted Billy and arranged to meet him in the bar. He switched on the tablet and checked his emails.

Email from Andy that the Panama liaison officer knew he was going and would meet up when he got to the city. A Radisson hotel was booked in Panama City for the first night, after that just book accommodation himself. No further usage of Filipe's phone but it was used in Panama City, Colon, Aruba and Margarita. Filipe had made a call to a hotel in Colon called Andros and called a number in Aruba on a few occasions which wasn't identified the same number contacted him again in Margarita and a number for a hotel in Margarita, The Imperial.

His phone rang, it was Billy in the hotel lobby. He went down to meet Billy and Alan, they went into the bar. They had recorded some bank account numbers and found books on North American Native Indians but nothing of any use and no further information from Josh's friend Marty but Alan had taken a statement. Billy had collected Josh's laptop for Walter to work on. After a large coffee, they left, Billy was driving Steve's car back to the office. Steve went back to his room and showered again. He sent a text to Jessica. "Radisson room 418".

At 8pm prompt, Jessica walked into the lobby of the hotel. Steve was sat waiting, drinking a glass of sparkling water. They met each other and shook hands, then Jessica keeping hold of Steve's hand, pulled him closer and kissed him on the cheek. Steve thought she looked magnificent, a short length red and dark blue patterned figure-hugging dress and matching heels, her dark long hair tied back in a ponytail. She was about five centimetres smaller in height than Steve in her heels. They left in her Porsche and went to Wilmslow. For the next three hours they had a meal and chatted to get to know each other and their relationship was developing.

On their return to the Radisson they both got out of the car. They embraced each other and kissed each other gently on the cheek. Steve promised that he would meet up with Jessica when he returned from his Latin American enquiry. He hadn't felt like this about any woman he had met. They kissed again and Jessica got into the car and drove away slowly. Steve made his way to his room, on his own. Not what he wanted. Not what Jessica had wanted either?

In the morning Steve had showered and dressed in lightweight travel clothing, he checked his emails but there was nothing new. After taking an early self-service breakfast, cereal, full English fry up with toast and lots of coffee, he had walked across the walkway from the hotel into the airport terminal and called the boss. Nothing new to report but the liaison man would meet at the airport in Panama City when Steve made contact.

He was now sitting comfortably in the window seat 57K of the Virgin 330-300 and waiting to complete the emergency demonstration prior to take off. He was approached by a male steward, "Mr. Bond." Steve nodded. "Jessica has a seat next to her in premium If you would like to make your way there after take-off please"

He gave a quizzical look to the steward, "What? Yes, I will".

CHAPTER 6

Monday 9th May

The lads walked together through the Tocumen International airport terminal in Panama City. They were both carrying their heavy rucksacks as they stopped to look at the departures board. The flights were on time so they headed for the Copa airline desk.

Filipe bought a one-way ticket to Aruba which would take off in just over an hour. He paid cash in dollars. At the same time, Josh was paying for his flight with his credit card for his flight to Los Angeles. There was just enough time for a small beer together before they hugged shoulders and separated, Filipe walking briskly to the departure gate. Josh watched him disappear through the gate then walked towards a restaurant for some tacos. His flight was another four hours to wait.

Susanna and Maria were sunning themselves on the top sun deck of the 'Alisios'. They were stretched out on the thick padded loungers next to the fresh water pool, with their mojitos placed on the nearby table. Both were enjoying life, happy with what they had completed and looking forward to further payment and probably more work. It was so easy money.

Later that day, Filipe landed in Aruba Reina Beatrix International airport. He took a taxi to the Brickell Bay Beach Club and Spa hotel, a mid-range hotel, on the beach just twenty minutes from the airport. As Filipe was booking in and paying cash in advance for his stay, Josh was in his aisle seat on the runway in Panama ready for take-off to the USA.

Filipe checked out the bedroom furnishings and used a plastic self-adhesive hook inside the rear of the drawers to hang a small bag containing his camera and cash. He thought this was safer than using the safe provided as he had done this throughout his travels.

Two days later, in the early morning sunshine the 'Alisios' slowly manoeuvred into the waters around Aruba and into the cruise terminal of Oranjestad. Filipe had taken a seat in the air-conditioned terminal watching the final phases of the ship being readied for disembarkation. It seemed to take forever until eventually the ramp was lowered to allow the passengers to leave. The tour coaches were starting to park up outside the terminal. Filipe took a seat outside the passport check to wait for Susanna and Maria. The short stay visitors were directed one way towards the coaches, those leaving the cruise walked towards passport control.

He saw Susanna and Maria approaching the desk, he slumped in his seat, put his head down and pulled his bucket hat lower over his face. Maria came through first and stopped and waited for Susanna. They were laughing and walking towards the exit, they would pass Filipe.

"Hola senoras, como estan" (*hello ladies how are you*)

They both turned and looked towards Filipe. He lifted his hat and started laughing. There was a look of puzzlement on the girls' faces and then Susanna walked over and hugged him tightly and kissed him on the lips and both cheeks. Maria kissed him on both cheeks. Filipe explained that Josh had travelled to the US. The terminal was busy and their movement was stopped by the volume of passengers and some tourists taking photos of everything and waiting for directions for which bus to board.

Susanna gave Filipe her mobile number and told him she would contact him later that afternoon when they knew where they were staying. They both wanted a cold drink; Filipe opened his wallet and gave them some US dollars in small bills which could be used for the drinks and tipping. He left them to get into a taxi before the queue outside got too big. They all hugged and they exchanged kisses on the cheeks.

Susanna hadn't spoken of Filipe since they boarded the 'Alisios'. In fact, she hadn't thought about him, it was supposed to be a one-night experience. She had enjoyed the night and was now starting to look forward to another night or maybe two together.

Susanna and Maria eventually left the terminal building and saw that the two suitcases had been put onto the coach. It was the same group of people from Panama all enjoying this short break. They boarded the coach and as usual, the passengers had taken the same seats as if personally prior booked. They were told by the holiday representative that they were staying at the Holiday Inn Resort. Susanna wrote a text and then sent to Filipe. She then deleted the text record.

Filipe had just walked into the foyer of the hotel from the short taxi ride when his mobile vibrated. He read the new message. He replied, "your hotel bar 3".

That afternoon Filipe met Susanna in the bar, Maria was spending her time on the sun lounger on the beach. Susanna was wearing a bikini with a white sarong wrapped around her slender waist. They went outside to the beach bar and sat at a table overlooking the turquoise sea. Filipe ordered Mojito's and they chatted about the sailing to Aruba, the quality of the cabin and the experience on board. Nothing was mentioned about the luggage exchange or how much she would be paid for this holiday. They were there for three nights and Susanna was going to enjoy every night. It was decided that the girls would enjoy the sun and sea during the day and meet up with Filipe on the evenings. Filipe was happy with the arrangement which would allow him to explore the island and hopefully get some photographs of the birds and wildlife.

Josh had an enjoyable flight to Los Angeles. He was sat next to Maddison. She had been to Panama on business as an I.T. consultant from her employers in California. They both shared experiences and chat during the course of the flight which shortened the flight time. They exchanged mobile numbers and email addresses before the flight had landed. Maddison was being collected by her employers when she landed but agreed to meet Josh if they got a chance. She was single and lived in Santa Monica. Josh thought she was about his age. He was attracted by her intelligence, manor and appearance. After passing through immigration checks, he again met Maddison who had waited for him with a cold Pepsi. He took a selfie of himself with Maddison on his mobile. They shook hands, holding a little longer, then parted. Maddison waved as she left the terminal building.

He was going to drive to Satwiwa Native American Cultural Centre. He had planned for a ten-night stay camping in the area to study native American history. He was on his own, he enjoyed the solitude at times. First, he wanted some comfort. He had booked a room at Boutique 444 Venice Beach for three nights to explore Santa Monica.

For Filipe, the next three nights went by too fast. It was living in Paradise; it was loving in Paradise. Maria did not come out with Susanna on the evenings and chose to stay in the hotel at the paid for bar. Filipe and Susanna spent the time visiting local bars before returning to Filipe's room in the early hours. They both knew that they would never see each other again so they made good use of the time together.

Early in the morning of Saturday 14th May, after a coffee Filipe walked to the Holiday Inn hotel. It was 07:30, it was bright and hot. Susanna and Maria were leaving the hotel and walked towards the coach. Filipe greeted them and kissed Maria on both cheeks. Susanna embraced him strongly and there was one light kiss on the lips. They were laughing but there was a sadness in Filipe, he really liked Susanna and wanted more from the relationship. He had good memories, he had his camera and asked one of the tourists to take a photo of the three of them together and one with Susanna. They were happy photographs. The girls got onto the coach, in the usual seats and were smiling and waving as the coach was driven slowly away from the front of the hotel. Filipe waved until the coach was out of site. He then checked the quality of the photographs. He was happy. He decided to walk back to his hotel. He had to make travel plans.

It took two days before Josh contacted Maddison by email. He had seen what he wanted to see in the area, but he really wanted to see Maddison. She replied that she would meet up with Josh at 'Santa Monica Seafood' on Wilshire Boulevard that evening and would book a table.

Josh was early, he had bought a new shirt, trousers and shoes. Looking at his reflection in the polished window, he felt good and thought he was looking good but was unusually nervous.

He stood outside the building in the warm breeze. A taxi stopped near to the restaurant and Maddison elegantly got out of the rear of the cab. Her long blonde hair was straight and over her shoulders, she was wearing a flower print dress that had style and grace and red heeled shoes. Her smile was warm. They greeted each other with a short hug. They stayed in the restaurant and bar for three hours. For Josh it felt like ten minutes. They got to know each other well, family members, friends, career plans, hobbies, likes and dislikes. They certainly liked each other. There was just the short matter of several thousand miles between them in just a few days' time. They had respect for each other and a want for each other. Josh suggested that Maddison could attend his sister's wedding with him in New Zealand to see first-hand how distance can be compromised and his heart jumped when Maddison said she would consider it if it was possible.

He was sorely tempted to forego his planned journey into the hills and live the life of a native Indian. Josh explained that he would be working as a volunteer with the local tribe, living in the same conditions of over two centuries ago. There would be no modern-day, hi-tech assistance or machinery for approximately ten days or more until the work was completed. That would include no mobile or internet contact with the outside world. Josh payed the bill for the restaurant and as they walked towards the door they held hands. A taxi was parked waiting outside the restaurant. They walked to the cab together, Josh opened the rear cab door. Maddison grabbed hold of Josh and they kissed and hugged lightly. She got into the car and waved as she was driven away.

The next morning, Josh drove to Satwiwa Native American

Cultural Centre. He took on a volunteer role in the community and handed his mobile phone into the safe keeping of the administrators. There was no mobile signal or internet in the mountainous area.

CHAPTER 7

Saturday 14th May

The 'Alisios' had arrived in Fort Lauderdale and the passengers were disembarking. Frank and Eleanor Carlson were waiting for their car to be delivered to the terminal meeting point. They looked like most passengers on the cruise, mid-fifties, tanned, well presented and the appearance of wealth. Their luggage was next to them, delivered by the ship's crew on a trolley. They were under observation by several DEA officers. Their car had been electronically tagged and a camera had been hidden inside the dashboard of the vehicle.

The vehicle was driven in by the attendant, it had been valeted and was gleaming. The white Chrysler 300 SRT 8 has a large boot, big enough to take the 4 suitcases. The attendant placed the luggage into the boot and handed the keys to Frank Carlson. Frank examined the vehicle and handed the attendant $20. The attendant opened the front passenger door for Mrs. Carlson. Frank started the engine, the attendant closed the passenger door and smiled at Mrs. Carlson as the vehicle was slowly driven away into a line of other vehicles exiting the quayside and dock area.

Six DEA officers had boarded the cruise ship and with the assistance of the ships purser they made their way to the identified crew's quarters. They detained two Latino crew who put up a brief struggle before being subdued and placed in handcuffs.

Frank was driving at a steady speed staying in the traffic flow. He was heading away from the docks. The traffic was light. A phone call was received in the car. Frank was heard to say "1961 Oakland Industrial Park ok." He then spoke to Eleanor "Not long now. Just drop and go".

Drug Enforcement Agency officers made their way to the area of Oakland Industrial Park in unmarked police vehicles. The command room made use of the CCTV coverage in the area and contacted the commander and told him of some activity in the area of the location given. The Enforcement helicopter was overhead at a discreet distance not to draw attention. There were four men seen at the warehouse building. It was a single-story building in the middle of a block, it had two large drive-through overhead doors, one to the front and one at the back and a pedestrian access door to the front of the building near to what was expected to be the office. There were two windows from the office which overlooked the front road and access to the building. One man was seen sitting in the driver's seat of a black Dodge MPV on the entrance to the estate. Some of the buildings nearby were occupied and there was a low level of activity in the area.

The ground commander deployed his foot team at a covert location 500metres distance from the building as the secondary team were following the Chrysler with the tracking device. The foot team made a circuitry route to specific points encompassing the building, avoiding the observer in the black Dodge and being wary of other spotters that may be in the area. They were all armed with assault rifle carbines, Sig Sauger 551 or HK G36K, Sub machine guns 9mm HK MP5 and semi-automatic pistols, Glock or Sig Sauger 9mm. They silently moved into specified radial locations with firing lines on the building and the exits.

After twenty minutes, Frank drove the Chrysler passed the Dodge MPV into the estate. The electric roller shutters to the front of the building were slowly being opened. A man in denim jeans and jacket waved towards the Chrysler, directing Frank to drive into the warehouse. Frank drove the car under the shutters which were closed behind the vehicle. There were three men in dark coloured suits stood inside and were smiling as he stopped the car in front of them. One of the men approached the car and opened the driver's door, "Ola Amigo". Frank was smiling as he swung his legs out of the door, ready to shake hands. He was shot three times, at close range with a silenced automatic handgun. Twice in the chest and once in his face. Franks skull, brain and blood cascaded over Eleanor who screamed briefly. It was all being recorded. Then the sound of two more muffled shots and silence. The black MPV was now being driven towards the building and the doors were being raised, the DEA snipers were in position on the roof of the units opposite the front and rear of the building.

"Nobody leaves that unit unless they're handcuffed. They are armed and very dangerous if need be, if you get a shot take it." The Commander spoke.

The doors were open, the MPV was parked under the doors. The commander could see the road was free of traffic towards the warehouse, he gave the order "Strike, strike, strike."

The response was immediate, four armour protected cars entered the road at high speed. The man in jeans exited the building with an AK47 and pointed it towards the front vehicle. One shot from the sniper and he was thrown off his feet with a blood explosion from his chest. Another, the driver of the MPV who was partially hidden by the vehicle aimed his Glock at the fast-approaching cars. Another shot exploded and he thumped onto the floor quickly surrounded by a flow of bright red blood, the Glock dropping from his grasp onto the concrete floor. The sounds of the gunfire made those in the immediate area take cover inside the buildings.

The Carlson bodies were quickly dragged out of the Chrysler and dumped on the concrete floor by the men in suits. The rear unit doors were now opening, slowly, too slow. Two unmarked DEA cars were already parked up, the officers had ordered everyone inside, they didn't need telling twice. The cars were side on to the doors with the officers taking aim at the doors from behind their vehicles, other officers were in cover to the right and left of the doors. The Chrysler came out at speed scraping the roof of the vehicle against the bottom metal bar of the opening door, the loud screeching noise of the metal scraping noise was piercing. The three men inside the car immediately started firing their weapons rapidly and wildly at the DEA officers through the open side windows as the car was clearing the door. The noise was now deafening. The officers returned more precise rounds into the limited space inside the car, the windscreen shattered and blood was spattered inside the vehicle and out onto the bonnet. The shots stopped and the car continued at speed across the road into the rear of another warehouse and came to a hard, stop against the wall in a cloud of brick dust and debris. The officers ran to the car with their firearms aimed at the vehicle. There was steam billowing from the engine and dust from the impacts in a shroud around the vehicle. The front passenger was hanging halfway out of the passenger door, blood covering his head and body wounds. A quick check. Dead. The driver was trapped behind the steering wheel and airbag with half of his head missing. Still check to make sure. Dead. The suited man lying across the back seat was a bloodied mess across his body and spattered across his face and head. He was motionless and silent. Quick check. Still life. They removed the weapons from the vehicle.

Commander "We have one subject still alive need urgent medical team, multiple wounds to the body and legs, unconscious but breathing at this time."

"Can you confirm the area is secure for the medical team evac."

Commander "The area is secure for evac procedure. We want 4 officers to secure and keep the injured suspect safe with the medical team. No news to be given of the persons killed and we want total isolation for the suspect"

"Yes Sir"

The boot of the vehicle was opened and the four black cases were still intact.

It was a result and hopefully what the DEA had wanted.

Sixty kilos of pure white cocaine, street value $6 million. Six dead, two arrested and the closure of another transport route. One possible information source detained if he lives. This route had been watched for months. Identified every cruise from Panama involving the two arrested males. It was anticipated at least one cruise a week into different ports in the USA.

$312 million a year. That was going to upset one of the cartels.

Later a coded phone call was made originating in Fort Lauderdale to Cali, Colombia.

CHAPTER 8

Saturday 14th May

The Copa Airlines flight touched down in Cali later that morning, the sun was still bright. The girls left the airport, waved goodbye to their fellow holiday makers and both got into a waiting car. Their two suitcases were placed into the boot by the driver. It would be a fifty-minute drive to their destination. The time passed quickly as they relaxed, nearly snoozing after the alcohol consumed on the flight. The car turned off the main highway and onto the single track road that led to the Hacienda. A 5-metre-high stone wall surrounded the immediate perimeter of the Hacienda. A large modern Villa as one would expect to be owned by leader of a multimillion-dollar empire, it was very well protected by a large number of armed guards. The electric gates opened and the vehicle slowly approached the parking area. The girls had been before and were not in awe or had reason to be scared of the place.

Maria and Susanna got out of the vehicle and walked towards the open doors of the building. They were greeted by a smiling man, not tall, very well groomed and dressed in a dark suit. "He will be with you shortly in the meeting room." He directed them across the large entrance hall and opened the door to the room, he offered them a cold drink and asked them to take a seat.

The room was square in shape with two sides of full length glass curtain doors, they gave a beautiful view over the surrounding walls of the forest and mountains. One wall was all highly polished tiles and had a door which led to the bathroom facilities. In the middle of the wall was a large screen television. The room was furnished with a large oblong shape table made from Ceiba wood, a tree that had been felled during the clearance to build the Hacienda. There were eight chairs spaced dow one side of the table and three larger chairs centrally positioned on the opposite side, all made from the same tree.

The girls were given a cold glass of water and took their seats together in the middle of the table facing the three chairs. They sat and waited, both having two more glasses of water

He walked into the room flanked by his two colonels, Paco and Borja. Very typical business style, groomed and styled. Borja was carrying a small case.

"Buenas tardes chicas,"(*good afternoon girls*) Manolo gestured to the girls to stay seated. They were smiling as they took the three seats opposite Maria and Susanna. Paco holding the chair for Manolo to sit before they took their seats.

"Now, did you enjoy your little expenses paid holiday Susanna?"

"Yes, we did thank you very much"

"Did you have any problems or maybe suggestions for the future Maria?"

"No, no problems it was as you said"

"The delivery was done, OK?"

"Yes, it was again as you said"

"Susanna was there any sign of police in the area?"

"No, there was nothing."

"That is good, we have used this method many times and we wouldn't want to lose this route"

Manolo waved his left hand and Paco pressed a button on a control pad on the table. Another man walked in to the room, he was dressed casually. "Amigo, take a seat at the end of the table please"

"Do you know this man?"

Susanna and Maria looked towards the end of the table. They recognized the man and looked at each other.

Susanna "Yes, he was on the holiday."

"Do you know why he was there?

"No."

"He was watching my investment…….and you two"

Paco pressed another button and the television screen opened with a photograph of Susannah and Maria with Felipe and Josh with their arms around each other.

"Now please tell me who these gringos are?"

Susanna" They are just two men we met on the holiday, they are nobody"

"And what do you know about them?"

Susanna" They are on holiday, that's all"

Paco pressed and further photographs appeared of them in company with the gringos, on a canal cruiser, in a booth in Arecifes, Susanna walking through a hotel foyer with Felipe. Standing next to four black suitcases at a bus in Colon. Susanna being given American dollars in Aruba.

A picture was forming in the heads of Susanna and Maria and it was not a good one. They were starting to panic.

Maria "We have not done anything; we have said nothing to anybody?"

"How did he know to meet you in Aruba?"

Susanna "He saw the cruise liner he could have found out from Colon"

"Susanna. Why did he give you money in Aruba? Did I not give you enough?"

"Yes, yes you gave us more than enough. He was just being kind, for drinks it was nothing"

"They could have been FBI, CIA, DEA, what do you know of them?"

Susanna, "No, no. They were not American they were from England. They were not police"

"Are the Americans and British not partners in stopping us?"

Susanna "Yes, no. Felipe and Josh were just on holiday having a good time not the police or FBI, CIA."

"This Felipe had a good time with you, and you?"

"Yes, yes just good time, I never said anything, anything to anybody"

"And Maria what about you and, Josh is it"

"I only saw him on the canal cruise and in Colon. I never said anything we both didn't say anything"

"And where did Josh go after Colon?"

"He said he was going to" she then paused.

"Yes, where did he say he was going to?"

"United States. I didn't say anything, please believe me".

There was a long pause, as Manolo looked at both girls.

"There is a problem. The shipment arrived safely in Fort Lauderdale but can I trust you?"

Susanna and Maria "Yes, yes, yes you can trust us"

"A little time later my cousin Pepe and his collection team were ambushed and killed by the DEA. Two of my workers were arrested on the cruise ship. And. Importantly, my valuable shipment was seized and the route compromised. This is costing me lots of money. I am running out of cousins"

Susanna "No this had nothing to do with us, please believe me"

"Could you still provide a service for my business, that is the question"

Susanna, "Yes we can, I will do anything for the business"

"Ok, I want your mobiles now, Is Felipe's number in it.?"

Susanna, "No I deleted it. But I know it."

Paco gave Susannah a pen and a piece of paper. She wrote the number down. then passed the paper back to Paco.

"What about Josh?"

Maria "No, I'm sorry I never took his number or gave him mine"

"Does Felipe know your number Susannah?"

"I did give it to him, I'm sorry"

"Is your phone switched on now, he could be tracking your phone"

"No. No. I haven't switched it on since I left Aruba"

"OK. That is good we will have it checked"

Manolo continued "I cannot have you working near to the distribution until I can trust you again. And, of course I cannot give you the payment that I promised as I have lost a lot more than you. Borja show them what they would have earned"

Borja opened the small case and it was filled with used American dollars.

Maria "You can trust me; I will work for you to prove my trust and honour. I would not take the money."

Susanna "I would rather have your trust than money. I will do anything"

"OK. You will both work in the service area of my plantation for free for one month. Then I will decide if I can use you again."

Susanna "I will work to prove my trust"

Maria lowered her head, "Thank You"

Manolo waved his hand; Paco pressed another button.

The man returned and escorted the girls from the room, they were in tears.

As they left the room Borja slid the small case to the man sitting at the end of the table.

Manolo "Good job Sergio, there is your bonus. Leave"

Sergio left the room. The door was closed behind him as he walked towards the large wooden doors to leave the hacienda.

"I want those two fucking gringo's dead, I want them to know not to fuck with us, I want their bosses, friends, family to know not to fuck with us." Manolo spoke quietly with force and meaning in his voice. "I want it done now." He looked into the faces of Paco and Borja. They looked directly at Manolo and nodded. They got up from the table and replaced their chairs quietly and walked together to leave the room. "I want to know as soon as it is done" Paco turned to face Manolo and again simply nodded.

Two hours later, Susannah and Maria had been showered. They were in separate rooms. They were ready to start to do service for the farm workers.

CHAPTER 9

Thursday 19th May.

After take-off, Steve walked into Premium class and stood at the seat next to Jessica. To be fair, he thought, it was a better seat, wider and more leg room. He stood and looked into her face and without speaking asked the question.

Jessica," I can explain"

"I'm all ears." Steve sat down in the comfortable seat and stretched out his legs.

"After we spoke last night, I contacted Mr. Newton to ask if he had heard anything from Josh or his friends. I told him that the police were sending someone to Central America to make enquiries. He suggested that maybe I should go to keep him updated and he would finance the travel expenses."

"First, who has paid for this upgrade?"

"That's me, my own money"

"Why?"

"It's better than sitting on my own"

"Has my boss, or force been told that you are going?"

"Not that I'm aware of"

"Are you intending to follow me around while I do enquiries in these countries?"

"I would like to be close by"

"How do I explain that to the International Liaison officers? How do I explain you to the Boss?"

"Just say I'm a volunteer translator"

"Do you speak Spanish?"

"Si, perfecto"

"Really?"

"Yes, I'm fluent in Spanish, French, German, Arabic, Russian and a little bit of others"

Steve paused and looked at Jessica who nodded.

"We cannot do this, it's not right. There could be trouble,

violence"

"I can help, I know I can, I won't interfere with your investigation?"

"The boss will go apeshit"

"Don't tell him"

"I cannot hide you; I can't look after you"

"I'm not asking you to look after me, oh by the way I've ordered a bottle of champagne which should be coming soon, which is about now" as she saw the steward walking towards them.

"Thanks very much. What? That's another thing I'm on limited expenses. I won't be going to fancy bars and restaurants. I'll be with a liaison officer in some dive probably."

"I think Mr. Newton might mention it to your Superintendent"

"When is he going to do that?"

"Probably when we are on this flight"

"Shit, shit, shit. He trusts me. If he thinks we have set this up there will be fucking hell on"

"Language Jimmy"

"Don't you, effing start"

"Oh, here's the champagne, would you like some pretzels?"

"Yes please. Woah wait. For a starter, please do not call me Jimmy"

"Ok. I'm sorry Steve".

"I will have to call the boss and just tell him the truth. I didn't know you were going. I didn't ask you to go. Mr. Newton has asked you to travel at his expense to liaise with him concerning the safety of his son Josh from any information that might be gathered in central America. We are not involved in your safety. We are not involved in travel arrangements and we are not involved in accommodation. Is that correct?"

"Yes, I can agree to that statement"

"I will call him when we land in the states. Where are you staying anyway?"

"The Radisson in Panama City"

"Oh, fucking hell, better get another bottle of champagne"
"We might as well enjoy the flight."

Steve put his earphones in, reclined the seat and listened to his rock music and drank free champagne. He looked at Jessica and gave a little smile and a shrug.

Six hours later they both exited the plane into the transit terminal and Steve switched his phone on. After a few seconds there were constant beeps from the device. He waited until it stopped and opened the first message.

From Billy
YOU ARE IN THE SHIT
From Alan
Bigstyle shit Jimmy
From Andy
You might be in the shit Jimmy
From Sarah
He he, don't do anything I wouldn't do!
From Lauren
Might have email from Josh
THE BOSS,
RING ME

Steve looked at Jessica "I think they know"

Jessica gave a wry smile "No way Sherlock".

Steve walked away from Jessica and pressed the numbers for the Boss. It took a while to ring but was answered immediately. "What the fuck is going on Jimmy? You had better not have packed any swim shorts? We are not paying for Love Island holidays. When was this arranged?"

"Boss honest, I knew nothing about it until I was on the plane and the steward asked me to go and sit with Jessica in the premier seats."

"What, who the fuck paid for that? Who arranged this I'm not happy Jimmy? This is a serious murder investigation not a fucking jolly holly. I'm expecting you to do what you do best, work thoroughly, investigate this murder, liaise with our International colleagues, be professional get the job done and give some answers to the Lopez family. You are not babysitting a private security officer."

"Yes Boss. She paid for the seat and drinks, shit"

"Jimmy I'm going to take that shovel off you. I'm telling you now, I want answers to questions and I don't want any interference from a security officer. Do you understand."

"Yes Boss"

"I did get a call from Mr. Newton, who holds the security guard in high esteem for some reason and he told me he was paying all her expenses. Her expenses Jimmy. You do not have expenses for her, understand. I told him in no uncertain terms that she was not to interfere with our enquiries and she would only be given information after I had agreed with the release. I'm aware he is very concerned about the safety of his son but at the moment we are trying to clarify where Filipe has been murdered and who may be responsible"

"Boss, this is me Steve, eh Jimmy. I will do my job thoroughly. I will not abuse your trust and the funds of our force. I have met the Lopez family and I want to get this crime detected just like every other crime I investigate. Jessica will not be a problem, I promise."

"Do not compromise yourself, the force or British policing by making unwanted news Jimmy. Comprende! If you have to have a relationship with Jessica please let it wait until you get back to the town"

"I totally understand Boss"

"Billy and Alan say she's worth one, a keeper and Lauren said she was a lovely and has a nice car. Please leave her out of the way of the enquiry."

"I will Boss I will only tell her what you say."

"I haven't told HQ so I'll try and keep the lid on it. Don't let her get into trouble but you're not her minder. I think Sarah has something for you wait on the line." He shouted, "Sarah come and talk to shagger."

The sound of approaching high heels, "Hiya Jimmy, are you going to take some photos and send us them, happy days eh!

Billy and Alan are well jealous"

"Sarah, is that what you wanted to tell me"

"Ok, ok. We have recovered an email from Josh to a Maddison at a company address website arranging a meet after he landed in Los Angeles. They were to meet at a seafood restaurant in Santa Monica but there's been nowt since then. We are presuming Maddison is a woman"

"So, he is still alive"

"Well he was then. We are going through the protocol of investigating Maddison as much as we can before we or the U.S. cops contact her"

"That's something I suppose. Have you asked his parents?"

"No Jimmy we wanted to know a bit more before we did"

"He was quick enough to contact the Boss about Jessica flying to Panama"

"The lads say she's a cracker, you've done well there mate, fancy car as well. I think Lauren is a bit upset though."

"No, eh really, you joking. I thought Lauren wasn't interested in men now."

"Not men Jimmy, a man. You know what I mean?"

"Sarah, I trust you, we go back a long way. I never arranged this, the flights, hotels anything. It's been done by Mr. Newton. I have not asked him to do it, in fact I have never spoken to the man."

"Jimmy is she stopping in the hotel with you as well?"

"Quiet Sarah. Can anybody hear you?"

"Just the boss"

"Awe shit. Sarah they're shouting for our next flight, sorry my next flight, I'll have to run. Keep up the good work, I will do the same. I will phone when I get to Panama City in meantime if anything comes in pass it to the liaison officer in Panama.

CHAPTER 10

Saturday 14th May

Paco made a call to the farm. "Do not let the two new girls start work with the workers until we arrive. Let the workers wait. No one is to touch the girls. No one"

Susanna and Maria were waiting in the two rooms either side of the hallway in an old farm building on the edge of the jungle. They were the only residents in this building. It was one of six buildings used by the many farmer workers for shared living accommodation. Each of the girl's rooms had a large bed covered in brown sheets with stains, lots of stains, there was a small mirror on the wall, a water pitcher and hand bowl. It was an old building with red tiled floors which had not been brushed and washed for several days. There was only one door to the front of the building. All of the windows had elaborate fancy metal bars, allegedly to stop people breaking in, the windows had light drapes to create some shade. There was a ceiling fan over the beds in the two rooms. There was a large fan in the hallway where the Jefa (*boss lady*) sat in an overly large chair next to an oblong wooden table which was waist high in the middle of the room. Another door led into the basic shower room and toilet. It was her who answered the call from Paco.

There were now seven workers sitting in the shade outside of the building. An hour had passed since the call and the workers were getting frustrated, especially as they knew the service was free. The queue was growing.

A large white 4X4 luxury Toyota stopped outside of the building. The Jefa immediately opened the rear nearside door then ran around and opened the other rear door. A large man in a dark suit holding a semi-automatic weapon got out of the front of the car, the driver remained in his seat. They surveyed the area before Paco and Borja got out of the vehicle. They entered the hall of the building and the door was closed behind them.

The Jefa had clean glasses and fresh cold water in bottles from her fridge which she gave to her VIP's.

Paco went into the room of Susanna, Borja went into the room of Maria, the doors were closed behind them. The farmers were moved in to the shade 50 metres from the building, but they stayed in the line that was formed.

The two men were about to make a physical statement of power and control by fear.

Paco slowly took his trousers off, then sat on the bed. He didn't speak. Susanna got on her knees in front of him and started to masturbate him, he was quickly aroused and erect. He had no thought of giving pleasure to anyone. He stopped Susanna and indicated that she should kneel on the bed. He dragged her backwards towards the edge of the bed, lifted her cotton skirt over her back and pulled her close to him. He entered her with force and gave himself pleasure for a few moments before he released inside her. He washed himself with the fresh water in the hand bowl, he dressed and walked out of the room into the hall without speaking to Susanna.

Borja had instructed Maria to take all her clothes off with a wave of his hand. She lay on her back on the bed. Borja removed his trousers and sat on top of her across her waist, Maria gently touched his penis until it was erect and masturbated him for a few minutes. He stopped her and ordered her to get on her hands and knees in front of him. He had forceful sex briefly before ejaculating inside her. Maria collapsed onto the bed and wanted to cry but stifled her pain and anger. Borja cleansed himself with the fresh water using the hand bowl before he walked out of the room into the hall.

They were both offered more of the fresh drinking water which they accepted graciously. They dismissed the Jefa to the outside of the building and asked her to close the door behind her.

Paco called for Susanna and Maria to come to the hall. They both entered the hall from their rooms simultaneously. Borja placed a 15cm double-bladed knife in the middle of the dark wooden table in the hall. Borja stood at one end of the oblong table, Paco standing at the opposite end. Paco instructed Susanna and Maria to come and stand at the sides of the table facing their rooms.

Paco looked at the two women. "Ladies this is your life now, you know that. You have cost lives but most of all you have cost Manolo millions of dollars. How can you fix this? We now both know you can fuck and give pleasure to a man, even if you don't want to. We want to know; can you kill a man if we tell you to? Susanna show me how you would use that killing knife."

Susanna slowly picked the knife up by the handle with her right hand and twisted her wrist showing the blade to Paco and Borja then jabbed the knife quickly forward on three occasions. She then put the knife back in the middle of the table with the handle towards Maria.

Paco asked" Maria, show us how you could kill with the knife". Maria reached for the knife with her right hand and took a firm grip on the handle. She then quickly grabbed Susanna by her long hair and pulled her backwards and down onto the table with her facing the ceiling and instantly stabbed her in the throat and then the middle of her chest on two occasions. Dark blood poured from the throat wound down onto the table and seeped from the chest wounds through her flimsy white loose top. Maria let go of her friends' hair and looked down at her face as she lay motionless on her back on the table for a few seconds then slid onto the floor with her head cracking a floor tile. Maria placed the bloodied knife on the table. Susanna was staring directly up at Maria.

Maria bent down to her friend and said quietly, "Goodbye my friend no more pain" She was fighting to stop the tears and shaking.

Susanna was unable to move and dying, it would very soon be over. The Jefa had some work to do in the hall but the body would be taken care off.

Paco" That was good, and very quick but we want you to do it our way. Do you think you can?"

Maria "Yes of course" she said confidently, as if it was an everyday occurrence.

"If you do this there will be no more work here for you. You will be well rewarded. Did you have sex with the gringos in any hotel anyone of them?"

"No, the blonde gringo didn't want to have sex I think he is a gay boy."

"Could you get the other boy to have sex with you?"

"Of course, he is a stallion, so I was told, who can he fuck now? Me"

"We will make the plans; we will get your passport and travel. First we want to see you kill a man our way"

They called for the Jefa. She entered the room and upon seeing the bloodied mess closed the door immediately behind her. Borja addressed her, "We apologise for this mess, you will be well paid to clean it up and keep your tongue fastened. Is there a man in the queue you do not like, just name him and we will do you a favour. You might have to clean up again so we will give you more for your troubles."

The Jefa identified one of the farmers, a big man, strong arms." He is a pig, his breath stinks and he roughly abuses the girls. I call him El Cerdo, *(The pig)* all the girls call him El Cerdo."

The Jefa started cleaning the hall, it had never been that clean. The body was dragged into Susanna's room.

Paco told Maria precisely what she had to do with El Cerdo.

Paco and Borja went into the room with the body of Susanna and closed the door.

El Cerdo was ushered to the front of the line and directed into the room of Maria. Maria looked at him, he was a big man but do as they say it should be easy. She had to do this. He picked Maria up and threw her onto the bed he kicked his soil covered sandals off and took his filthy trousers and vest off, his body odour was disgusting. Maria immediately took hold of his penis and pushed him onto his back. He was a strong man with big legs and arms. She was massaging his penis, he was relaxing and laughing. She slowly moved her body around his side and sat on his chest her back to his face, he began to enjoy this new experience. Her legs were now over his arms, he was wrapped up. She took the knife from the new cut in the side of the mattress and while still giving him pleasure, she completely sliced through the base of his penis with the razor-sharp blade. The bright blood spurted upwards towards the ceiling and sprayed in all directions from the wound. She was immediately covered in his warm sticky blood down her face body arms and legs. She threw his penis onto the floor and pushed back and down onto the head of El Cerdo who was attempting to push her off with his strong neck muscles and then one swift stab into his heart, and then another. He struggled for a few seconds then collapsed open mouthed not knowing what had happened. Paco and Borja walked into the room and looked at El Cerdo and Maria, both covered in blood and the blood spattered walls, floor and ceiling. Borja said "Not quite perfect. You need to listen. Good result".

Paco "You need to get cleaned up you are coming with us now."

Twenty five minutes later, Maria Luiza Valencia, was sat in the back of a black Toyota 4x4 behind two protectors, they were both large men who didn't speak or look in her direction apart from the occasional glance in the mirror by the driver. They were following the white vehicle which contained Paco and Borja. The vehicle was cooled by the air conditioning from the external high heat of the day. She had been showered at length. She had washed her hair four times to get rid of the sticking blood from the butchered El Cerdo. She had cleaned her nails to remove any trace of his blood, she examined the nails again but they were still not clean. She was wearing a fragrant spray and deodorant and yet her nostrils were full of the stench of El Cerdo.

Who am I, what have I just done? I am 28 years old; I am an intelligent young woman. I have had loving parents, brother and sister. I have had many good friends as a kid, in school, University. I enjoy life and living, having fun and laughing. I have had sex with 2 young men, one at University and one in my home town of Buenaventura. I can remember both of them fondly. I have been taught how to defend myself and how to use a knife but I have never been in a fight in my life. Who is this person that has stabbed my best friend Susanna 3 times, slicing her throat, punching a dagger into her heart twice? Who is the woman who was sodomised by an old Colombian drug master, which hurt so much, the first man to take me as he wanted against my wishes? I hate that man. I want to kill that man, sometime his time will come. Why am I thinking about killing? I've just killed a man I don't know because Paco and Borja said I had to in a way they wanted me too. What more do I have to do? How many more do I have to kill? Will I ever be free? I will kill Borja sometime. He will suffer, I promise Susanna, and Paco will follow. Will I be killed? Probably. She nodded her head.

CHAPTER 11

Thursday 19th May

The camp fire was lit, the volunteers were leaving their tents and traditional round Indian huts made from sturdy tree branches, interwoven and covered in a mixture of large bark strips and animal hides. They were starting to congregate around the fire. Josh had showered in the improvised outdoor bucket shower and felt fresh and clean but he was still aching from the ten hours of physical work completed during the day. He had felt challenged today. The large timber construction of a bridge without any hydraulics or lifting gear. It was down to the basic brute strength of the number of volunteers and speed of others placing the blocking timbers. This was history being used again, just like centuries before. True, the bridge could not withstand 20-ton vehicles passing over, people, horses, carriages but now even a heavy 4x4 would safely cross the bridge.

A large cast iron pot was in place over the fire and the smell of cooking food was so good. Rabbit, beans and vegetables anything that could be gathered or hunted. There was also fresh cornbread on the flat plate. His diet was varied, deer, salmon, trout even green chilli. He would have liked a cold beer or even a coke. What he really missed was his mobile phone and contact with Maddison. He hoped that she was thinking of him and missing him as much. It was stupid, they didn't really know each other, his thoughts were interrupted as he was nudged on the arm and passed a bowl of piping hot rabbit stew. Just five more days and the project would be finished. He was enjoying the work, the experience, the people, he would have stayed longer had he not met up with Maddison. Now he had something to leave for, he hoped. The stew was good.

The next morning Maddison was sat at her workplace, a clean desk space with a large Apple screen in the middle of her desk. It was a large open office but there was a sufficient distance between each desk for each employee to feel they had their own space and not cramped but not too close to have a conversation. The office was on the ninth floor, with floor to ceiling glass exterior. The air-conditioning kept a healthy 18.5-degree temperature. There were twenty people working in the office, some wearing headphones and talking to clients on the telephone, some working on spreadsheets, some typing emails and other documents.

Maddison was formulating a flow chart for her Central American clients and colleagues. Her phone rang and she picked up the call. It was the floor leader.

"Hi Maddison can you come to my office please?"

She finished off the document and saved it onto the server. She stood up and straightened her navy knee length skirt and white blouse and walked to the office. The office had a glass front as was the theme of the office, everything visible. The floor leader Dwayne was sat at his chair and another man was sat facing him. As she walked to the door Dwayne waved her to enter the office. She opened the door and entered.

Dwayne, "HI Maddison can you close the door please?

"Yes. Sure"

Dwayne was mid-thirties, knew more than most about the company they worked for, a very friendly man and an excellent manager. He had a permanent smile.

"Maddison can I introduce you to Officer Simons from the police department, there is nothing for you to worry about. He needs your help to trace someone and that is all I know. If you don't need me, I will leave and let you two have a chat. Is that OK? I won't be too far away, maybe in the coffee room."

Maddison was puzzled by the visit, "Yes that's ok, I hope I can help"

Officer Greg Simons stood up and shook Maddison by the hand. Not too firm. Greg was in his early forties, shaven headed, smooth dark brown skin with an infectious smile. He was 1.88m tall and stocky, African American, his polite manner was ideal for the role of liaison officer. He was wearing a brown jacket, light-coloured trousers and brown brogues. A white shirt and cream and brown striped tie.

"Please take a seat Maddison"

They sat facing each other on the two leather chairs on the opposite side of Dwayne's desk. The officer took his wallet out and showed his I.D. to Maddison.

"To the point, do you know an Englishman by the name of Josh Newton?"

"Is he ok, yes I do."

"I hope so, that's why I'm here. Do you know where he is now?"

"No, not exactly, not really, no I don't"

"How do you know this man?"

"I was returning from an appointment in Panama City and he sat next to me on the flight"

"Is that the only time you have met?"

"Why do you want to find him?"

"We think he might be in danger. He is not a threat to you or anybody here that we know of. He might have got caught up in something he doesn't even know about"

"Is he a bad guy?"

"No, not at all but we need to find him. Have you met him or been in contact with him since the flight?"

"Yes, we met up in Santa Monica. He's really a nice guy"

"Have you spoke since?"

"No. Josh was going to do some volunteer work on a native Indian reservation in the mountains and he didn't have any access to a phone or internet"

"Is he going to get in contact with you at some time, soon?"

"Yes, he would contact me when he left the reservation and we were going to meet up."

"Did he mention his travel partner, Filipe at all?"

"Yes, he told me that they had travelled through Central America together and then split after travelling through the Panama Canal."

"What was the reason for the split?"

"As far as I know they were always going to split, so Josh

could do his work with the native Indians and then travel to New Zealand for his sister's wedding"

"What did Filipe do, did Josh say?"

"He did mention that when they split in Panama City, Filipe had booked a flight to Aruba to hopefully meet up with a Colombian girl that they had met on the canal cruise. She was on a cruise holiday from the canal to the island and he hoped to meet her as she left the cruise"

"Do you know if he met up with the girl or if he got a flight?

"Josh told me that Filipe had got the flight a few hours before Josh got on our flight. I don't know anything else about Filipe after that."

"Did he mention the name of the girl or the name of the cruise ship?"

"Not that I can recall. But it did leave Colon to go to Aruba the day we all got flights from Panama City"

"Do you know of any form of communication between Filipe and Josh since that time?"

"No. There might have been but Josh never mentioned anything to me. Is Josh in danger or trouble?"

"I have been asked by the English police to visit and ascertain what you know about Josh and Filipe. At the moment it is their enquiry. From what you have told me, Josh has not been with or seen Filipe since Panama, so I can't think that he would be in any trouble from the law. He might be able to give some information to assist with their enquiries. I may have to get back in touch with you if that's ok?"

"Yes, that's fine with me"

"Do you have any idea where Josh was going to do the voluntary work? Did he mention a tribe, location anything that might help find him?"

"No. I'm sorry. Have you tried locating his cell phone before it was switched off?"

"I haven't but I'm sure the English bobby's will be working on that one"

"If you get the authority I could maybe help with our new

systems."

"I will mention that in my report. "

He handed Maddison his contact card. "Please get in contact with me or ask Josh to get in contact with me as soon as he gets in touch with you. It is very important."

"I'm guessing something bad has happened to Filipe. Josh couldn't have anything to do with it. He hasn't seen him since Panama airport"

"I can't say Maddison, just ask him to get in touch with me or go to a police building near where he is as soon as he can."

Officer Simons stood up from the chair at the same time as Maddison. He again shook her hand gently "Thanks for the help Maddison. I'm sure Josh will be ok. I apologise for the intrusion in your office."

"Where in England is the enquiry from?"

"City of Newcastle Major Crime unit"

The officer spoke to Dwayne and shook his hand then left the floor.

Dwayne walked back into his office. Maddison was still sitting in the chair and faced Dwayne.

"Do you need to get away, take some time off. The officer didn't tell me the nature of his business. Are you ok?"

"I might need to take some time, but not now. I have things to do, occupy my mind. I will continue on the cell tracking project if that's ok?"

"Yes, that would be good if your head is clear and have no distractions. Are you sure you want to be here?"

"I'm sure. Thanks Dwayne."

Maddison returned to her desk.

Officer Simons returned to his office in the Police Headquarters on Olympic Drive in Santa Monica. He poured himself a coffee from the machine in the kitchen area and made his way to his desk. He acknowledged two fellow officers who sat at desks near to his. He took off his jacket, his side arm was in the holster under his left arm, and opened his portfolio. It was now 10:40. He picked up his desk telephone and pressed in the dialling code for the UK then checking the email the remaining numbers and waited for the answer.

"Hello, Newcastle Major Crime Team, Sarah speaking how can I help you?"

"Hi, I'm Officer Simons from the Santa Monica Police Department, California, USA."

The American accent quickly registered with Sarah.

"Well hi Officer Simons, what's your first name?"

"Greg Maam"

"Hiya Greg, I take it you've been doing an enquiry for us about Josh Newton with Maddison?"

"Yes, that's correct Maam."

"Just call is Sarah, I'm not your mam. How did you get on?"

"Hi Sarah, what is your role in the department in regards to this enquiry?"

"Greg, I'm the lead intelligence and liaison operative in the Crime Team, that is how you have rung my telephone number. If you have a look at the email address you should see sarahcrimeteam. I sent the email to your Police department."

"Yes, I can see that Sarah, thank you for your patience"

"Well I'm all ears Greg." There was a pause. "I'm waiting to hear what you have to report."

"Yes, Sarah sorry, Are you English, Scottish it's just the accent?"

"Don't worry, we all talk different but it means the same doesn't it"

"Yes, I guess so. I have seen Maddison who is safe and well. She has met Josh, on a flight from Panama on the 9th May and met him once more at a restaurant in Santa Monica a couple of nights after the flight but she hasn't seen or heard from him since."

"That's a good start Greg. Do you know where he is now?"

"Apparently, he left the day after they last met, to work as a volunteer at a Native Indian Reservation as a volunteer for ten days or more. Apparently, he will not have use of modern technology, cell phone, email, social media for the duration he is there"

"Bollocks, sorry Greg. Can you go to the reservation and visit him, see if he is safe and if he is can he help with our investigation"?

"It's not that easy, Maddison didn't know which reservation or which tribe he was staying with"

"Do you need another email request or can you carry on our International cooperation?"

"I will talk with our Native Liaison officers and see if they can help. Not all tribes are one hundred per cent non-technology, process of elimination really."

"Did you ask Maddison about any information that Josh gave her about Filipe?"

"Yes, I did. Josh had told Maddison that Filipe had caught a flight to Aruba just a few hours before Josh caught his flight to Los Angeles from Panama City. Josh had told her that he was planning to meet a girl, lady, who was Colombian and they had met on the canal cruise and was going on a cruise ship to Aruba. He was going to surprise her when she arrived."

"Did she know the name of the lady or ship she was on?"

"No, she did not. I think she was more interested in knowing about Josh"

"That's great Greg. I really appreciate, the department really appreciate what you're doing. What's the time over there? Have you got time to write a short concise report and email the important bits back to me? I think I'll be going home in about an hour and it's stotting down."

"Which town did you say?"

"No, I meant, it's raining heavily and I will be leaving to go home soon."

"It's just going on lunch here Sarah. I will continue on with the request and if there is anything else, I will include it in the email"

"Thanks Greg you're a star. I will speak to you again no doubt"

The phone call was ended. Sarah had been writing down

notes as she was talking to the officer. She shouted to Andy who came to her desk and she passed on the information. The information was then filled into the occurrence log both paper and electronic. Andy then called the Boss and gave him the information.

It had been a productive day in the office.

Walter and his team had sourced the phone records of both Filipe and Josh.

Filipe had last used his mobile in Margarita, a call from an unknown number. He had also contacted the Hotel Imperial in Margarita.

Josh had used his phone in Santa Monica on Thursday 12th May. that was the last location

Lauren had been working on the travel and financial enquiries of Filipe and Josh.

Josh's financial enquiry revealed that he had used his credit card to pay for his flight from Panama City to Los Angeles. It was again used to hire a car from the airport. He used it further to book and pay for the 444 Boutique Hotel in Santa Monica and also at the Santa Monica Seafood restaurant. There had also been $400 withdrawn from an ATM at a bank in Santa Monica.

It was known that Filipe had taken cash out of a bank in Panama City but there were no more financial transactions or traces for transport.

Sarah had been preparing a time line, starting from the Canal trip from Panama City on Sunday 7th May and incorporating all known facts,places, movements, phone calls, hotels. There were too many gaps. Work to be done tomorrow.

There had been no money taken from either of the two accounts which would possibly explain a motive for Filipe's murder.

CHAPTER 12

Thursday 19th May.

It was just passing 18:00 when Steve and Jessica were leaving the baggage area of Panama City Tucuman airport. They had a dry flight from Atlanta just drinking soft drinks and coffee. They were both awake and alert. They had both freshened up on the plane prior to arrival.

It was decided that Steve would meet the liaison officer in the airport police office and later introduce Jessica. They were hoping for a lift to the hotel and an early night before commencing first thing in the morning.

Steve entered the police office leaving his case with Jessica who sat in a seat in the corridor with a view of the office door.

Steve walked to the empty reception desk inside the office. As he did so an internal door behind the desk opened and a tanned male, in his late forties, about 1.80 tall, wearing a dark blue suit, well groomed, slightly greying hair, approached the counter. He had a large smile on his face, "You must be James?" There was a notable Yorkshire accent.

"I take it you have been speaking to my boss. Yes, please call me Steve."

"And where is your undercover partner?" with a smile on his face.

"I don't want to get off on the wrong foot here, I don't mind a joke, taking the piss, that's what we police do. But I've only just met you, I've had a long flight and I'm tired. So, can we save the piss taking until tomorrow eh"

"Yes, sorry Steve. Ok."

"Ok. And you are?"

"Hi, I'm Martin Chapman. I'm one of the liaison team in this part of the world" He held out his hand and they shook hands firmly and politely.

Martin was now 49 and was in his final year of a three-year secondment to Panama in his role as liaison officer. This was his second secondment in Latin America having previously worked in Colombia for three years with a two-year stint back in London NCA sandwiched between the two roles. He spoke fluent Spanish which he had learnt from his time in Colombia as assistant to the liaison officer and security for the embassy staff. He was single, having been divorced ten years earlier, and enjoyed his life in South America. The weather, vibrant cities, lifestyle, cheap alcohol and beautiful women had been the major attraction. The job was paid well and the expenses payed for everything, well almost. Marty had bought himself a Pursuit OS 345 Offshore fishing boat with twin Yamaha V8 engines which he had moored in La Playita de Amador Marina, just over the causeway to Perico Island from Panama City. It was more luxurious, fitted with every need that he wanted and far better than his small fishing boat tied up in Whitby, on the Yorkshire coast. The fishing was for bigger and better species and cruising the warmer waters was so beneficial in many ways. He was planning on retiring in Panama next year and then spend more time onboard 'Pasion Del Mar', his Passion of the Sea, it held more appeal than Guisley and Yorkshire in winter.

"Right, now that we have met, how did you pull off this all-inclusive holiday for two, apparently the office is well jealous"

They both started to laugh.

Martin continued, "Seriously, there is quite a bit for you to catch up on and I want to start really early in the morning with a trip to the canal cruise site. I can give you the updates on route if you don't get them on your email account. I'm not expecting any sort of problems at the ferry site but at the same time I do not expect a great deal of information from the crew. It's the norm for over here."

Steve, "Have you started any enquiries over here?"

"No, I haven't to be honest. I haven't had anything to make enquiries about until a few hours ago when I got the updates from your office. Some very interesting stuff but I'll keep it till the morning. I'll take you and Jessica to your hotels; have a drink and sleep and I'll pick you up at 6:15. I will not be able to spend the day with you tomorrow, especially with Jessica being with you, it might be better for you both, you can enjoy the canal cruise. I expect to be busy in the office but I plan to finish early for the weekend."

"As it happens, we are booked in the same hotel but different rooms. It is a professional job by both of us. I'm investigating a murder and Jessica is gathering information about the safety of Josh Newton. She is not involved in my enquiry"

Martin looked into a television monitor where Jessica was centre screen sat on the bench seat then looked at Steve. "I have no problem with her coming tomorrow, as I say I can't see any problems at the site. But she cannot get involved, agreed."

"Agreed"

After introducing Martin to Jessica, the group took a lift to the lower ground floor where they got into a grey Chrysler Town and Country car. After a short drive, during which time, Martin gave a briefing on crime and the dangers in Panama and Latin America. They were dropped off at the doorway of the Radisson hotel in Panama City.

"Don't have nightmares, see you both at 6.15"

They were met by the concierge who placed their two suitcases onto a large trolley and then directed them to the hotel reception desk, they carried their own shoulder bags.

They each booked into the hotel for two nights and after having their passports checked, used separate credit cards for confirmation of payment.

Steve went to his room with the concierge who opened the door and placed the suitcase on a luggage table. He handed the concierge a $5 note who placed it into his trouser pocket, thanked Steve and then left the room. He sat on the bed and took the laptop out of the shoulder bag. After a short while, after accessing the hotel Wi-Fi, he was able to read the emails from the office. He showered and had a bottle of cold beer from the room fridge.

Jessica had also tipped the concierge $5. She had taken a small bottle of chilled wine out of the room fridge and poured it into a wine glass. She stripped off and took a warm and then cold shower. She wrapped herself in the extra-large and comfortable white hotel towel and lay on the bed.

Then the alarm sounded.

◆ ◆ ◆

Friday 20th May

Martin had gone to his office at 05:00 and immediately began searching through the information data base for any incidents on the canal cruise over the last six months. Nothing other than a few tourists having wallets or cameras stolen while left unattended. Any incidents reported from Hotel Andros in Colon. There were two reported robberies of tourists staying at the hotel but not at the hotel.

Steve and Jessica were sat in the breakfast room of the hotel having coffee with some fresh fruit and tortillas with scrambled egg when Martin walked in. Martin helped himself to a mug of black coffee and a banana and sat next to them at the table.

"Good morning hope you both slept well"

Steve, "Yes we did, in separate rooms. Are there any updates?"

"Nothing of note. I've done some enquiries this morning for places in Panama and found nothing."

Jessica " Is there anything I can do?"

Steve, "It's best you keep out of the way"

Martin, "I've been thinking about that. You're not a police officer so you're not bound by rules and regulations. Would you be amenable to travelling on your own but we'll keep a close eye on you?"

"I'm a grown woman you know."

"Yes, I can see that. That on its own can be dangerous. I have questions to ask in Spanish from the locals, we must ensure we don't cause the locals any problems and they us. We don't have any powers in this wonderful country. You were saying you speak Spanish, can you understand the dialect, it is sometimes better than in Spain itself."

"Yes, I can fluently, I studied languages before I went into the forces"

Steve, "You're ex forces. You didn't say?"

"You didn't need to know? I was an intelligence analyst"

"Where were you based?"

"Cyprus, Falklands, Afghanistan, Iraq and Lincoln"

"I was in Afghanistan in 2006, 45 Commando"

"I was in Helmand then"

Martin, "Sorry to interrupt the reunion but we do have work to go to"

They picked up their shoulder bags and walked towards the car parked outside of the main hotel door. They were all dressed casually, Martin and Steve wearing light coloured shirts with collar and cotton trousers. Jessica was wearing a plain turquoise T shirt and three-quarter length cream trousers.

Jessica got into a taxi waiting in the hotel taxi rank and in English asked the driver to take her to the canal cruise terminal.

Martin followed the taxi at a discreet distance.

When Jessica arrived at the cruise terminal, she noted it was similar in appearance to the one in the last known photo of Josh and Filipe. She paid the taxi driver in cash and gave him a tip. She was directed by the taxi driver towards the cruise ticket office.

"Hello, do you speak English?"

"Yes, off course."

"Great, can I have a ticket for today's cruise, the full day please"

"If you paying with a card or dollars it will be 150 or 140 English pounds"

"Yes please, my boyfriend did it a few weeks ago and told me I must do it"

"If you have a look in the bar area you might see his photo of recent passengers"

"That's great can I pay in English please"

Jessica passed her the card and received her ticket and boarding card. She made her way to the gantry of the MV 'Reina del Canal'. She showed her boarding card to the crew member and boarded the ship. She noticed that there were CCTV cameras installed looking down onto the gantry entry and exit positions. She made her way to the refreshment area and took a free orange fruit juice.

Martin was accompanied by a Panamanian police officer who was in uniform in the front of the car. Steve was a rear seat passenger.

Martin with Steve and the officer approached the entrance to the gantry. They spoke to one of the crew who radioed a message to the ships control. After a short wait one of the vessels officers came down the gantry and spoke to the officers. He invited, the three on board and into the refreshment area where he offered them a cooling drink.

After an introduction by the Panama police officer, Martin spoke in Spanish to the officer.

"We are trying to trace two Englishmen who we know travelled on this vessel on Sunday May 8th. We know they both got off the vessel in Colon. There is nothing to suggest that anything untoward happened on this vessel. We would like to know if they possibly met someone on the cruise and if you have any CCTV or photographs of the passengers. Possibly if any crew member can remember them."

"I can get you a copy of the CCTV we have if it's any good. I'll get it prepared for you. Do you have photographs of the men?"

Martin showed him the photograph of Josh and Filipe standing in front of the vessel the day they did the cruise.

"I don't know them but I am up on the bridge. The other deck hands and bar restaurant staff might remember them. We are leaving in five minutes. You can have a free cruise if you want but we cannot miss our slot in the canal"

"Steve will stay with you if that's ok. I must leave with the police officer. I will collect him in Colon if that's ok?"

"Do you speak Spanish Steve?"

"No, I'm sorry Sir"

"Yes, I will help with Steve no problem. I will see you in Colon, can you please leave now. I have things to do now I will ask someone to come and help you ok"

The last of the passengers were on board and as soon as Martin and the officer had left the vessel the ropes were cast off and the vessel drifted away from the mooring.

Steve stayed in the refreshment area near to Jessica but they never acknowledged each other's presence. The room was full of activity with passengers getting drinks and snacks, whilst the safety announcements were being made. It was not a good time to talk to the crew they all appeared to be very busy.

CHAPTER 13

Friday 20th May

It was 3pm and Sarah was sat at her computer running links to known places in the enquiry. A can of cola sitting on top of an NUFC coaster. Her desk phone rang.

"Hello, Newcastle Major Crime Team, Sarah speaking how can I help you?"

"Hi, my name is Maddison Roberts"

Sarah recognised the American accent

"Eee, hello Maddison how are you? It's lovely to speak to you"

"Hi, I'm ok thank you."

"I was just talking to Officer Simons yesterday and he told me you are a lovely lady"

"Well thank you Sarah, Greg is a nice guy."

"He sounds a lovely fella. How can I help you, what do you want Maddison?"

"I'm concerned about Josh, is he ok, I don't know if you can tell me but is he a bad criminal that's wanted, I'm worried, I like him"

"No, not at all Maddison he's a lovely lad. We just want to make sure he is safe. Something has happened that I cannot tell you about it, we don't believe that Josh had anything to do with that. We just need to make sure he is safe."

"Ok that's good. I may be able to help. Can I ask do you have to give out information where you get information from?"

"That depends, not all the time and not if it could cause grief to the informant if known. Do you have something?"

"The last sighting location for the cell phone used by Josh is on Lynn Road, that is L Y N N Road. Which is near to Thousand Oaks in California to the North of Los Angeles. There is a native Indian reservation there from the Satwiwa tribe. S A T W I W A"

Sarah was writing down the message as Maddison was saying it

"How do you know this Maddison?"

"It's a development research that I'm working on for my company. Let's just say I ran a trial"

"That's fantastic Maddison, thanks very much, why did you not just call officer Simons?"

"There are legal implications about that kind of stuff"

"Yes, I'm sure there is. Just a lucky guess I suppose, Greg might have it written down somewhere as well. Thanks Maddison I'll set the wheels in motion. Anything else we can help each other with?"

"No, thanks for your help Sarah, please find Josh?

"Well, we have a head start now. I'll let you go now and I will get things going. It's been lovely talking to you. Have a nice day now, cheerio."

"Andy, I've just spoke to the girl in America, Maddison Roberts she has given us a possible location for Josh".

Lauren, "I've got something as well that looks very interesting"

Andy, "I'll speak to the boss and see if he wants a meet"

Andy went into the boss's office and walked straight out, "Get everybody here in thirty minutes for a briefing. If you can both tighten up what you've got and we'll have a run through the lot. Sarah phone Jimmy see if he's got anything for the briefing. Anybody for a cake or sandwich from the bakers? When the lads come in get them to make a pot of tea and better tell Walter."

Andy disappeared to the bakers.

Lauren telephoned Alan and told him to both get back in twenty minutes. She then wrote down her report on her new information.

Sarah made a call to Steve. It took quite a while to connect and ring then Steve answered.

"Hi Steve here"

"Hiya Jimmy it's Sarah how you doing?"

"I'm fine, I'm on the canal cruiser attempting to ask the

crew questions about Filipe and Josh but not getting much joy at the minute"

"That's good, I just hope you have the right boat. How long have you got before it leaves?"

"It's left Sarah, I'm stuck on board. I don't think I will be able to ask any questions until after we get through the locks. The crew are too busy"

"Is Jessica with you on the boat, you're having a canny time?"

"No, she isn't." He lied. "This is a police enquiry. She will not be asking any questions. Is there any more info come in?"

"We're just about to have an update but it looks like Josh is ok on some red Indian reservation in Cali-for-nia. Do you know that Filipe is supposed to have met a Latino lass on the canal boat?"

"No, that's the first I've heard. It's not on the emails."

"It was on the briefing note I sent to the liaison officer late last night"

"Why didn't I get the email?"

"I thought he would have shared the information with you when he saw you. Sorry Jimmy my fault"

"Yes, its ok. I'm pleased you mentioned it though. Anything else significant he might not have told me?"

"The boss is having a briefing in about twenty minutes. Can I phone you later?"

"Yes Sarah, even if there's nowt, I want to know. There's just been a little mix up this morning. I thought I had the latest updates."

"Will do. What's the trip like, is it bonny and sunny? How's Jessica?"

"Everything is lovely, sunny and hot. Jessica is ok I'm sure. Phone me later ok." Steve ended the call.

Andy had returned with a selection of sandwiches and cakes. The lads came in and had a bag with two pasties each. There was a large tin of biscuits placed in the middle of the briefing table, Walter had put the kettle on and was making a large pot of tea and two coffees for the boss and Lauren. Sarah and Lauren were still writing up their updates at their desks, Andy had placed a pile of A4 paper on the table. They began to take their seats around the table as Walter poured the tea into pots and passed them to the appropriate person, one coffee was given to Lauren and the other coffee was placed in front of the boss's chair. Each had their own cake or sandwich on a sheet of A4, the lads were eating their pasties from inside the bag so not to drop crumbs on the table. Walter had a handful of biscuits; a custard slice was put next to the boss's coffee.

The boss was wearing an open collar shirt and had removed his tie, having returned from a meeting at HQ.

He took his seat. "Carry on with your cakes and pasties, I'll pay for the them Andy. Right, I do believe we have some updates. What I would like to do is start from the beginning and see if we can fill in the missing bits. If you have something relevant just shout up ok. Andy do you want to start or Sarah?" The boss started on his custard slice.

Andy, "I'll start. The enquiry is concerning two men Filipe Lopez 24 and Josh Newton 25. Filipe is from up here in the town and Josh is from Alderley Edge in Cheshire. They are both from reasonably wealthy families and have no criminal convictions. They met at Newcastle University, became friends and had planned this holiday touring Central America when they were at the Uni together. They were then going to split up with Josh travelling to the USA to do some volunteer work at a native reservation, Sarah I believe has something on that for later. Filipe was going to continue into South America visiting special sites and some beaches. They were then going to travel to New Zealand for the marriage of Josh's sister." He took a drink of tea from his mug. Just a plain white mug with Andy hand written in large capitals in red marker pen. "The last photo we have of them is when they boarded a Panama Canal cruise vessel, the 'Reina del Canal'. Jimmy is on board the vessel now attempting to ask the crew some questions. Sarah has established that

Filipe met a lady of Latin American appearance on the trip, that he was planning to meet in Aruba when she docked there three days later. It would be interesting to get a photo of this lady and identify her. Lauren you have something to share."

"There was only one cruise ship that sailed from Colon to Aruba on the 9th May. That's also the day that Filipe caught a flight to Aruba and Josh got his flight to Los Angeles. The ship was the 'Alisios'. I've done a search on 'Alisios' and it made news in Florida, when two passengers were murdered by a Colombian drug cartel in a warehouse unit in Fort Lauderdale, shortly after they had disembarked. They had been observed by the DEA who had information on the route used by a cartel. They were under surveillance, which ended up with 5 bad guys being shot and killed in a shoot-out at the premises. No police officers were injured. A substantial amount of high purity cocaine was recovered in the suitcases of the two named passengers. I haven't confirmed this information with the DEA as yet."

Boss, "Good stuff Lauren, my office when we've finished. Continue"

Andy, "We know that Josh met Maddison Roberts on the flight to L.A. He hired a car, stayed in a hotel in Santa Monica. He had an evening with Maddison at a restaurant in Santa Monica and then went to the reservation. Sarah"

Sarah," I have spoken to Officer Simons of Santa Monica Police department and he located Maddison at her work place in Santa Monica. It was Maddison that informed the officer that during discussion with Josh he had told her that Filipe had met the girl and was going to Aruba to meet her. I got a phone call today from Maddison herself. She is doing some work on cell site recognition for her company. She has used her research to possibly identify the native reservation as the Satwiwa tribe reservation near to Lynn Road near Thousand Oaks in California, not too far from L.A. I have not pushed this further yet"

Boss, "Likewise see me after this meeting"

Andy," We have not traced any hotels for Filipe in Aruba as yet, there are no financial transactions, likewise in Margarita, or flights purchased with a card or accommodation. We do know he was using his mobile phone in Aruba to make and receive calls from a number we can't identify. We know that he did call The Imperial Hotel in Porlamar on the Island of Margarita"

Walter," One of my lads has been looking on Social media sites and Trip Advisor and unless The Imperial has had a facelift it is definitely not the hotel where Filipe was murdered. The furnishings are totally different. We know which one it isn't so I've got three of them looking at other hotels in that area to try and identify which one is most likely."

Boss, "Good work Walter pass my comments onto the lads."

Andy," The last call Filipe received was on Margarita Island at 21:42 on Sunday 15th. The last message was the WhatsApp message to the Lopez family on Monday 16th from Caracas in Venezuela. I think we can assume that Filipe was murdered by a female between those times. We still have no motive, no body, or weapon. The suspect is a female with dark hair, Latino coloured skin if I can say that, and looks fit."

Boss "Some good work done there team. Anything to add lads?"

Billy, "No boss. We are continually checking the mates of Josh but there is still no contact or extra information."

Boss, "Very interesting about the DEA involvement and a cartel that could explain things but where is the link. Sarah can you contact the Santa Monica officer and give him the information of Josh's location. We need that acted upon urgently to make sure Josh is safe and hopefully get more information. Do that now. Walter keep the lads at it, they're doing a great job. Lads stay in the office I might need you, Andy, Lauren we will go into my office"

They entered the office and closed the door. The boss gave Andy a ten-pound note," Keep the change for the office kitty. Right pick your seat. Like I said Lauren, that's good work and hopefully it will be something. So how do we extend this enquiry at speed. I want a passenger list from the Cruise ship especially those joining the cruise at Colon and departing at Aruba.

Did the two murdered passengers get on at Colon or Aruba. Get the lads onto that, it might be easier if they liaise with NCA but try the company straightaway and we might get away with a few nice emails. Any problems let me know. We need to liaise with DEA in Fort Lauderdale to get the truth about what happened not the paper's version. Again, NCA might be the go-to agency but no harm trying ourselves first, speed is of the essence. Lauren find the relevant office telephone numbers in the police almanac and I will give them a ring initially, if you can be the liaison officer after. Andy ask Sarah to contact Martin Chapman in Panama and the other liaison officers to see if he or his colleagues have anything of use and pass on all of the updates we have on Josh. Andy you make a call to Steve about 7.45 for any updates and give him anything we have. Office closes at 8 drinks at 8.15, if we are done. That's it, get cracking."

CHAPTER 14

Friday 20th May

They had been on the 'Reina del Canal' for an hour and Steve and Jessica had not acknowledged each other. They had both made a tour of the decks of the small vessel and had found nothing of help in their investigation.

Jessica had taken a seat on the bar deck with a view over the canal. She was regularly approached by the waiters bringing soft drinks and fresh fruit. She made no attempt to speak Spanish and gave no impression that she understood the language. She smiled and encouraged their interaction.

Steve was approached by an officer of the vessel just as they were approaching The Miraflores locks. The officer introduced himself to Steve. He gave his name as Alvaro. He spoke good English and apologised for the length of time it had taken to come and help him. They shook hands. Alvaro gave Steve a DVD disk from the CCTV system which he had downloaded, it's what we have I don't know if it's any good. Steve placed it inside his shoulder bag. Steve explained he was attempting to trace two Englishmen who had gone missing after visiting Panama. The last known location was on board this vessel and then disembarking in Colon. He was wanting to speak to the crew to gather any information about anyone they might have met on the vessel, if they were involved in any disturbance on the vessel. Steve took an A4 size photograph of the two from his shoulder bag. Filipe and Josh were standing in front of the vessel at the dock in Panama City. Alvaro did not recognize Josh or Filipe but he spent most of his time in the bridge.

Alvaro then accompanied Steve around the vessel and stopped at each one of the crew, Alvaro spoke to each one in Spanish. He always got the same reply. "No" and a shake of the head.

After fifteen minutes Steve and Alvaro entered the refreshment area and approached a waiter near to Jessica. Alvaro spoke to the waiter, "This is an English policeman, he wants to know if you have seen the two English men in the photo, if they met anybody. It's very easy to say no and continue in your work if you understand. Have a good look and say no." The waiter took the photograph and had a look and like the other crew said "No". Jessica overheard the conversation. They then approached the other waiter in the area and the same conversation was repeated with the same answer, "No".

After Alvaro and Steve had left the refreshment area the two waiters stood close to each other and within earshot of Jessica they discussed having served the two men who were with those two Colombian good-looking fun girls on the front seats of the vessel. One said that he had taken a photograph of the four of them with the dark-haired man's camera. It was better not to get involved.

After another ten minutes, Steve returned to the refreshment area and poured himself a cool pineapple juice and took a plate of savoury snacks. He took a seat with a view of the magnificent industrial locks. He received a text on his phone.

JESSICA   officer not helpful told crew to say no. the 2 waiters served both with two Colombian girls. 1 took a photo of them all. They will say nothing. When we getting off.

Steve replied: I had feeling good job I will phone Martin.

Steve then made a call to Martin Chapman.

"Hi Steve. You enjoying your trip, some nice views. Any good"

"Basically, one of the officers took me around the crew, spoke to them in Spanish and told them to say nothing"

"Yep, that's about the norm"

"But Jessica overheard his conversation and then heard two waiters discussing having seen them on the vessel with two Colombian girls. Good looking apparently."

"Two, that's interesting." He lied. "There have been some developments they will be on your emails. You need to get off the trip at Gamboa. I'm off for the weekend, out on my boat, but an officer will be waiting for you or one of the staff will be there.

Just enjoy the downtime. You're going to be busy"

Steve sent a text to Jessica "Gamboa. c u away from the boat"

They both continued on the cruise acting ignorant of each other's presence and enjoying the views of the canal.

Martin was at his desk with the aircon in the office making the room comfortable against the external heat. His office was within the British Embassy on the fourth floor of Humboldt Tower, in Panama City. It was a modern office, he had received a call from Sarah with the full current update and was actively chasing up enquiries and committing some items to his memory. An email would follow. Martin had confirmed that Filipe was on the flight list from Panama City airport to Aruba Reina Beatrix International Airport on Monday 9th May A further search revealed he had left Aruba on a flight to Margarita Island, Porlamar airport on Saturday 15th May. He took a mobile phone out of his middle drawer and switched it on. Making sure there was no one in earshot he made a brief call.

◆ ◆ ◆

Officer Simons was driving down Lynn road towards the entrance to the Satwiwa Native American Indian Culture Centre. He slowed his unmarked vehicle as he drove onto the dirt track that was the road towards the car park. This was adjacent to the timber building of the reception centre. He got out of the car and took his jacket off the rear seat and put in on, straightening the back. He collected his black leather portfolio. He closed the car doors and walked to the reception centre.

There were no public in the centre and he made his way to the reception desk.

A young native American Indian lady dressed in traditional clothing sat behind the desk. Officer Simons showed his Identification badge and introduced himself. "I would like to speak to the person in charge of the Centre if possible, quite quickly"

"Yes Officer, can I say why?

"No, but it is an urgent matter that needs dealing with now.

"I will contact the Chief now; he is not in his office"

"Will this take long?"

"Not now, we use radios not smoke signals". She gave a smiling smirk.

"Sorry, it's just, urgent"

"She picked up the radio and relayed the message and took the reply"

"If you want to have a look around the exhibits, he will be here in 10 minutes"

"Yes, thank you I will"

After 25 minutes a brown MPV stopped outside the front of the reception area. A tall native male with black and slightly greying hair tied back in a pony tail and wearing a brown leather native style pullover top and trousers got out of the vehicle. He walked in to the centre and straight to the reception desk, he handed some paperwork to the receptionist and he was then directed towards Officer Simons.

He walked to the officer and they shook hands." Would you please come into the office? Would you like a drink, you must be thirsty after your wait"

"Thank you, coffee please, black"

The receptionist nodded and they walked into an office adjoining the reception desk. They both took a seat. The chief sat behind his plain empty desk with a view out onto the mountainous park. Officer Simons sat facing the Chief.

"I am the chief of the National Park, our land, The Satwiwa. Forgetting politics, please call me John. And you are?"

"I am Officer Simons, Greg Simons from Santa Monica Police Department"

"That's the formalities done. What brings you here, we don't get many police officers visiting other than on our request?"

"It's an urgent enquiry from the police in England."

"England, it must involve Josh I presume"

"Why do you say that?"

"He is the only English person here. Is he in trouble?"

"No, not at all. There is a concern for his safety"

"I can assure you he is very safe and has been all the time he has been here."

"There is no thought of him being in danger here. It's from outside, from other, uhm, groups shall we say."

"Is he taking refuge here and putting our members at risk?"

"No, he doesn't know he is in danger."

The receptionist brought in two black coffees. There was silence until she left the room.

"I need to see Josh to speak to him and hopefully clarify a few issues. He is not going to be taken away from here unless he wishes to go or agrees to go."

"Drink your coffee and I'll get it arranged. It will take him a short time to get here." The chief left the office and spoke to the receptionist and returned to the office. "OK, Greg did you play football?" The two sat and talked football for about 35 minutes.

There was a knock on the door and the receptionist guided Josh in to meet the two men.

Chief, "How Josh"

"How Chief"

"Josh this is Officer Simons from Santa Monica Police Department. He needs to speak to you; he says in private. You can do so in this office; I will be in the reception area if you need me"

"Yes, thank you that's ok."

The chief left the office. "Hi Josh I'm officer Greg Simons. I have some information that you need to know and I need to ask you some questions"

"Am I in some sort of trouble, do I need a solicitor, lawyer?"

"No. Please take a seat." Josh sat down.

"Your friend Filipe, has been murdered. Are you aware?"

Josh sat open mouthed looking at the officer taking in what had been said," No, no. When?"

"It's believed between the 15th and 18th"

"Where?"

"It's believed in Margarita. He was stabbed by a young Latino woman"

"Susanna?" He said quizzingly.

"Who is Susanna?"

"She was a girl we met on the Panama Canal trip. They got on together. I thought they did."

"Can you explain more?"

"On the canal cruise we met two girls Susanna and Maria. Filipe took a shine to Susanna. We met up after the cruise in Colon in a bar. Later he took Susanna to her hotel room and they, you know, he told me."

"What about the other girl Maria?"

"She came back to my hotel but we had a few drinks in the bar nearby and we slept in our room. We just cuddled, hugged together and went to sleep"

"I need to know. Did you have sex with, Maria?"

Josh asked, "Why, is it relevant?"

"It may be" Greg replied.

"No, it wasn't like that, we both enjoyed the company but took it no further."

"When did you last see the girls?"

"The next morning that would be Monday about the 9th. We were at their hotel, The Raddison, when they boarded the bus for the cruise to Aruba"

"Do you recall the cruise ship?"

"Yes, the 'Alisios'. It was berthed in Colon next to the Arecife bar we had been drinking in"

"What happened after they left on the bus?"

"We took a taxi to Panama City, its quicker than the ferry. I got my flight to L.A. and Filipe caught a flight to Aruba to meet up with Susanna"

"When was the last time you were in contact with Filipe?"

"That day. Unless there is something on my phone. I haven't used it since I got here."

The door opened and the Chief brought Josh a small bottle of water. Josh took the water and asked for this phone. The Chief left the office.

"Do you have any photographs of the girls?"

"No, I don't but Filipe had a few on the canal cruise and some at their hotel"

"They don't have possession of his phone. It's believed the female took it"

"No, his camera. He always hid his camera, cards and passport in his room"

"Where would he do that?"

"Usually he stuck a hook at the back of the bottom drawer on the cabinet in the room. He did that everywhere we stayed."

The Chief brought the phone and a charger into the room and plugged the charger into a socket. He then left the room.

Josh asked, "Why would Susanna kill Filipe, was it a fight, what. I can't work it out in my head"

"Did either of you get into any disputes, arguments or fights with any of the Latino people on your vacation?"

"No. We just had a great time exploring and seeing sights. That was the first time we had even spoke to any girls anywhere on our travels."

"Did you buy any narcotics, drugs, cocaine?"

"No way. Beers and tequila, mojitos, rum. No drugs"

The phone started to charge and then a constant stream of sounds emitted as messages started to filter through. Josh picked up the phone and checked the incoming texts, messages, missed calls and WhatsApp messages. He looked for Filipe. There were three WhatsApp messages.

One showed a photograph of Filipe and Susanna on a beach on Aruba, with the message "Look who I met in Aruba" dated Tuesday 10th May.

The second showed a photograph of Filipe and Susanna outside the Amsterdam Manor Beach Resort.

"Susanna going back to Colombia our last photo" dated Saturday 14th May.

The third was a message dated Saturday 14th May. "Flying to margarita"

Officer Simons, "Josh I need to take possession of your phone it has a lot of information that may be vital to the enquiry. I also need to take a written statement. I would appreciate it if you could come to Santa Monica with me to complete these details. I will arrange accommodation where you will be safe."

"What do you mean, safe?"

"We have been asked by the English police to ensure your safety, whilst this murder of your friend is investigated, at least until you fly from the U.S."

"Why should I be in danger?"

"I am not aware but that's what has been asked and that's what has been approved. Ok"

"Can I use my phone now?"

"No, I'm sorry. You can use the phone at the police headquarters when we get there as much as you like. I do not want to risk any information being lost from your phone. Can you collect your clothing and travel gear and we will get off straight away?"

"What about my hire car?"

"It will be collected and taken to the hire company by one of my colleagues. Please gather your bags so we can go. I will make a call to Newcastle police while you do this."

Josh left the room. Greg Simons made a call to Newcastle.

Sarah was at her desk working on the computer when the phone rang.

"Hello, Newcastle Major Crime Team, Sarah speaking how can I help you?"

"Hi Sarah it's officer Simons from Santa Monica"

"I knew it was you straight away by your lovely accent. Have you got something for us?"

"First, Josh is ok."

"Eee, that's great news Greg. I took it you found him easy enough"

"Yes, after your precise information it was straight forward."

"Right, howay then, spill the beans"

"Pardon Sarah"

"Yes, I mean what have you managed to find in your enquiry Greg?"

Greg then went on to give the information about the two girls Susanna and Maria. The hotels and Arecifes bar in Colon and also in Aruba. The WhatsApp messages and photos. Where Filipe hid his camera. They didn't have any problems on the holiday. They did not use narcotics. He had taken possession of the phone. He was taking Josh to Santa Monica to a safe hotel and would take a written statement from him in an hour or so. The last contact with Filipe was on the day he was flying to Margarita. Was it ok to allow Josh to make phone calls, which was agreed. He would forward the photographs from the phone when they were safely downloaded at police headquarters.

"Eee, Greg that's fantastic. You've done a good job there, thanks a lot. I'm going to tell the boss straight away and I'm sure he will send an email to your Police Department singing your praises. Can I get back to you later if need be and can you email a secure copy of Josh's statement as soon as possible, I know you will."

"I will do Sarah, it may be a few hours before its complete"

"Listen that's champion, I'll not be going home until it's done but don't hurry it. We are desperate to see the photo's as well. You're just great. We will contact Josh's family you can let him know because they've been worried as well, it's spoiling their cruise."

"Got to go Sarah, Josh is packing to travel"

"Cheers, Greg like I say thanks a lot you've done all we could ask for"

Sarah put the phone down, "Andy the yankee cop has come up trumps"

CHAPTER 15

Friday 20th May

Martin was at his desk when he could feel the mobile vibrating in his trouser pocket. After a quick look to confirm there was no one in the area, he took the phone from his pocket and pressed the green receive button and held the device to his right ear. His eyes were constantly scanning the door of his office whilst listening for footsteps. He listened very carefully to what he was told. He replied "Si" and closed the conversation. Another job to be done. More complications. He placed the phone inside his trouser pocket and walked out of the office and leaving the air-conditioned building he walked into a park and sat at an empty park bench.

Martin again checked for observers before taking the mobile out of his trouser pocket. He felt uncomfortably hot and not because of the 34-degree temperature. He pressed the numbers and was quickly answered by a man sitting in an airconditioned car in the port of Gamboa. It was a short message, no doubt.

The 'Reina del Canal' was mooring in Gamboa. Alvaro had come down from the upper decks to say farewell to Steve and was apologetic that they could not help. He had given Steve a DVD of the boats CCTV recordings for the last month, which might help. Steve thanked him, took an exhibit tag out of his shoulder bag and asked Alvaro to sign it and gave him a biro pen. Alavaro signed and dated the label and gave Steve his pen back. He put them both in the shoulder bag and checked to ensure it was closed fully. Jessica was finishing off a large fruit juice as the crew lowered the ramp onto the concrete jetty. She walked passed Steve and Alvaro without acknowledging either man and thanked the crew for a very interesting cruise and made her apologies about it taking longer than expected. She then walked towards the small town. Steve shook hands with Alvaro and lied as he thanked him for his help. He then left the boat to find his transport. Jessica waited until she was out of sight of the boat then waited for Steve.

Steve spotted the grey Chrysler Town and Country car with the driver inside in air-conditioned comfort. The driver, who was not in uniform got out of the car and opened the two rear doors for them both. Jessica sat behind the driver and Steve had more leg space behind the front passenger seat. The driver said it was just a 40 minute drive and started to drive towards Panama City. The road was a dual carriageway with the canal to the North side and Jungle on the South. It was still bright sunshine but the aircon was cooling. The driver was making good progress. Steve noticed that the driver had removed his gun from his right-side holster, he thought this would stop a rear seat passenger taking it off the driver and would possibly be in his training. He then became more aware of the driver and his actions; he was getting mixed messages and became more alert. He noticed the driver regularly checking his mirror, more at the passengers than for any road manoeuvres. Why was he not in uniform there was no need to hide his identity, it wasn't the same driver as before?

Jessica was also picking up on certain signs. The drivers' neck was sweaty, despite the cool interior of the car. Without speaking they both formed the opinion they were not in a good place and more than likely in real danger. Military training and survival instinct were coming to the fore.

The driver started to slow and said there was a fault he would have to stop. He started to turn off the carriageway towards a heavily wooded area and the canal. There were no other vehicles that could be seen on this dirt road. It had to be now, what could be waiting, strike fast. Seat belts ready to be loosened. Jessica saw the drivers left arm move from the wheel down towards the door well.

Go.

Jessica wrapped her right arm around the drivers' neck and pulled him tight back against the headrest choking his throat with her right arm across his carotid artery and securing the hold with her left arm. Steve saw the handgun in his left hand coming across the drivers stomach towards him. He jumped forward and pressed the barrel of the pistol down into the drivers' groin with his left hand. There was the explosion of a gunshot and a spray of deep red blood up into the roof of the car and onto the inside of the windscreen. The car was still travelling at pace when it crashed between two large trees and into the thick jungle. The initial impact activated the drivers air bag into the body and face of the driver. Jessica somehow managed to keep the choke hold on through the impact, her head and right shoulder hitting into the back of the headrest and seat, the driver was pulling and scratching at her right forearm with all his dying strength to no use. He suddenly stopped fighting at the final impact front on into a thick tree trunk, his head slumped forward onto her arm. The blood flow eased from the driver. Steve got out of the vehicle and pulled open the drivers' door, it was apparent he was dead or very close to death. "Jessica you can ease off now. You OK"

The car was completely hidden from any road or path by the thickness of the jungle.

"No apparent injuries, what about you?"

Steve was checking the driver out in the wrecked car," I'm Ok, I'll check him over." There was a pause feeling for a pulse on his neck. "He's gone," the driver's seat well was full of dark red warm blood. "Have a look in the car for any other weapons. I've got a phone from his pocket." He left him holding the Glock pisto.

"Do you think he is on his own?" Jessica recovered another Glock 19 automatic handgun from the glove compartment. Looking in the boot she found two shotguns, another Glock pistol and two boxes of ammunition. "Do you want to start a war?" she asked. There was an unopened 8 litre bottle of water. Steve poured water over his hands to wash away the blood and washed Jessica's forehead that had been spattered with blood. There was a first aid kit which Steve opened and saw a large bandage inside a self-sealing plastic bag. He took out the bandage and threw it away, then placed the recovered mobile phone inside the bag and sealed it up. Jessica picked up a tube of antiseptic cream which she opened and used liberally on the scratch marks and friction burns from the air bag on her forearm. She then pocketed the cream.

They both looked shaken, but they showed no outward signs of being in a violent confrontation, other than the large amount of blood splattered across their upper clothing. Fortunately, it was not their blood. They would not be able to change their clothing and it would be needed for protection in this hostile environment.

They looked at each other, then both automatically threw themselves at each other in a massive hug, then stepped back from each other and surveyed the immediate area. They had survived on instinct. They looked around and picked up small parts of vehicle debris that were visible and placed them inside the wrecked vehicle which was partially hidden by the jungle mass. They then pulled more jungle debris which was in abundance and thick to conceal the damaged vehicle and the now dead unknown driver.

Steve, "I don't know what's going on but we have to move and we have to move fast away from here. We have to get by on what we've got. There could be others coming or nearby. Get all of our stuff." Steve picked up the handgun, the shotguns were too difficult to conceal and carry.

Jessica had already taking their bags from the rear of the vehicle. Their phones were still intact and charged. They had their passports, money, cards and now had weapons. They did not trust anyone in this country, not now. Jessica took a folded map from the glovebox. She had one pistol, which she checked to find it fully loaded, and pushed in the back of her trousers, safety catch on. She placed her bag over her shoulder.

Steve checked the pistol; it was fully loaded. He checked the safety catch which was on then placed the pistol and ammunition boxes into his shoulder bag. They made a quick sweep of the area for anything else that would be useful. Nothing.

Steve picked up the water bottle and they both set off at a slow jog away from the scene towards a tarmac strip of road. They then headed East away from Panama City.

As they were walking quickly and silently along a pathway that run parallel to the route East in the general direction of Colon, Steve felt his phone vibrating in his pocket. He picked up the phone and saw the office number and answered, he and Jessica walked from the path into the trees for cover.

CHAPTER 16

Friday 20th May

Andy spoke, "Hiya Jimmy, how's things going in paradise mate?"

"Sorry Andy, is the boss there; I need to speak to him now"

"Ooh, got something have you?"

Steve spoke more deliberately and slightly louder.

"Andy, I need to speak to the boss, now."

"Yes, sorry mate. I'll transfer you to his office phone. Boss, I'm transferring Jimmy to your phone."

Detective Superintendent Colin Tinkler was relaxing in his black leather swing chair looking forward to a few drinks with his team when he heard Andy's call. The phone rang and he picked it up straight away. "Hello Jimmy, what have you got to report?"

"I've just killed a Panama police officer. I think"

The Super knew it wasn't a joke. "Wait Jimmy." He shouted for Andy who walked directly the short yardage to the boss's office. "Andy shut my door, stay outside the door, no visitors, none" He picked up his A4 paper lined book, opened a clean page and picked up his favourite Mont Blanc pen.

"Are you ok, safe?"

"We, are ok and safe for the time being, but obviously there are problems"

The Super took a deep breath, "Right, from the beginning"

Steve started, "I have a feeling that Martin might be batting for the other team"

"Tell me about the Panama cop first"

""This morning Martin met us at the hotel after breakfast. The plan was to take the boat trip from Panama to Colon and hopefully gain some intelligence on the two lads. Apparently, he hasn't passed on all the intel updates to me that he was given from the office. Anyway, Jessica and I get on the boat separately. I'm introduced to an officer on board by Martin who would help with some questions to the crew. Jessica was just to listen to the Spanish crew to hear if they were talking about it. After a while the officer took me around the boat talking to the crew. Jessica overheard the conversation which was, the police man wants to know about the two English men, it's a lot easier to say you know nothing. They all said nothing. But Jessica heard two members of crew who had seen them with two Colombian girls. Martin told us to get off the boat at Gamboa. We did. He told us there would be a driver waiting for us. He was taking the weekend off. There was this officer sitting in the car I had travelled in to the terminal this morning, a different guy had been the driver then. We both got into the back of the car as he had opened the rear doors for us and he set off towards Panama City.

Colin said "Yes go on"

"Somethings just didn't feel or look right. His gun wasn't in his holster, he was continually looking at us in the mirror, he was sweating a lot. The car was ice cold with the aircon. Then he pulled off the main road onto a jungle track, he slowed down a bit and pulled his gun out with his left hand. Then we jumped him."

"Take this bit slow, starting at he pulled his gun out and WE, emphasise WE"

"Yes, We, that is Jessica and I reacted. Jessica was behind the driver; she saw his left arm start to rise from the driver's door well. I saw the barrel of the pistol coming across his lap towards me."

The Super is acting out the description given.

"Jessica jumped forward and put her right arm around his neck in a choke grip and her left arm over his left shoulder and pulled him back onto the headrest to stop him turning towards me. I jumped across his chest and pushed the gun downwards away from me and then the gun went off. The bullet went through the artery at the inside of his right leg and he was losing a lot of blood but still struggling. Jessica kept the choke on and then the car crashed into the trees in the jungle.

"Are you sure you are both ok, no injuries

"Yes boss

"Continue"

"I jumped out of the back seat and ran to the driver's door; Jessica still had the choke hold on. He was still. I checked his pulse and found that he was dead"

"What killed him, the gunshot wound, or?"

"The gunshot boss, severe loss of blood, the drivers well was inches thick of the stuff"

"So really this guy has shot and killed himself, is that right Jimmy?" This was more of a statement than a question

"Yes, boss"

"It sounds like the young lady may have saved your life Jimmy. Where did she learn how to do that hold?"

"Ex forces like myself Sir."

"Keep it to boss Jimmy please. What's the situation now?"

"I recovered a mobile phone, not police issue I suspect from the drivers' body. I've bagged it. We took possession of two Glock pistols and ammunition from the car. We have enough cash and cards, our mobiles which will need charging soon. We are on a jungle path not too far from a main road heading towards Colon. I didn't think it's wise to head back to Panama City."

"I need to get you safe and out of there and fast. I can't trust the Liaison officer in Panama and don't know about the others. I'm going to have to go to HQ and probably further with this. Can you two look after yourselves and keep low profile for a while, holiday makers or something. If you are right about Martin, he probably won't broadcast that his car is missing but he will use other means."

"Our intention is to stay alive and get out of here by any means. Just had a thought the driver had no ID that I could find. He may not have been a cop."

"Save your battery unless you need to use the phone. Turn it on, on the hour. Someone from here will ring."

"If you don't know, Filipe may have been killed by a drugs cartel for some sort of interference in a shipment from Panama. I've got calls to make. Stay safe and thank Jessica for her actions from me."

"Will do boss"

The call was closed.

◆ ◆ ◆

Colin kept his door closed and made a call to Fort Lauderdale Police. "Can I speak to assistant Chief karen Ostrowski please, it's Detective Superintendent Tinkler from Newcastle,England", there was a short pause.

Hi Colin, sorry I didn't get back to you, you know how it is. Nice to speak to you English bobbies at any time. How can I help?"

"Can I call you Karen?

"Of course, Colin, it's more friendly that way"

"We are investigating the murder of a young man; we think on Margarita Island?"

"Wow Colin, that's a fair distance off your beat as they say?

"Yes, I agree but it's a strange circumstance."

"Aint they all. Go on, tell me more. What is the connection with my police department?"

"Very briefly. A local young man from Newcastle, England, of Mexican descent and his friend went on an Americas holiday. What is known is that they met two Colombian girls, as yet unidentified on a small Panama Canal cruise boat. The two girls were on a cruise holiday from Colombia which culminated in them boarding the 'Alisios' in Colon and getting off in Aruba."

"Did you say Alisios?

"Yes, I did, interested?"

"Hmm I maybe. Go on"

"It so happens that Filipe, the Mexican descendant, met up with the girls again in Aruba when they disembarked. When they left, he left the Island and went to Margarita. Shortly after the time of the drugs job on the 'Alisios', this young man was murdered by a Latino woman in a nasty way. The murder was recorded on a mobile phone and sent by WhatsApp to his parents, here in Newcastle."

"And you think both incidents may be linked?"

"The young man has no connection with crime or drugs but appears to have been blamed for something."

He continued. "More pressing. I have two officers in Panama in hiding, who have just started tentative enquiries and have had their lives endangered. I believe that there is some form of Police involvement, possibly International police involvement. They are the only persons who know of their presence"

"Are you alleging that it may be from my Department or my Country getting involved?"

"Not at all, Karen. But you might have a source or sources close to the 'Alisios' job that could shed some light. They are in need of assistance now, not tomorrow. I'm asking for help and it is urgent that is why I have come direct, to save time. I can fill in forms later, can't we?"

"We, possibly could if there are forms that need filling in Colin. Can I get back to you, how long are you there, I promise I will this time?"

"Yes of course I will be here all night".

The call was closed.

Colin sat back in his chair and looked to the heavens. Now to phone the Chief.

Karen Ostrowski was in her late forties. An attractive and intelligent police officer and well respected by the officers and the local public. She stood a full 1.70 and had gained a few comfort pounds but carried herself well. She always wore her uniform for her work. She was a police officer and wanted everyone to know that. She pressed the call button to her secretary, "David, I want Major Watkins here a.s.a.p."

◆ ◆ ◆

After making the call to the Chief. He had argued successfully that he needed to remain in his office for contact purposes after passing all available information to the Chief. She wasn't happy to say the least but promised all positive action and backing for Colin. She had to contact the Home Secretary's office to make them aware of a possible National incident and arrange a press blackout. One big question, why was a female from Cheshire with Jimmy in Panama on a possible murder enquiry? That had to discussed at a later time.

Colin shouted, "Andy" and his door opened immediately, "Yes boss"

"Is everyone here, the drink is cancelled."

"Yes, ok boss. Sarah and Lauren are still prettying themselves in the ladies. The lads are at the briefing table"

"Get the girls, everybody in the room and then lock the doors."

Andy left the room to go to the ladies' room but bumped into them both in the corridor. They both looked bright and cheery, their makeup applied and hair put into place. The smell was intoxicating. They had both changed, Sarah was wearing a two toned blue patterned round collar short sleeved blouse, short length light blue skirt, showing of her long-tanned legs and dark blue 4inch heeled shoes. Lauren was more conservative with a knee length red floral-patterned dress and short heeled red shoes. Andy couldn't help but smile his approval, "You two look absolutely stunning. The drinks cancelled; something is up. Meeting in the room now"

The girls said nothing, looked at each other with a shrug of the shoulders and it was back to work. When they walked into the office Andy locked the door from the inside, which caused both girls to look at him and they knew something serious was happening or had occurred.

They were all sat around the briefing table. Colin had his pad open in front of him. Andy, Sarah, Lauren, Billy, Alan and Walter picked up a sheet of A4 and a pen out of the multicoloured spotty plastic pot in the middle of the table. There was silence and they were all looking at the boss in anticipation.

He began, "To the point, Jimmy and Jessica have killed a guy purporting to be a Panama cop, in self-defence......and are currently taking evasive action to avoid detection and further attempts on their lives in the Panama jungle"

The reaction was as expected, looks of shock and puzzlement. Billy broke the silence in a manner that was also expected, "What the fuck?"

The boss continued "Jimmy is of the opinion that the Panama liaison officer Martin Chapman, may, that is may, be involved."

They were still staring at the boss with a look of despair and disbelief.

"We are no good here unless we are all doing something active" Colin knew he needed this team to get their brains working, to think, to be active and not to be scared. "Are you with me on this, it could well be us who can save them both?"

A collective "Yes boss" from around the table

"Andy, my apologies but I will lead on this ok?"

"Certainly boss" Andy was relieved at the decision.

"Let's start. We have to be quick we have fifteen minutes before I can call Jimmy again, he has limited battery life on his phone. Sarah what have you told Martin about our enquiries?"

"He has got a full write up Boss, everything. You told me to tell him."

"What is everything and when did you give him it?"

Sarah was going on the defensive by her tone, "It is all documented as usual on emails and phone call logs it can be checked"

"I am asking you to check, now Sarah"

"Yes boss, sorry boss" as she stood up and walked to collect the call logs and emails that had been sent from her station. She could still hear the nearby conversation at the briefing table.

"There has to be a connection. Filipe is murdered after having a fling over a few days with an unidentified possible Colombian woman in Panama, Aruba and probably Margarita. He is possibly murdered by the same woman. Only possible, there are a lot of women, keep our minds open. The cruise ship the Colombian girls were on is used to transport cocaine into Florida. There is a hit on the cartel in Fort Lauderdale at a location where the two elderly mules were killed in the car and the cartel gang are wiped out by the DEA in a gunfight. The drugs are seized, millions of dollars lost by the cartel and several cartel members. Where, could Filipe and possibly Josh fit into this scenario. Open question?"

After a short pause. Lauren, "Why should we think that Josh is involved or in danger?"

Alan coughs and the boss nodded in his direction. He continues, "Just possibly like, if they are linked, what I'm thinking is that the two girls were maybes part of the drugs team you know. They could have carried the drugs on the cruise ship in Panama, Colon is it? They had the fling with the lads in all innocence, well on the lad's behalf anyway. When the deal has gone down bad in Florida, the head honcho is wondering how the fuck has that happened. It's like, howay man, we've done it loads of times and it goes wrong now. He thinks what's different and he thinks of our two lads. Cos it is different, possibly. Or maybe it was just the boss's lass he was shagging"

Billy joins in, "Aye but, we don't know the girls are involved in the drugs and if so, how would the honcho geezer know about the lads?"

Andy," Good question Billy"

"Thanks Andy" Billy said and he gave a little unconscious nod.

Lauren, "What if they told him or he had the girls watched. It was a lot of coke."

Andy, "That sounds reasonable as well."

Lauren continues, "Just maybe he thought they were undercover coppers. Maybe informers for cash and they found out what the lasses had been doing and he wanted revenge."

Walter asked, "What if it wasn't the girls, we know about who killed Filipe, it's possible. Nice lad but we know he has gone off with one lass already?"

Andy, "Yes I could understand that"

Alan," I bet it's that twat in Panama"

The boss, "Good theory but let's not get carried away as yet. I think there has to be a link with the Fort Lauderdale incident. But where does Jimmy fit in? The only person who knows he is there is the liaison officer or the boat crew"

Andy, "Is Jimmy getting too close to the organisation. Well not so much Jimmy but this enquiry?"

Sarah came back to the table with her documents. The conversation and guessing stopped and they looked at Sarah. "Right, it's all here in chronological order when I made contact with Martin. He knows everything that we know and he knew within a very short time of our briefings. He knew more than Steve knew as he was supposed to brief Steve on the latest info about there being a Colombian girl and the fact that Josh had been traced by officer Greg Simons. He knew about the possible connection with the drugs bust in Fort Lauderdale everything, well apart from where Filipe hid his camera and wallet in the bedroom"

Colin looked all around the table, "Who knew Jimmy and Jessica were in Panama City?"

Sarah," Only one man, Martin fucking Chapman, the twat."

The boss looked directly at Sarah, "Now, now Sarah. He probably doesn't know that we have been in contact with Jimmy and know what has happened. I want you to call him as you usually would in your lovely Geordie manner and just ask him if he knows where Jimmy is, as we can't reach him on the mobile. If he asks why tell him the boss needs to speak to him about complications about Jessica."

The room went silent, Walter attached the recording device to the phone. Sarah dialled the Panama number. There was no reply. "I'll try his mobile" After five rings the call was answered. "Martin Chapman"

"Hiya Martin, its Sarah again. Sorry about ringing your mobile, I tried the office first, how are you doing, I bet its hot and clammy over there?"

"Hello Sarah, "raising his eyebrows "Yes you could say that, what is it you are after?" without thinking crossing his fingers.

"Do you know where Jimmy is, I've been trying to get him on his phone but he's not answering?"

"Jimmy is on the canal cruise; he will probably be in the middle of the lake and he won't get a signal out there until he gets off at Colon. Can I help is it important?"

"No, not really, well maybes you can. I'm all dressed up here waiting to hit the town with my mates, I could send him an email but if he hasn't got his computer, he won't get the message. Will you definitely see him or speak to him at Colon?"

"Sarah of course, you can depend on me." He raised his eyebrows.

"Right then, just let him know that Josh has been found and that Jessica has to return to England. I'm sure he will be dead disappointed"

"I'm sure he will be", again crossing his fingers. He continued casually, "Is Josh now at Santa Monica Police Headquarters Sarah?"

Sarah gave a quizzical look and the boss rolled his hands; signalling keep it going.

Sarah thinking quick, "Yes he is for now but I think they're going to move him somewhere out of the way soon for safety you know"

"Too right Sarah. I will let him know, keep me in the loop it would be great to see the job finish well. You enjoy tonight, is the Toon still as crazy?"

"It certainly is Martin, its manic man, speak soon."

The call was closed. Again, there was silence quickly interrupted by Sarah, "The lying bastard". Then imitated spitting on the ground.

The boss," Everybody keep your thoughts going. I'm going to phone Jimmy it's nine."

In the air-conditioned bar 'The Blarney Stone' on Calle 47 Edif Aquarius, in Panama City, Martin took another drink of iced cuba libra and allowed himself a little smile. He ordered a Shepherd's Pie with additional chips from the barman, Lionel. He indicated one more cuba libra then picked up his glass and walked to an empty booth and took a seat. The booths either side were vacant. He took the other mobile phone from his trouser pocket, checked and saw no calls. He then pressed a number from memory. "Josh está ahora en la sede de la policía Santa Monica" *(Josh is now at the Santa Monica Police Headquarters)* a pause. "Si, el oficial es Greg Simons". *(Yes, the officer is Greg Simons.)* He put the phone in his pocket, sat back and relaxed.

Colin had returned to his office sat back in his recliner and keyed in the numbers on the desk phone. It seemed to take an eternity to ring. It was answered immediately, "Hello". Steve and Jessica took shelter from the heat in the shade of the trees just off the rutted pathway and sat on the lush grass

"Hi Jimmy, it's the boss are you still both ok?"

"Yes, we've kept moving towards the East and Colon, not too far from Gamboa again. We're going to get some clean clothing and food hopefully somewhere there."

"No sign of being followed?"

"No, nowt. I think we are ok but need to make a plan, that is after we have food and some change of clothing"

"I think you are correct about our liaison officer." There was a pause and then he continued, "He is lying. He has just seconds ago told us you were in the middle of a lake floating towards Colon and not accessible by phone"

"Aye, that's probably wishful thinking. He must know by now what happened to his hit man?"

"Possibly not Jimmy. If he wasn't his hit man if you know what I mean. He probably thinks the deed is done and that's the end of it. When you don't get off at Colon, he will start an action looking for you both, kidnapped or your dead bodies, give him a bit more time, alibi's search areas, your bodies might never be found. He will be profoundly guilty that he let you go by yourselves of course."

"No boss, he will be profoundly guilty. Full stop."

"As long as he thinks you're both dead the both of you are safe. Do you have the business credit card with you?"

"Yes, I've got the lot. Mine, Jessica has hers and the business card."

"I think I have a plan, put the phone on speaker if you can I need you both to hear what I say.

Speaker was switched on "Jessica are you there?

"Yes, I am"

"Thanks for helping my good friend and I really mean it. He is a good friend. Now listen both of you, if you have any questions ask as we speak"

Colin then went into detail of a plan that had jumped into his head after hearing Martin on the phone. It took a short while with very few interruptions and a course of action was planned.

There would be no more communication from the office phone until 12:00 tomorrow Newcastle time, 06:00 Panama time. It was now 21:10. The office phone would be manned 24 hours should they need to get in touch.

Colin sat back deep into his comfortable chair and ran his left hand through his hair. He allowed time for himself to think the whole incident through. He shouted "Sarah, here".

Sarah walked at pace knocked on the door and walked into the boss's office.

"Urgently. I want you to contact Officer Simons. You tell him in no uncertain terms he is not to return to Santa Monica Police station or wherever he goes. Get him to go somewhere that would be safe. We need to get Maddison located and into protection away from that area. I will contact the Chief and liaise with Santa Monica Police Department while you do that. I will sort out authorities and paperwork. You get that message done now. If there is a problem, tell me"

" Yes boss." Sarah quickly walked back to her desk.

He stood up and walked back into the squad room. "It looks like it might be a long night. Does anyone need, want or have to go. No one is under any pressure to stay; I know it's been a long few days and it's possibly going to get longer." He opened his arms in front of them, hands open facing the ceiling.

There was a mixture of "No boss" and shaking heads. "Walter what about you, you're not on my budget but I can get it sorted. I think you will be needed"

"I'm ok to stay and help out, I want to help out, we all do"

"Thanks Walter. First can you nip down to the Persia kebab place, I'll have a mixed lamb and chicken with full salad and chilli and garlic sauce."

For the first time in a while in the team laughed. Walter took an A4 sheet from the pile and a pen from the multi-coloured pot and started taking down everybody's orders.

After giving Walter their orders they all went to their own part of the office and made phone calls to loved ones and friends.

Colin found the number for the Santa Monica Police HQ and made contact.

Sarah pressed the number for Greg Simons. It took a few seconds to connect and start to give a ringing tone.

"Greg Simons"

"Hi Greg it's Sarah from Newcastle. This is very important"

"Go ahead, please continue. I must tell you that I'm on my car speaker and I have Josh sat next to me if that makes a difference."

"No that doesn't matter." Speaking slowly and clearly, she continued. "There is a current possible danger to you and Josh. A real danger. Do not go back to Santa Monica Police HQ. Can you go to another safe location for protection?"

"I can if it is really necessary, I'm in Malibu now. Wait," there was a little pause for thought, "I'm thinking about Oxnard that's in the opposite direction."

"Greg that would be great. My boss is presently contacting your chief at Santa Monica to explain and hopefully assist"

"Is there a danger to Miss Roberts?"

"My boss is arranging for Maddison to be taken somewhere safe now as we speak. Josh I'm pleased you are safe. Just do as the officer says please."

Josh, "Yes of course, I don't understand any of this."

"It's very difficult Josh but everyone is working hard to get things sorted. First, we need, you, Maddison and Officer Simons to be safe."

Greg Spoke, "We are turning around now, we should be there in 40 minutes. I will inform my control room."

Sarah knocked and walked into the boss's office. "I've spoke to the officer with Josh. He is taking him to a town called Oxnard. Josh is ok"

"Thanks Sarah. I have contacted Santa Monica, it's sorted I will write it up in the log. I've got a couple of emails to do and have to call the boss. I will be in the room shortly."

While waiting for the food delivery the squad were busy checking emails for replies from Cruise companies, tapping fingers waiting for International telephone calls, they returned to the briefing table one by one with no further update. It was understandable they were four hours ahead of where the replies were coming from, still in their working day.

Sarah spoke to the boss across the table, "Boss is there any way we can get in touch with the other liaison officers without Martin knowing or arousing suspicion. They might be finding evidence we need, which might or could incriminate him or identify the murderer of Filipe."

"Thanks Sarah, I've been so busy thinking about Jimmy, I nearly forgot how this all started. That is a very good point. I've been in contact with NCA. There is action in motion now which I know but I cannot elaborate on." Looking around the table, he continued, "I trust you but you do not need to know. Sarah can you get me a can of coke from the refreshment room and bring it to my office."

"Yes boss"

They walked away from the table, the boss walking into his office and Sarah carried on along the corridor, opened the locked door and went on to the Second floor.

CHAPTER 17

Friday 20th May

The Sun was high and beating down on the jungle path, that ran between the roadway and the canal. From the path they could hear the large ships moving slowly through the canal towards the entrance to the large lake before making for Colon and the Atlantic Ocean. After a short time, they came across a clearing with several car parking spaces spread around, each one next to a purpose-built barbeque and seated area made from large stones and concrete, it offered a wide view of the canal and passing shipping. In the distance they could see families at the canal edge fishing, relaxing in the sun and playing an assortment of ball games

Steve removed his shirt and Jessica took off her blouse, she had a white sports bra covering her breasts. For a while they stayed in the shade watching the families move between the cars, the barbeque and the open play area nearer to the canal. They made their way to the nearest car, a small Beige coloured Nissan Murano. It had shields inside the windows to keep out the heat. No one saw them or took any notice; they were at least 150 metres from the canal and the family were having fun in a baseball game. Jessica tried the boot and found it to be open. Steve raised the boot no higher than the height of the car. Jessica examined the contents of the boot, there were cold bags of raw chicken and fish but also crisps, tacos, fruit, cheese and bread there was also cola, beer and water. The other bags had spare clothing for mam and dad and the two boys. There was also a handbag which on quick inspection had what looked like a key for the car. Jessica gave Steve a clean Tee shirt and picked up a large oblong piece of material patterned with exotic birds, parrots and forest flowers. She took two small cans of cola and after a brief discussion decided against taking the car. Steve gently replaced the boot door and they both walked away continuing towards the main road to Gamboa.

Once they had covered the open ground of the parking and picnic area they walked into the cover of the trees. Steve discarded the bloodstained shirt he was carrying and after cleaning himself with the water that was left in the bottle put on his newly attained blue tee shirt. Steve then watched as Jessica washed herself down, emptying what water was left. She then took the oblong piece of thin cotton material and tied two of the ends together to form a circle of cloth, then twisted the material in the middle into a figure eight, then looping on end over her head and the other over her back and arms made what looked like a designer top in seconds. Steve was impressed at what Jessica had done but more impressed with Jessica. She discarded her old top, all of their old blood-stained clothing was concealed well into the densely wooded area. Her back was now naked above her waistline. She removed the Glock and placed it into the shoulder bag.

They both looked at each other and inspected the clothing, Steve said "You just look great."

"You don't look too bad, you will do."

Steve asked, "Are you ready for this holiday now?"

"I think we deserve one. Are we now booking into double rooms, I think it would make sense?"

"I thought you would never ask. For safety reasons eh".

They came back onto the dirt road and walked the few kilometres towards Gamboa, crossing the single bridge over the Chagres river and into the small town. They found a bus stop which offered shelter from the sun near to the town post office which was still open. Jessica examined the timetable and a bus to Colon should be passing by in twenty minutes.

Steve sat in the shelter of the bus stop canopy whilst Jessica went into the post office. She returned after a few minutes with new hats for them both. Jessica gave Steve his Light blue Panama straw hat to match his new shirt and she was wearing a wide brimmed off-white ladies panama hat. They were beginning to look like tourists. She had also purchased two sticks of bread, two bags of crisps, two bag of nuts and two, one litre bottles of water. They sat together and had their first holiday picnic. They discussed the events of the day and the new plan until the coach arrived, they boarded for the onward one-hour journey into Colon.

CHAPTER 18

Friday 20th may

Colin had finished his conversation with his NCA contact and was writing the updated log when his desk phone rang. "Superintendent Tinkler."

"Hi Colin it's Karen, you are working late."

"Hello Karen it's good to hear from you, I hope you have some good news for me"

"I may have. I have been speaking to the officer in charge of the operation which involved the 'Alisios'. Obviously, I cannot disclose sources but they had been working on this one for a while. They had observed one previous importation which was allowed to run, the couriers were not murdered in that instance and they are now in a state penitentiary awaiting a trial. My teams know the dangers of arresting our Colombian friends and were well prepared. What I can say is, the source is unknown, the intelligence has originated in Panama. There have been two authorised payments of substantial amount of dollars to this person"

"When you say the source is unknown, do you mean to you or the officer receiving the intelligence?"

"That's it precisely Colin, both the officer and I do not know the true identity."

"How do they communicate? How can they trust the information?"

"Like I said Colin, they did have one test run, speculate to accumulate. The information was perfect. The second occasion was even more detailed"

"In what respect, if you can tell me"

"There were photographs of the exchange on the Quayside in Panama with the two known cruise employees and two Colombian girls although you couldn't see their faces, then named the couriers on the cruise"

"So, it's safe to say that the source would have been at the port when the exchange took place."

"I guess you could say that"

"Would it be possible to have copies of those photographs with the two Colombian girls Karen? They would not be released to the press from this office and could be vital in our enquiries."

"Yes, I would like to act in furtherance of International Police Relations"

"I would really appreciate that, thank you Karen. How did the informant, receive his or her payment?"

"The payment was paid in dollar bills by our Panama agent using the code number given at a meet. The informant was Panamanian or Latino, I cannot give any more information that would lead directly to the identity of the source Colin"

"Are there any mobile phone numbers you could give to me to help in my enquiry."

"I believe so Colin but you would have to go through the appropriate channels for that information, again it would possibly identify the source which we will not do, certainly not over an open phone conversation"

"Yes Karen, I appreciate that formalities must be adhered to but what you have given us is a good start. I hope I can keep in touch and I will keep you updated on our enquiry and certainly if there is any cross intelligence that may be of use to you and your teams."

"Is this pointing in the direction you were thinking of Colin?"

"Karen, I couldn't possibly say, but it certainly helps. I have now involved NCA, it is more than one murder enquiry now. I will include the contact details of the officer in charge in my email. Possible joint effort and cooperation would be beneficial to all. All intelligence will be coordinated from there. We will just work on the murder enquiry but all of our intelligence will be accessible by NCA."

"Go expedite Colin, keep in touch." The line went dead.

Colin sat back into his chair, rubbed his hand across his face, realising he now needed a shave and mouthed to himself, "The bastard." He took a drink from the Coca-Cola can and then leant over his desk picked up his Mont Blanc pen and started writing the phone call update. He shouted, "Sarah"

"Yes Boss" He could he the heels tapping on the floor as she approached his office door. "Come in Sarah take a seat" she sat down and kept her knees together with her short dress halfway up her thighs. She carried in the kebab the boss had ordered and placed it on the small coffee table.

"Is the Santa Monica police officer back at the police station with Josh yet?"

"Well if he isn't, he shouldn't be far off boss. What you after?"

"I want Josh and his girlfriend, ehm." He opened his arms towards Sarah.

"Maddison Roberts boss",

He continued "Yes, I want the pair of them given 24/7 protection."

Sarah asked "Maddison as well?"

"Yes Sarah, we don't know what might happen but I would rather that we had them safe"

"Should I speak to Greg about it or will you contact his Boss"

"I've sent an email and spoke to the Chief of Santa Monica and he has offered us full assistance in the matter. They have a safe house set up somewhere but we're going to do some distraction work."

"Ahh, ok boss."

"If you can speak to Josh when he gets there, go through the niceties with the officer first, but there is a slight possibility we could have the girls on film at the port in Colon when they're getting to the cruise ship."

"Well, if we can find Filip's camera there should be loads of photos of them all."

"I've progressed that, wait we'll have a chin-wag again, is

everybody there?"

"Yes boss, the lads have been trying to hurry up the cruise company but it's not working yet, Andy is doing up CARD system, Lauren is getting some authorities for phones and stuff and Walter is researching phone companies in Panama"

Colin and Sarah walked into the squad room towards the briefing table, the smell of garlic, onions, cooked meats and grease was hanging from the ceiling. "Someone open the windows a bit please?"

They all took their seats around the table. The boss at the head of the table, with his warm kebab in the white polystyrene box in his hand. Billy and Alan sitting next to each other as usual down the left side Andy sitting opposite the boss, Lauren next to Andy on the right side, Walter in the middle and Sarah next to the boss.

"Thanks for stopping everyone and thanks for what you have all done and achieved today, it's not been easy." He paused for a few seconds. "This is where we are now, Josh is safe in the care of Santa Monica police, we should get confirmation soon that he is in fact at the police headquarters. It's intended that after making a statement that Josh and Maddison Roberts will go into police protection for a period of time to assess the threat level against him and now possibly Maddison. As we speak Mick Mather from Venezuela liaison has been contacted by NCA. They have given him the possible hotel that Filipe stayed in and now the possible location of a hidden camera. He is under the strictest orders not to communicate with Chapman. As protocol, he will contact NCA and the information will be passed to this office with no delay. Another NCA liaison officer Winston Jones is in Aruba but I'm not expecting to get a great lot of information or intelligence from there. As far as I'm concerned nothing of note happened there. I have received information that the informant for the 'Alisios' job is from Panama City but, no one can give any information on the informant, other than probably Latino. Which could rule out Martin Chapman. Now, Jimmy and Jessica are safe, uninjured and should be heading into a town in Panama and bedding down for the night later." Billy and Alan gave each other nudges whilst Sarah and Lauren just looked at the two naughty boys and didn't need to speak. The boss smiled at the group; it was a good team. "There is not a lot we can do now here, lads if you want to get away comeback at 7 in the morning, keep your phones on. I want to get away for a few hours, I'll be back for 6.30. Andy can you cover until that time," Andy nodded. "Sarah, Lauren are you both up to speed with what your both doing?"

They replied "Yes boss."

"I want one of you to stay with Andy, Sarah can I ask you to stay for liaison with Santa Monica you have spoken to the cop over there, he should be phoning soon and help Andy with anything that might come in. Lauren might as well get a few hours' sleep and come back fresh in the morning again, 7 ok"

The boss stood up, "Right then any questions?"

Walter raised his hand. "Oh, sorry Walter, I hadn't forgot about you. Is there any chance you can trace locations on a mobile phone in Panama?"

"I have been looking into that and there is a possibility that Maddison might be able to help as well. Other than that, there is a new app, which might be useful. I'll try it out in the lab"

"Can you stay on please; I would like to know where Chapman is at all times if possible. Just about now, I think our two friends Jimmy and Jessica are going to be reported as missing by Marty Chapman".

"Certainly boss, no problem. I don't need much beauty sleep anyway"

Sarah and Lauren gave Walter a sour look and a laugh.

"Ok those of us going, let's get went"

They picked up bags tidied their desks and left in a hurry. Colin was taking his kebab home.

CHAPTER 19

Friday 20th May

The sky was starting to darken as the coach pulled in to the terminus in Colon. It was a run-down city Steve thought. Not a city you would expect Ocean Cruisers calling, certainly not glamorous that he could see. The traffic was very busy in the small city and the terminus was full of people carrying their daily shopping in baskets in a rush to get their transport home. It was very lively but no one noticed anybody else, they were all concentrating on their own life. The canal cruise would have been arriving in the port after its long water crossing around the same time.

Steve and Jessica took their time with the other passengers and alighted from the bus into the rush of pedestrians. It was hot and the smell of diesel was very strong and unpleasant. They walked off in the direction of the Free Zone shopping area which was just believed to be a short distance away. Jessica stopped a passing taxi to free herself from the hustle of the pavements. Steve jumped into the back and Jessica sat next to the driver, both thinking, I'm not making that mistake again. Jessica spoke to the driver in Spanish and he set off in the heavy traffic, it was a lot slower than walking but at least it was comfortable in air-conditioned air. The driver ignored them both and listened to his radio playing the loud local radio station music.

They got out at the entrance to the large enclosed area of warehouses known as The Free Zone, a tax-free enterprise. Jessica gave the driver $5 and they made their way to the first warehouse store.

In the next hour, they had bought two holdalls, an assortment of lightweight clothing and footwear, toiletries, a DVD player two new mobile phones, two SIM cards and two portable mobile phone chargers.

As they left the enterprise area, they saw the Radisson hotel.

A large white building with a red roof which stood out against the other aging buildings in the area. It was on the dockside. There was a large cruise liner docked immediately behind the hotel. They made their way to the hotel reception.

The reception area, was quiet compared to the activity outside of the hotel and gave cool comfort. It was typical of all modern hotels, wood panelling and lots of glass. The reception desk was flanked by bars to the right and left and it appeared that several passengers from the cruise ship were making good use of the cheap alcohol on offer. The hotel staff were smiling and looked smart in their uniforms, short sleeved white shirts and black waistcoat style jackets.

Jessica approached the reception desk and speaking in Spanish arranged a double room for one night and explained they were on holiday exploring the area. Steve handed the Northern ventures credit card to validate the booking. They handed over their passports for examination. Jessica explained that they would be eating out and asked for directions to a nearby restaurant and were told 'Arecifes'. Jessica was given the key to a non-smoking room on the fourth floor overlooking the harbour. They took the lift to the fourth floor and used the electronic key to enter their room.

It was a large room with a double-glazed door which opened onto a balcony with a view of the Cruise Liner 'Southern Freedom', which looked majestic in freshly painted white and blue livery and then beyond the liner the industrial port. The sun was setting but there was still activity inside the harbour. There was a King-sized bed with an array of white pillows spread across the top against the wooden headboard. The bathroom was clean and bright with a large shower room and deep bath, the towels were, large, white and soft. Facing the bed on a long set of dark wood drawers was a 40inch flat screen television. A full wall of fitted dark wood wardrobes and a full-length mirror in the middle.

The only apparent fault was a smell of dirty water. Possibly that was Steve and Jessica. They both had the oppressive dirty feeling and needed a full body cleansing.

Steve suddenly felt embarrassed about washing, changing and other bodily functions that were needed. Jessica could sense the awkwardness in the room and silence. "Why don't I use the bathroom first, ladies first, unless you have any urgent toiletry requirements and you can sort out the phones and stuff. You could pour a couple of cold beers for when I come out"

Steve, "Eh yes, I was just about to suggest that, good idea. I'll see if I can fix up the DVD player and charge the new mobiles."

Jessica walked into the bathroom and closed the door behind her but Steve listened and never heard her lock the door. It felt good in her company, he had never met anyone he had a feeling for like Jessica. After looking at the door for a few seconds he turned his mind to work and plugged the mobiles into charge and fixed the USB lead into the rear of the TV and into the DVD player. He connected the DVD player to the electricity supply; the green light came on and the lid opened. Removing the pistol from the shoulder bag he put it inside the bedside cabinet, on his side, the right side he thought. The DVD was took out of the bag and out of the protective plastic sleeve and placed it into the DVD player and closed the lid. He picked up the TV remote control and selected the correct media connection, HDMI2. Steve pressed play and sat on the bed, he had to fast forward the disc to the correct date and pressed play.

Steve was not expecting to see anything on the DVD after the reluctance of any of the staff on the canal cruise boat to be helpful at all.

Sunday 8th May 0610. There were four images in squares on the television screen. Top left had images from the boat down the boarding ramp onto the concrete harbour. Top right was a black screen. The bottom left image showed the lower level where the food, coffee and soft drinks were served. The bottom right showed the bar area. The on-board images were of staff placing the food and fruit onto the serving tables and cleaning down the bar area. There didn't appear to be any passengers on board at this time. Steve concentrated on the upper left image which showed the passenger boarding ramp. He could see that it was a sunny day. At 06:19 the first of the passengers appeared, a group of four who walked across the concrete area and were greeted by the staff member who inspected the boarding passes. There was a steady flow of passengers walking to the boarding ramp.

At 06:32 a yellow taxi stopped about 10 metres from the ramp and Steve saw Filipe and Josh get out of the taxi. They got their rucksacks out of the boot of the taxi and the driver took a photo of the two lads. They then walked up the boarding ramp showed their passes and walked on board. Steve watched the other segments but did not see Filipe or Josh enter the restaurant or bar area.

Steve continued to watch the boarding ramp segment. 06:48 a brown tourist coach stopped approximately 20 metres from the ramp. The passengers started to get off the coach and walk to towards the ramp and stopped at the bottom of the walkway. A man was seen to get off the coach carrying a brown clipboard and walk passed the waiting passengers to be met by the crew at the top of the ramp. "Fuck me". Steve paused the recording and without thinking opened the bathroom door and walked in.

Jessica was wrapped in a long white towel and was leaning forward towel drying her wet long brown hair, she looked at Steve "Sick of waiting, are we?"

"You have got to see this"

"Well that's an offer a girl can't refuse"

"Come on, have a look at the telly"

They both walked out together and sat on the bed looking at the image in the top left segment.

She said "That's him, definitely." She turned and looked Steve directly into his eyes, "You are not getting anywhere near me until you have showered and shaved. Hurry up, don't keep a girl waiting"

◆ ◆ ◆

It was just after midnight in Newcastle and Andy was sat at a desk leaning back with his feet on the desk, he was twisting but he could not get comfortable against the rigid black plastic of the seat. Sarah was making two cups of coffee and waiting for the kettle to boil, she was thinking, and talking to herself 'I've put too much water in for just the two of us.' The phone rang and sounded panicky loud in the empty office. Andy and Sarah walked to the central desk where the phone was located, they were both looking at each other. Andy gave Sarah a calm sign with his hands. Both hands open, palms facing down and pushed down towards the floor. Sarah nodded. He then indicated quiet, she was not there she was in the town with her friends. Again, she nodded. Andy Picked up the telephone, it was on speaker and being recorded.

"Newcastle Major Crime Team, DS Andy Bacon speaking"

"Hi Andy its Martin Chapman from Panama, we might have a problem"

"What kind of problem Martin?"

"Steve Bond and his female companion Jessica have not got off the canal cruise at Colon"

"Excuse me Martin, there's no stops on the cruise along the canal is there?"

"Well there is one at a place called Gamboa in the middle of nowhere really. But I told Steve that he would be picked up in Colon"

"Are you in the office Martin can I call you back?"

"No Andy, I'm in Colon at the ferry terminal. I'm on my mobile, Sarah has the number."

"Have you checked the ferry, spoke to the crew"

"I have but they are definitely not on the ferry. They have either got off at Gamboa or."

"Why would they get off at Gamboa then?"

"I've no idea Andy. I will head back that way but it would have been 4 or 5 hours ago that they would have stopped at

Gamboa and I'm sure we would have heard from them. I am very concerned for their safety. They wouldn't be the first tourists to be kidnapped in Latin America"

"It doesn't sound good Marty. There's nothing we can do this side can you do what you can over there. I'm working through the night, the boss is in early doors, I'll tell him when he comes in. Let's hope that they're both ok and sleeping some drink off somewhere. Sarah tried to contact them earlier and didn't get a reply, I tried about an hour ago and got nothing. I presumed he was still out of range"

"I will be busy over the next few hours, I will try and retrace their steps, I'll start off in Gamboa. I will keep in touch"

"Thanks Martin. I will keep trying his phone from this end. I will let you know if he gets in touch."

Andy replaced the receiver. "Sarah phone Walter see if he got a location for that call?"

He picked up the phone and dialled Jessica's mobile phone.

Jessica was using the hairdryer on the dressing table next to the television when her phone rang. She looked at the number and recognised it was a 191 a Newcastle number, similar to Steve's desk number. She pressed the green button and placed the phone to her left ear.

"Hello"

"Hi Jessica, I'm Andy, Steve's mate"

"Hello Andy, we have some information to pass on"

"So have I, but first can you ensure that Steve's phone is switched off, I take it he is with you" Jessica picked up Steve's mobile in her right hand and found that it was switched off.

"Yes, he's here just getting a shower, we have had a dirty day, if you know what I mean."

"Yes I do, can you get Steve out of the shower I want to make this a quick call. Does Martin have your mobile number?"

Jessica was walking to the bathroom door, "Not that I know off, wait just one Andy" Jessica pushed the bathroom door open; Steve was showering with his back to the door. Jessica could see a jagged scar down his left hamstring from his left bum cheek.

"Steve" he half turned and looked towards her, "Andy needs to talk to us now"

"Ok, I'll get a towel." Jessica walked back to the bed and sat on the end she was joined shortly by Steve. The phone was on speaker. "Hi Andy what you got then?"

"First you can't use your mobile ok. Martin Chapman has just phoned the office to report that you haven't got off the canal cruise at Colon."

"Is he here now?"

"Walter is checking that now and I'm waiting for an answer from Sarah who is talking to Walter. As a matter of course I'm expecting Chapman to ring your phone several times to justify that has looked for you both over the next few days and certainly next 24 hours"

"We have bought some new phones here, we will be using them but they're not fired up yet. I've got the SIMs but they're in the box, I'll give you all contact numbers later when I call the boss."

Sarah had finished her call to Walter, she looked at Andy and said, "He's in Panama City"

"Chapman was in Panama City when he made the call a few minutes ago. It looks like you and Jessica are dead and not going to be found. He has suggested that you both may have been kidnapped. Jessica said you had some information to pass on"

"Certainly do mate. The crew on the boat were working to instructions and they all said they knew nowt basically. However, one of the officers gave us a DVD of the day the lads were reportedly on the boat. Low and behold there they are walking onto the boat up the ramp after getting out of a taxi. A little while later there's a coach stops and about 40 get off with a few girls that might be the two we're looking for. But. The bus driver, tour rep, gets off the bus with the boarding passes and walks up the ramp into full view, guess what."

"It's Chapman"

"No, but close, only the guy who tried to top us off."

"You're sure, can't be mistaken.?"

"As sure as eggs is eggs mate"

"Kinnel. They've got to be linked. Steve I'll let you get on with what you're both doing. But switch both phones off to be safe. Have a good night you deserve it"

"We will try, but got some more work to do first."

The call was closed and Jessica switched her phone off. She turned to Steve and pushed him back onto the bed, with very little resistance and they embraced and kissed before Jessica told him to hurry up and get dressed she was starving.

CHAPTER 20

Friday 20th May

Mike Mather was the British Police Liaison Officer in Venezuela. Now 44 years old, nearly 1.90 tall, with an athletic build and still kept his natural dark hair in a short style. Mike had started his police career in Thames Valley and later developed his talents in the National Crime Squad before it became the National Crime Agency. A natural ability to talk and listen to anyone, would push him into the intelligence department where he would gather information at ease. Later he was posted as a covert human intelligence source handler to the Caribbean. His wife was Spanish and he had picked up his Spanish from her and her family. The Liaison post had become available and Mike was generally pushed into applying for the role. Surprisingly, he was offered the role on a three-year posting. He enjoyed his job in Venezuela but he missed his wife who stayed in Aylesbury with their two children. The family did visit occasionally on short holidays and they would spend time and not a lot of money on the fantastic long golden beaches. Playa del Agua was their favourite choice on Margarita Island. Venezuela was not a good place to have a family in the present political turmoil. He was wearing a sand coloured lightweight suit and white cotton shirt when he walked into the reception of the Imperial Hotel, in Porlamar, Margarita Island.

The hotel is the typical white painted four-story hotel with a loop drive to the reception doors. It had seen better days but tourism was at an all-time low. It has a small reception area with a grey marble wooden panelling on the desk and concrete pillars. The digital clock on the wall behind the counter was showing 19:18. There was one lone female working behind the desk. She was wearing the white blouse and black skirt as would befit her position of Senior Receptionist. The red rimmed glasses which she was wearing were halfway down the bridge of her nose. She appeared to be a local of the area, light brown skin and black wavy hair down to her shoulders. Quite an attractive woman Mike thought, possibly younger than him about 40, those deep brown eyes, but to honest he had not seen many women on the island that were not attractive. She was wearing a name badge, Maria Gonzales. She watched every step that Mike took towards her desk. He was carrying a small black leather shoulder bag over his left shoulder.

"Buenos tardes" she said. (*good evening*)

Mike spoke back in Spanish with a slight recognisable English accent.

"Buenos tardes. Would it be possible to speak to the person in charge of the hotel this evening" the conversation continued in Spanish.

"Yes, it is, and you are. How can I help"

Mike showed his police identification badge. He knew it had no power and often caused more problems but it was protocol and had to be done. "Please, call me Mike". He gave Maria a pleasant natural smile.

"Ok hello Mike. What brings you to our hotel?"

"I'm trying to trace a young English man by the name of Filipe Lopez"

"An Englishman, Filipe Lopez, interesting". Maria screwed her face in surprise.

"He is of Mexican parents. He stayed here not so long ago about 15 to 17 May"

"Are you sure he stayed here?"

"Yes, he stayed here"

"I will have a look at the registration book. Has he done something bad?

"He has been murdered."

"Madre Mia. Not here I hope" She looked straight at Mike in the eyes.

She had opened the page for the date and was sliding her finger down the list of registrations and stopped at an entry that had a red line around it.

"Yes, he did stop here in room 215 on the second floor and he left without paying."

"Well possibly you could get your payment. How many nights did he book in for and stay"?

"He booked in for five nights and payed $100 deposit and owes another $100."

"Do you own this hotel?"

"No, stupid. Do I look like I own a hotel?" and gave Mike a smile.

"Well I could give you the $100 if you could show me the room he stopped in"

"Actually, it was $150 for deferred payment" she replied, again with a smile.

Mike replied with a smile and a nod of his head, "OK 150, can we go now?"

Maria shouted across to the bar and told the barman to look after the reception for a short time. She took her glasses off and placed them under the reception counter. They took the lift to the second floor, Maria stood in heels and was just about the height of Mikes collar, she could smell his aftershave and looked up to his face. She had a thought in her mind. When the lift door opened, Mike indicated for Maria to exit first and she nodded her thanks. Maria stepped out and walked on to the room. Maria stopped at the door and said "150 please".

Mike opened his wallet and took out 3 crisp $50 bills and handed them to Maria, she pushed them deep inside her white lace bra under her right breast. She opened the door with key, no electric cards here. Fortunately, no one had been allocated the room, but the hotel was quiet, not many people in Venezuela took holidays now and the gringos didn't come anymore in numbers. There was not much earned in tips, you get what you can.

Mike knew where to look. He saw the dark wooden set of three drawers below the mirror at the end of the bed. Maria watched as he got on his knees and pulled out the bottom drawer fully. As he had been told, at the back of the drawer cabinet, hanging from a white plastic hook was a camera and a small mesh bag containing plastic bank cards, a small amount of American Dollars and a passport. Mike took some photographs of the find with his camera and his mobile phone. He put on a pair of evidence plastic gloves. He opened the passport and saw the face of Filipe Lopez looking at him. Another look but there was nothing else to be found. Mike took out two self-sealing plastic exhibit bags. He placed the camera in one bag and sealed it and then placed the bank cards, passport, cash and the white hook he had pulled from the back of the cabinet into the other bag. Again, he sealed the bag. After writing his signature over the seal on each bag. He stood up and looked at Maria, "Thank you Maria you have been most helpful" He placed the bagged exhibits into his bag, he removed the gloves and dropped them in the bag and closed it.

Mike then took some photographs of the room, Maria made sure that she was not in any of the photographs.

Maria asked," Would you like to examine anything, anyone, in the room for just a small bill, say another 50?"

"Maria, I would enjoy that and possibly you could help. Yes, that would be good. Not now though, possibly some other time." Mike smiled at Maria and continued, "I could give you another 50, if your memory is poor and you forget about me finding these" as he tapped on his shoulder bag.

Maria," You, I have never seen you find anything" she smiled and held out her right hand. Mike took another $50 note from his wallet. Maria was leaning toward Mike as she put her right hand inside her bra and pulled it away from her left breast and slowly put her head and eyes towards her breast. Mike had folded the note and pushed the note deep inside her bra. She put her hand over his hand pushing it against her bra and breast. "That feels good, 25 possibly?" she said while looking with a sad face towards Mike.

Mike slowly and gently pulled his hand away from Maria's ample breast and said in English, "Not tonight Josephine" and slowly shook his head whilst keeping a smile. Maria looked puzzled.

"Which days do you work here?"

"I'm here every day, I can be here anytime you want to visit"

Mike took some photographs out of his bag and showed them to Maria, "Do you recognise this hotel from the bedroom furniture?"

"And if I do, do you want me to take you there?"

"I just may do"

Maria thought for a while, "Possibly, Hotel Colinas. Not a lot to look at, we should visit"

He gave her a smile and placed the photographs back into his bag.

"What happened to his bag and clothing, do you have it in storage?"

"No." She laughed and shook her head. "He left it; people here do not have a lot. You know"

"It may be worth something if it was found, just for a look you never know"

Maria stepped back from Mike and gave a shrug of her shoulders. "OK". Maria opened the room door and they walked out together in silence. They then took the lift to the ground floor. She pointed towards the exit and walked back behind the reception desk. There had been no further conversation between them. She watched as Mike walked out of the double glass doors and out of sight. The digital clock on the wall above her head was showing 19:47.

It took just 20 minutes for Mike to get back to the airport in the taxi. The flight is only 50 minutes, he should be back in the Caracas office shortly before 10 o'clock.

◆ ◆ ◆

It was now 00:50 on the clock in the IT room. Walter was still in the office. Despite the time of day and the fact he was working, alone and sat at a large computer screen, Walter was still wearing his white coat. There were now considerably more pen markings above his left breast pocket where he kept his growing number of Biro pens. The multi coloured spotted mug on the briefing table was nearly empty. On the screen was a map of Panama City Centre and one red mark on Calle 47 Edif Aquarius. There was no movement and had been no movement since the call from Chapman that Andy had answered. No more phone calls of desperation for assistance to track down Jimmy and Jessica. Walter was joined by Matty at 01:05 who took over the watching and recording duties to allow Walter to get home to some sleep.

In the Squad room Andy was writing up the information received in the log book and incident file. Sarah was making another two cups of coffee. There was an audible tone for an email being received on the group network. Sarah carried the coffee back for Andy and sat down to see the incoming email. It was from the Cruise line company with an attachment of all passengers who had been on any part of the cruise. It was downloaded and printed. Sarah collected her coffee and waited for the whole print out. It gave full names, nationality, terminal of joining the cruise, terminal of departing the cruise and room type and number. Andy joined Sarah to look over the document. It didn't take long to identify Frank and Eleanor Carlson. USA, Fort Lauderdale, Fort Lauderdale, Mini Suite D316 on Deck 9 Dolphin. They then looked for passengers joining at Colon and departing Aruba. Approximately 40, mostly couples. One particular pair caught their attention. Maria Luiza Valencia and Susanna Piqueta Cuadrado. Colombian. Colon, Aruba, Balcony D306 on Deck 9 Dolphin.

It was just after 05:04 in the morning when the phone rang on Sarah's desk. Again, Andy answered the call. It was Mike Mather. "Hi Andy, Mike Mather I'm back in my office in Caracas, is Sarah there I was told to liaise with her?"

"No Mike you're stuck with me, she has gone for some well-deserved sleep. Did you manage to find anything?" Sarah was making coffee again with the last of the milk.

"Yes, it's late, or early over there. I did. I found his passport, cash, bank cards and his camera."

"Great stuff"

"What's more, there are quite a lot of photographs on his camera memory. I'm going to send the lot. I don't know what you're looking for. I've forensically downloaded the memory card and produced three copies. I will email them in bunches of date order. What date do you want to start from?"

"Sunday 8th May would be ideal he was in Panama City then."

"One more thing. I have been told the furniture fits the description of a hotel called Colinas, which I believe will be the Hotel Colinas del Sol in Porlamar. I didn't have the time to go there and get back here tonight to view the rooms but I can go back tomorrow, if I'm not directed elsewhere by London."

"That's great Mike. Yes, I'm aware NCA are running the show now. I doubt if there would be any forensic evidence there now. That's if you could identify the correct room. Are the local police very helpful on the island?"

"I have some contacts there. They are not as bad as you might think but they do not like creating problems for the island. If you get my drift?"

"Yes Mike, thanks a lot for today. If you send the photographs, they will be useful. Someone will contact you tomorrow, we have all your contact details"

"Yes, I'll do that. All the items are packaged for examination and I'll put them into storage here, as we believe it has happened here."

After 10 minutes the emails arrived with the very clear photographs of Maria and Susanna.

CHAPTER 21

Friday 20th May

Steve had charged the new mobile phones and inserted the Sim cards. Jessica ensured the other mobile phones were switched off and took the battery out of each one.

They were clean and dressed casually in a holiday style and were both in need of food. They left the Radisson and walked the short distance to Arecifes. They took a seat inside so as not to be on public view and ordered beers and a seafood mix for 2 with some ceviche as a starter.

Jessica saw the board on the wall with a collection of photographs of recent visitors. They walked across to take a look. There were approximately 60 photographs, all the same size but at obtuse angles, overlapping. All showing the patrons having a happy time, dancing, drinking, kissing or just smiling. They were there, near the top right corner, Filipe, Josh and two females. They were in a booth together, holding drinks and smiling towards the photographer. The staff was too busy to notice or care that Steve removed the pin from the photograph and put it into the small grip bag that Jessica was carrying.

They stayed in Arecifes for over two hours. The ceviche was very spicy and tasty, the food which had been barbequed was delicious and plentiful but the ice-cold Polar beer was very much needed and enjoyed. They talked through the events of the day and what the plan of action was. They knew there was work to be done and they had to get back to the hotel room.

They walked the short distance back to the hotel quickly and went immediately to their room. Jessica took two cold beers from the fridge and opened the bottles. The new mobiles were fully charged and Steve placed a new SIM card into each mobile and passed one to Jessica. After installing the cards, they went through the process of activating the phone then obtaining the hotel web access from the information book inside cover and they could now contact the office.

Jessica placed the DVD back into the player and Steve switched the TV set on to the appropriate setting to view the recording. The images were stopped at the point where Filipe and Josh climbed the walkway onto the small canal cruise boat in Panama and Steve took a photograph of the image, which showed time and date. It was again stopped at the best images of the driver of the coach and the man who they had left dead in the canal side jungle. Steve again took several photographs of this unknown man. Jessica forwarded to the point where the two girls walked onto the canal boat and Steve took photographs of the captured image and a photo of the four together in 'Arecifes'.

Steve sent the images to the office in Newcastle as attachments to emails.

They sat looking out over the port from the balcony of the room in the warm evening air with a slight soothing breeze picking at the small selection of assorted nuts courtesy of the hotel. Steve went to the fridge and opened two more bottles of cold refreshing beer and took his seat again with his feet raised onto the top safety bar of the balcony and gave Jessica a bottle which they chinked together. They could hear the music playing on board the nearby cruise ship 'Southern Freedom' and the voices of the passengers enjoying the music and effects of alcohol. The mobile alerted a message had been received, Jessica picked it up and saw that is was from Andy acknowledging receipt of the photographs. The message also confirmed 06:00 reception.

After finishing the beers, they retreated into the air-conditioned room and packed their new bags in preparation for tomorrow, still not knowing what their involvement would be but they would be prepared after a good sleep they hoped. The room door was double locked, the pistols were on the bed side cabinets, loaded and safety catches off. They went into a deep sleep.

◆ ◆ ◆

Sat in comfortable black leather chairs at a desk in a secure office in Oxnard Police Headquarters, Greg Simons was writing the statement of Josh. There were no distractions in the office, no photographs of graduation, no printed circulars on notice boards. Just plain light grey painted walls and bright overhead lighting. A plain oblong desk with 4 leather chairs. They both had paper cups with what once was cold water in front of them. Greg had told Josh of the murder of Filipe in some detail, to make him understand the possible threat to his life. Josh was searching his mind to recall and recount any small piece of information that may be helpful. There was a knock on the door. Greg shouted, "Enter". A uniformed officer opened the door and Madison walked into the room. Her face broke into a wide smile at the sight of Josh. Josh was taken back by how beautiful she looked. Her blonde hair was tied back, she was wearing a white Ralph Lauren polo shirt, sky blue canvas trousers and white training shoes. She still looked a million dollars in his eyes. Immediately, Josh stood to his tallest and they quickly moved towards each other and embraced. They held each other tightly without speaking. They eventually moved apart but still looked at each other.

Greg, "It is good to see you Miss Roberts". That appeared to break the spell.

Madison turned towards the officer," It's great to see you both, I've been very worried and I still am."

Greg indicated for the officer to leave the room and the door was closed behind him as he left. "Why don't we take a break from writing? Anyone want a coffee or tea possibly. We can just have a chat and chew over what's going on." Greg pulled up another leather chair next to Josh and he then left the room to get the coffees and sandwiches from the nearby coffee store frequented by the local officers.

CHAPTER 22.

Friday 20th May

It was 20:18 when the Copa Airlines flight was landing at Panama Tocumen International Airport from Cali. Maria was preparing to leave the aircraft and take a taxi into Panama City. She was travelling alone. She had purposely watched all of the passengers that had also boarded and had committed to memory, their faces and clothing. This was a business trip and she had one small pull trolley case; she did not intend to stay long.

It took 50 minutes from landing at the airport to walk into the reception area at the Hyatt Place hotel in downtown Panama City. She had chosen the hotel from an advertisement in the airport terminal. After checking in to the hotel, there had been no problems with her new identity passport, she took the lift to the fifth floor and entered her room with the room card. She discarded the small case on the metal framework luggage rack and draped her lightweight jacket over the back of the black fabric upholstered bucket seat. The shoulder bag was dropped into the seat. After checking the view onto the large avenue down below which was full of static traffic then the immaculate bathroom she flopped backwards onto the King-sized bed. She closed her eyes, memories and hatred came flooding into her brain.

Susanna was lying on the floor, blood gurgling from the wound in her throat, and slowly oozing out of the two deep stabbing wounds through her chest, staring upwards into her face. A look of disbelief and despair as her life drained out of her eyes. I did that, how could I do it, I loved her. I did it for her, I did it for her. Maria told herself. She would have suffered and would die in that place if not now but soon. I did it for her. How could I do it? The thought was reverberating around in her head. Those bastards, Borja, she saw the image of Borja in her mind, immaculate dressed in his suit sitting at the table in the hacienda. He fucked me, no raped me, I should have killed him, I was going to kill myself but no I killed Susanna. No man has done what he did. I will kill him, for me, Susanna, for them all. Her thoughts jumped to El Cerdo, the stinking, dirty, large hulk of a man who fought strongly and frightened her. Why did I kill Cerdo, because he told me? The man was a pig but I killed him because they told me and showed me. What am I? What am I? I'm a paid assassin, I'm now paid to kill anyone they want. She thought of the kind, good looking English boy. I acted like a butcher and killed Filipe. He was just a good guy, really loving me and I butchered him in the middle of passion. Fuck, fuck, fuck. I hate me. How do I get out of this? They know my parents, I'm not scared for me, what the fuck do I do? She lay there completely still, her deep dark brown eyes closed in deep thought. Tears were slowly rolling down the side of her face into her ears and down her neck towards the pillow, leaving small damp patches on the immaculate white Egyptian cotton pillows.

Her thoughts were disturbed by the tone of her mobile phone calling to be answered. She slowly sat up on the bed then stood and took the three steps to her bag and retrieved the phone. She took a deep breath then exhaled slowly and answered, "Hola". She listened to the instructions and answered, "Si, vale" (Yes Ok). The call was ended. It was Borja. No names but she knew.

The phone was thrown onto the bed as she walked into the bathroom and ran the cold water into the sink. She looked at her face in the illuminated mirror and shook her head, then washed her face with the cold water, removing the signs of the tracks of her tears. She shook her head and then ran her fingers through her natural curly hair which fell loosely into its place. She straightened her denim jeans and dark blue T shirt, threw her three-quarter length sleeve jacket on. She took the phone from the bed and placed it into the shoulder bag then left the room.

The Hyatt Place Hotel was only 200 metres from The Blarney Stone Irish bar.

Martin Chapman had been in contact with the Embassy to explain there may be problems with the missing police officer from Newcastle. It was his intention to wait at the hotel to see if he returned there but there was no urgency at the moment. He was still sitting in the bar, slowly sipping on his mojito. He couldn't recall how many he had so far but he wasn't counting. He would chat to the barmaid, Eva as she was known. He regularly wished about having a relationship with Eva, not a long one, maybe just one night. He was not the only one who had that thought but no one would get anywhere near her. Martin thought what a wonderful place to retire. He felt the phone vibrate in his trouser pocket and walked away from the bar towards an empty booth with no neighbouring drinkers and took a seat.

The call was precise. A trip had to be facilitated to meet at a similar location. A courier would give instructions. One more then it will be finished. Thank you for information. Where and when will you meet courier. Sunday deadline for meet.

Chapman had answered yes when he was supposed to and suggested Urraca Park grassed area near to the café area at 11:00. Chapman believed that area was wide open and a safe place to meet avoiding any harm. He asked Eva for his bill. He then thought this can't be on expenses, I'm not here, he took his wallet out of his hip pocket and paid in Balboas.

Maria was walking down Calle 47 as Chapman was paying his bill, also leaving a good tip and wishing Eva a good night. She walked passed the door of The Blarney Stone Irish Bar, which held no attraction to her and continued to 'Tacos de Finca' at the junction with Calle 45.

Chapman left the bar and walked across the pavement and stopped at the side of the road. He did not notice Maria who was walking away from him with her back to him. He got into a waiting taxi and gave the driver the instructions to take him to his apartment. The taxi was driven off and passed Maria as she continued walking towards her instructed destination. Both were none the wiser.

After another three minutes walking, Marie entered the 'Tacos de Finca' restaurant. It's a good quality South American restaurant and very popular with the locals and tourists, there were patrons sitting on the outside pavement tables and inside looked very busy. The smell of barbeque, cooking steaks, chicken, tacos, chillies was making Maria feel very hungry. She stood momentarily at the open doorway inside the restaurant, then saw the raised right arm in a long white sleeve beckoning her towards a seated area. As she walked passed the waiters in the aisles, she saw it was Borja.

Borja was sat at a corner table. On the wall behind him there was a large mural of a fearsome South American male skeleton skull with a crazy grin below a wide sombrero rim. There was a large cigar jutting out from the teeth of the face. Somehow Marie imposed Borja's face onto the skeleton in her imagination which brought a slight smile to her face. She was stood in front of the table.

Borja greeted Maria, "It is a pleasure to see you smile. You must be happy to see me. It has been a little while since we last spoke. I know you have been busy."

He tilted his head and gave her a smile then indicated towards the empty seat opposite him and waved his hand for her to take the seat.

Marie had already recognised two of his protection employees sitting just two tables away. The two tables between them had small reserved markers placed in the middle of the tables, Borja had his privacy in such a busy well-liked restaurant. There was no cutlery in front of the seat Maria was taking. She thought, this bastard doesn't trust me and is taking no chances. She was right.

Laid out on the table in front of Borja was the speciality, Volcanes Especiales. There were three tacos, one sizzling beef, a spiced and sliced chicken and another taco crammed with chorizo. They were accompanied with a green hot local sauce and a small bowl of diced chillies.

Borja, "This is good food I'm not going to waste it. You have another detail." He started to wrap the beef taco with the green paste and liberal quantity of the red chillies. "There is a small package for you my friend Emilio will give you when you leave. It has everything you need. When that is done you will have to see me for one thing I need." He looked up from his taco into the face of Maria and gave her a threatening smile. She understood what his need was. She gave him an agreeable nod and a slight smile. He indicated with his right thumb for her to leave. As she stood up, he said," I look forward to our next meeting." He then returned his attention to the tacos.

As Maria was walking passed Emilio, he gave her a padded protective envelope which she placed inside her jacket and held firm from the outside pocket. As soon as Maria believed she was in a quiet, unobserved area she placed the envelope into her bag. She then walked back to the Hyatt Place hotel. Entering the cooled air inside the hotel, a relief from the overbearing heat outside she made her way to the empty reception desk. The male receptionist, in his immaculate uniform appeared from the office to the rear. Maria ordered chicken tacos with a side of guacamole dip chips and two bottles of cola to be delivered to her room. She stepped inside the lift and opened the bag then took out the envelope. There was no writing or printed names to be seen. She put the envelope back into the bag and took out the room card.

As she entered her room, she felt the cooler air of the air conditioning which she had left on. She threw the bag onto the bed, draped her jacket over the chair, then stood on the heel of her Converse flat shoes and kicked them off. Taking off her jeans and tee shirt she threw them on top of the small fight case she then walked into the bright bathroom and turned on the shower before discarding her underwear. Placing the foot towel on the floor, she then stepped into the tepid, powerful shower. She stood with both of her hands against the wall and allowed the water to runover her head, shoulders and down her back. Cleaning away the dirt of the meeting and the man but nothing could clear her memory. It took a full ten minutes in the shower to feel clean before having the shock of the ice-cold water before she stood out and dried herself off and wrapped a towel around her head encompassing all her long black curly hair. She was still in the bathroom when there was a knock on the door. Maria wrapped a large white towel tightly around her body and put a grip knot just above her breasts before going to the door. After looking through the spyhole and seeing the room delivery with her order she opened the door. He placed the order on top of the unit and the drawers under the television. She tipped him and watched him leave before double locking the door and placing the safety catch over the lever.

She took the envelope out of the bag, pulled the chair into place at the unit and sat down. She opened the gummed envelope and poured the contents onto the unit top. There was a large number of mixed notes, US dollars and Bilboa's probably totalling about 5000 US dollars in the mixed currency. There was a black fountain pen. She checked inside the envelope and removed a folded white A4 paper with typing. Inside the folded paper was a smaller sealed flat envelope, there was biro markings crossing over the seal to prevent tampering. She began to read and started to prepare her tacos.

CHAPTER 23

Saturday 21st May

It was now 0600, in England and the Crime team office in Newcastle was occupied by Andy and Sarah who had updated the occurrence log on a written report and also electronically. The intelligence had been updated on the Crime Analysis Research and Development (CARD) system and produced a timeline with the various links in Newcastle, Manchester, Panama, Margarita, Santa Monica and Fort Lauderdale. The intelligence had now all been forwarded to the hub at NCA. The newly received photographs had been received from Jimmy with the images of the two Latino women with Filipe and Josh and the coach driver who was now dead.

At the same time in London at the NCA Headquarters, Rajid Badie was leading his team of analysts and intelligence officers who were currently liaising with offices in Margarita, Santa Monica, Fort Lauderdale, Newcastle City and the new Panama Liaison.

They were sat in a modern styled open plan office on the second floor of the building. It was on the corner of the building and had daylight coming into the office from two sides. The desks and seating were well spaced, the office furniture was new and had been designed to produce positivity in the workplace. Every desk had a central large IT screen and telephone extension. There was no hot desking here, this was a bright room to generate bright ideas. This was a room for work only and a plastic cup of water from the cooler. The tea and coffee room, was further along the corridor where the seats and tables were closer together to generate chat and ideas.

Working with Rajid was Gavin Williams who had established liaison with Santa Monica, Ayesha Majeed who was in contact with Fort Lauderdale, Antonio Perez with South America, Panama, Venezuela, Colombia and Aruba. Penny Harston liaison with Newcastle City Crime Squad and Aaqil Khan overall intelligence analyst. They all had a University background and between them spoke over 15 languages.

There had been four locations of activity which needed to be linked and if possible acted upon, it was time imperative to formulate the action plan based on good evidence practice. Rajid called his team together and Aaqil would present the intelligence PowerPoint and input newly gathered intelligence. They gathered in front of the large central office display screen and were sat in the ergonomic individually designed black cool material office chairs. The room was silent as Aaqil started the breakdown. He spoke slowly and read from the script. Each point was visually displayed.

"Venezuela.

It is known/highly believed that Filipe was murdered by a female on Margarita on or about Monday 16th May. It had been established he was on the Island; The last call Filipe received was at 9:42 on Sunday night from an unregistered mobile used on the island. The WhatsApp message to his parents was sent from Caracas on Monday 16th May. Not known by who. His camera, passport and cards were recovered by Mike Mather at the Hotel Imperial where he had booked a room. However, he never returned to the hotel and the bill wasn't paid. Photographs on the camera identify Filipe in Panama with 2 females known as Marie Luiza Valencia and Susanna Piqueta Cuadrado as recorded on the cruise ship manifest. It is highly doubtful that these are the correct names of the females. There are no significant photographs of Filipe with a female in Margarita, other than the final video. There is no record of his movements but he was not murdered at the Hotel Imperial. Mike Mather, the liaison officer is checking out a possible murder scene later today.

Panama.

Filipe and Josh boarded the canal cruise and met with two Colombian females who have now been identified as

Maria and Susanna evidenced from Josh and photographs from the recovered camera of Filipe. The girls were within a group of 42 who were on the same holiday package from a Colombia travel company. The same two girls were seen and photographed handing the suitcases to crew from on board the 'Alisios', these were later found full of cocaine in the trunk of the two couriers murdered in Fort Lauderdale. These cases have been forensically examined and several DNA samples taken but DNA samples from the females are needed.

The driver of the tourist coach is known to be dead after attempting to kill Steve Bond and a civilian associate in the incident. Is there a known link between the females and the driver? Steve Bond is in possession of this man's mobile which needs forensically examining a.s.a.p.

The recipient of informant payments for the Operations in Fort Lauderdale was a Latino person in Panama. No direct information as to the informant's identity has been given but we are asking.

Martin Chapman, police liaison, is known to be lying to Newcastle City Major Crime team concerning Bonds whereabouts, he also had not been passing on information to Bond. He has taken four days leave. He is known to be in Panama City believed in his apartment where the mobile phone is currently sighted. The mobile is being monitored by Newcastle City Crime team. He is currently under light surveillance by Panama National Police until a full surveillance unit has been mobilised. The driver who is dead is believed to have been dispatched by Chapman to meet Bond and his associate O'Brien, he was driving the car used by Chapman which as yet has not been reported stolen. The drivers' body has been recovered by the National police but it has not been reported. We hope to obtain his identity later this morning or early afternoon. Importantly there has been no reports of a missing Panama police officer, ruling out that the original dispatched officer has been killed. It is thought that Chapman has been spending quite a bit of cash in the build-up to his retirement next year. There is to be a full prolonged surveillance on Chapman which hopefully will be successful in evidence gathering. For your information, Steve Bond will be in with the surveillance team, do not pass this to Newcastle Penny. Bond will be in the Command vehicle; Northumbria Police and The Ambassador in Panama are aware of this action.

Aruba

It is known that Filipe travelled to Aruba on Monday 8th May

Photographic evidence from his camera shows him with the female believed to be Susanna, the female with the straight hair, in various locations on the island and also Bricknell Bay Hotel. Enquiries have revealed that the females were staying at the Holiday Inn with the other holiday makers. There are photographs timed around 07:30 Saturday 14th of the two females with Felipe outside of the hotel and the females boarding the coach for what would be the start of the journey back to Colombia. As far as we know nothing criminal occurred in Aruba. There is no urgency for actions in Aruba.

Colombia.

It is believed that the females are both Colombians. They were with a tourist group that travelled from there and returned there. They told Filipe and Josh their life story as such can be believed that they were from Colombia. The drugs seized in the Fort Lauderdale Operation are known to be from a cartel based in Cali, the MMV, ran very rigidly and ruthlessly by Manolo Martinez Valero and two lieutenants Paco Verdu and Borja Sanchez, his cousins. It is believed that this cartel use passage through Panama as its major distribution route. Interestingly Martin Chapman worked in Colombia for three years at the embassy in Cali before returning to NCA in London for 2 years then being seconded to Panama for the last two years. Also, the females did say they worked for their family in logistics and hotels in Colombia. Enquiries are to be made where the tourist party was booked, if any of the group had been on previous similar organised trips. Was there a link between the tourist organisation and the females? Identify the females.

Fort Lauderdale

It is looking that the operation that occurred against the cartel in Fort Lauderdale has been the catalyst for a series of actions of retribution or revenge. It is linked to the females, the dead coach driver and the cartel. There is no direct link with Felipe's murder other than possibly one of the females murdered him, probably Susanna, but it is believed that they were in Colombia at the time of his death. There was time for one or both of them to travel back but there is no communication track. We do know that there was a call to his mobile at 9:42 on Monday night from an unregistered phone but made from on the island. There had been two payments made to the informant but there may have been several drugs run completed before these two actions. We would like to identify the informant is it the driver, Chapman or someone connected to them?

Santa Monica

The only suggestion for the involvement of this location is that Josh is there. He was with Felipe when he met the girls in Panama but as far as we are aware it is to ensure the safety of Josh, there is no known direct threat against him. It is basically a belt and braces operation.

Newcastle

The Crime team have done a fantastic job up to this point where we now take over due to our International experience and overseas teams. We will not let them down. Steve Bond and his associate Jessica O'Brien are still in Panama and will be collected at their hotel by the Panama Surveillance unit around 5am. It's believed that Martin Chapman believes they are dead having been murdered and disposed of by the driver, it may become apparent that the driver is missing at some time which may create movement. The Newcastle office will still maintain the tracking facility on Chapman. They are also running a pattern spread of mobiles being used in the same location as Chapman, which is a recent development. This could identify another mobile being used by him if it shows up in similar locations to him on a regular basis. Any intelligence they get will be immediately sent here. We will give updates to the Super Colin Tinkler, if he is not there Sarah Pearson is the only nominated recipient.

Mobile Phones

We have not recovered the mobile of Filipe. It has not been used since it was used in Caracas on Monday to send the WhatsApp message to his parents. We have a full itemised use of calls and messages and one number was used frequently in Aruba and we believe that was Susanna. That mobile is no longer in use and was last traced in Porlamar. We are still awaiting WhatsApp history.

Josh is now in Santa Monica area and the phone has not been used while he was in the native Indian reservation. There is recent history prior to that to known identified numbers. Again, we are waiting for the mobile to be examined in Santa Monica and await WhatsApp history.

As stated, we have the mobile of the dead driver but it is possession of Steve Bond. This will be examined by Panama police later today.

Chapman is now having his mobile tracked. I don't believe he would be foolish enough to use his own registered mobile for criminal activity but hopefully the new development may help identify any other mobiles he may use.

Photographs

So, who are we looking at and talking about?

There followed a photograph display from the photographs recovered from mobile phones, camera, CCTV recordings and historic photographs.

First this is Felipe with Josh and the two females Maria and Susanna.

Josh is the taller of the two men with fair hair and Susanna has the long straight hair.

This is the driver of the coach, who attempted to kill Steve and Jessica. He is shown presenting the boarding passes to the canal cruise staff.

Here is Martin Chapman from his latest id card photo.

These are from the police surveillance photographs of Manolo Martinez Valero, Paco Verdu and Borja Sanchez.

Ok that is what we have at the moment, everything, any questions."

Raj asked, "When will we get the WhatsApp history, is there a problem?"

Aaqil, "It should be here now, the usual data protection requests. All the applications have been electronically delivered I will chase it up."

"What time are the full surveillance team starting on Chapman"

"They should be there for 0600 Panama time 12midday here. Antonio get that confirmed please." Antonio nodded and moved to his workplace.

"I want to keep Newcastle involved, Penny can you ensure that they have copies of all the photographs available and ask for a thorough examination of every one just in case there is something that might be important." She acknowledged Raj and nodded.

CHAPTER 24

Saturday 21st May

It was 06:18 in Newcastle when the phone on Sarah's desk rang, she had just returned from the local 24/7 with 2 loaves of fresh thick sliced bread, a large tub of butter and two, 2 litre plastic cartons of semi-skinned milk. She dropped the bag next to her desk and picked up the phone, "Good morning, Newcastle Major Crime team Sarah speaking."

She recognised the American accent straight away. "Hello Sarah are you still there? Have they got you chained to your desk?"

"Eee hello Greg nice to hear your voice again, how ya doing cowboy?"

Greg laughed at Sarah, "First let me tell you that Josh and Maddison are in a safe place in Oxnard Police Headquarters. But,"

"Oh oh, what's coming Greg, come on tell is"

"We have examined his mobile and there was a WhatsApp message from Filipe on Monday 16th May which read Looks good, where you staying"

"That's impossible I think, unless we're wrong, I'm sure Filipe was killed on the Monday. What time was the message?"

"It is recorded at 11:18 when it was received here that would be 13:18 in Panama and 19:18 in England."

"Give us a second Greg I'll just check the other info we have." Sarah opened the occurrence log and searched for WhatsApp message. It came on the screen instantly. 19:16 Monday 16th May, WhatsApp message received by Lopez family. "Greg, we have a problem, that has probably been sent by the murderer or persons involved with the murder."

"That's what I was thinking, would they have any idea where Josh may have been travelling to, or in fact if he was coming here?"

At this moment Superintendent Tinkler walked into the

office, he was looking better for his sleep, he looked fresh wearing a white shirt with the collar open, his suit jacket over his shoulder and carrying a white plastic bag that contained a sliced loaf of bread and a 2-litre carton of milk. Sarah raised her voice, "Boss, can you come here please Greg is on the phone from the states?"

Colin walked over, "What is it Sarah"

"Greg has just told me that there is a WhatsApp message to Josh and it was sent two minutes after the message was sent to the Lopez Family."

Colin waved with his fingers for the phone off Sarah, he took the phone, "Hello Greg, I'm Detective Superintendent Tinkler, I would like to thank you specifically for the work you personally have done on our behalf in Santa Monica. I have been in contact with the Senior Officers already to express our gratitude. This is an ongoing complicated case, of which you are a major part. This information you have given changes matters and it is now imperative that Josh is in a safe place at all times. There is a strong possibility that persons who wish him harm may know his approximate whereabouts. Do you understand the situation Greg?"

"Yes Sir, I do. I can assure you that both Josh and Maddison will have protection at all times"

"I will be contacting your own Headquarters very shortly but I wanted to thank you personally and give you advance warning of the threat level rising. Thank you very much Greg I will pass you back to Sarah." Colin handed Sarah the phone and walked towards his office, Andy walked behind him into the office.

Sarah "Greg, the boss is highly delighted with what you have done. I don't know everything but if he says there's danger, it's a warning. Is there anything else urgent cos I've got a briefing with the boss now? I can call you back shortly"

"Yes, that's good. There is nothing in the story of Josh that gives much information. I will send the statement to you and make arrangements here for Josh and Maddison. Speak later if you need anything"

The call was ended and Sarah made her way to the bosses' office. She knocked then walked into the office. "Good morning Boss"

"Morning, take a seat Sarah." She took a seat next to Andy." There are somethings you need to know and others that you don't." He paused, "This operation is now being run from NCA in London. It has nothing to do with how we have performed, in fact your work has been highly praised and I regard you both, well, all of the team very highly. It is not feasible for us to continue with the overall management of the operation, but we still have our part to play. It is now a multi-National joint enterprise, in which the links you have unearthed are the basis for the Investigation. What I really want is for you both to get home and have some sleep, that is after I've been briefed. First, Sarah forward that latest piece of info to London. Andy have they got everything else if not it needs doing now. Right then, who wants tea, coffee and toast. You two get done what has to be done, then go and freshen up a bit and I'll pop the kettle on and put the toast in, should have had a pan could have made milky coffee. Oh, did Walter go home?"

Andy," He did boss about one but said he'd be back for the morning briefing. He has Matty in monitoring the mobiles in the office."

Billy and Alan were the first to walk through the door with Alan carrying a white plastic bag holding a 2-litre carton of milk and a thick sliced loaf of bread. He took them out of the bag and put the loaf with the other bread on the table next to the toaster and kettle and just managed to fit the two cartons of milk in the small fridge in the improvised kitchen area. The boss put four more slices of bread in the toaster and loaded up two cups with coffee granules. Lauren walked in with her cup of McD's coffee and a paper bag full of croissants. The boss asked Billy to get everyone sorted with drink and toast while he contacted London and went to his office to make the call.

They all took their seat around the table with an A4 paper

plate of toast or croissant and hot drink of their choice. Walter had phoned in from his office checking that Matty had given him all of the information and would be there shortly. The boss returned from his call and took his seat and he enjoyed his coffee and toast with his team while they waited for Walter who walked in and quickly picked up his prepared coffee and toast and took his seat opposite Lauren.

The Super cleared his throat, "Keep enjoying your breakfast, I'm hoping we can have a better time together soon. We are no longer running this enquiry, we never could really with the many International implications, NCA are now the lead. You have all done an excellent job and some will still play a part. I have earlier spoken to Andy and Sarah, now they need to get home for some sleep. All of the information we have gathered some new, which you will not know about has been passed to London. They have asked for our team to examine quite a few photographs recovered from the camera of Filipe for anything that may be helpful, they've also sent photos of the females, coach driver, Chapman and some well-known Colombian Cartel members. It is probable that the murder did occur on Margarita Island which is not in our remit. Information from NCA will only be given direct to me, and, Sarah. Nothing against anyone but Sarah is our intel specialist. That's it in a nutshell. Walter there is a specialist role required by you and your team which I will discuss in my office. Ok, questions?"

Lauren, "Are Steve and Jessica safe?"

"Yes, they are, good point I should have told you. They are being protected, officially."

Billy "Should Alan and me look at the photo's?"

"Ideally I would like all of you to look at every photo. First, I want Andy and Sarah taking home then picking up later. Oh, this might tickle you lot, the chap in charge of the job on NCA is called Rajid Badie."

Lauren had just taken a drink of her coffee and nearly choked spraying her hot milky coffee across the fresh white coat of Walter sitting opposite. They all burst into fits of laughter, Lauren was coughing and crying with laughter at the same time as the rest due to the mixture of the term 'radgie gadgie'(Geordie name for a violent, bad tempered man) and the projectile coffee expulsion from Lauren on to the once clean white coat and Walters shocked face, what a picture.

The meeting was ended Billy was to take Andy and Sarah left with Alan.

Lauren sorted the photos into three similar sized piles, whilst the boss explained to Walter that he needed to keep contact with the mobile of Chapman and report any movement. Press on with the search in vicinity of his phone and record all visible numbers.

As Alan pulled up outside the home of Sarah he asked "Are you inviting me in for a coffee then?" and gave her a smile

"You've got no chance of coming in if that's all your after" and gave him a wink.

CHAPTER 25

Friday 20th May 23:30

Greg had completed the statement of Josh and his mobile phone had been analysed by the IT crime unit in Oxnard Police Headquarters and documented. The information and the statement had been electronically sent to Gavin Williams in the NCA London office. Gavin had acknowledged receipt of the documents. The original documents and the mobile phone had been packaged and placed into the exhibits store within the building.

Josh had recorded some of his contact numbers from the mobile before it had been packaged. He was able to make a call to his parents using the police landline and had a chat for a little time explaining that he was safe and did not have any idea what was happening or what had happened to Filipe. He mentioned that he had met Maddison and it was readily accepted that she could attend the wedding in New Zealand and his father would pay her expenses. At his father's request he sent a message to Jessica O'Brien to thank her for what she was doing and that he would be meeting her when they got back to Alderley Edge.

Arrangements had now been made for Josh and Maddison to stay at a nearby hotel overnight and there would be uniformed officers from Oxnard giving protection from outside of the rooms. A flight had been booked for Josh to fly from Los Angeles to London at 15:35 on Saturday afternoon but Maddison was undecided on her plans, however a seat had been reserved next to Josh on the flight for her with American Airlines. It would be a non-stop, flight to London Heathrow.

Greg had finished his job, for now and was feeling a sense of relief and pride that these two youngsters were safe and the paperwork was completed. He would return on Monday and arrange for the paperwork to be dispatched to the NCA office in London. He knocked on the interview room door, as a light warning that he would be entering, he then opened the door and walked in. Josh and Maddison were sat facing each other in conversation but they both stood up and smiled at Greg. He was just one of those nice guys, Maddison said, "Greg you will have to introduce me to your bad cop partner."

"Oh, I'm so special Maddison they let me work on my own" he replied smiling at her, "Hey, good news. Josh your flight is booked for tomorrow, American Airlines, Maddison there is a seat reserved and will be paid for if you decide to travel, you have up to the last call time but please make it sooner. You two just look like peas from the same pod. My jobs done now, I have to say it has been a pleasure, if you stay around here, I wouldn't mind meeting up again Maddison and have a chat about the English project"

"How do you know about that, Sarah? She does talk strange at times but I would like to meet her"

"I couldn't possibly say what Sarah says. I Like her, heck, I haven't even seen her but like you, I would like to meet up. At the end of this, I might just get an invite over"

Josh, "Well if you do, I will be there to greet you and thank you in style"

Greg exchanged a hug with Maddison and accepted a kiss on his cheek. He and Josh had a manly handshake. "Ok, time to go".

Greg opened the door and introduced the two officers who would be staying outside of their rooms for the night and they both walked through the double doors and out of sight towards the car park. Greg picked up his document bag and followed towards the car park. As he was opening his car door, he watched as an unmarked police car drove passed and Josh was waving, Maddison blew him a kiss, which he theatrically caught in the air then waved as they were driven out of the car park.

Greg got into his car and started on the journey back to Santa Monica.

Josh and Maddison were in deep conversation about the future possibilities, they didn't know each other, had only dated once and were now considering the possibility of living together in the UK. What would their parents think, what if they didn't get on, what about work prospects? At this time, they only had eyes and thoughts for each other and their futures, together.

The traffic was light on the freeway, it was almost midnight as the motorbike made to overtake the car, as it was parallel with the cabin of the car, the pillion passenger lowered an automatic rapid fire M16 assault rifle and aiming inside the darkened cabin opened fire and maintained shooting until the magazine was empty. The car was riddled with high velocity bullets, it violently swerved left towards the motorbike and then to the right and crashed hard into the roadside barriers then exploded into a huge ball of fire.

CHAPTER 26

Saturday 21st May

It was 02:27 on Saturday when the DEA intelligence officer in Fort Lauderdale received a mobile phone call from code number 89147. Another drugs run was being planned through Panama, different method, similar quantities and a major player involved. The informant demanded a higher payment as there would be risk involved and would contact again later when more information was known and would expect to hear a serious payment offer. The call was recorded and the mobile number was written down next to the information.

◆ ◆ ◆

Gavin was at his desk in London when his desk phone rang, he picked up the receiver and answered in a cheerful way, "Gavin Williams, good morning, how can I help you."

"Hello Gavin, I am Captain Ray Carroll speaking from Oxnard Police department." The Captain was speaking slowly, it did not sound promising. "I have some bad news. Shortly after Josh Newton and Maddison Roberts were taken from the police headquarters and Greg Simons left to return to Santa Monica, there was an attack on the vehicle. A pillion on a motorbike fired several rounds into the vehicle which eventually crashed at speed and burst into flames. Sergeant Greg Simons was killed instantly."

"Oh my God, that is shocking news Sir."

"I have taken the decision to have Josh and Maddison returned to Oxnard Police Headquarters where they will stay until the flight tomorrow. They are both now booked to fly. I have relayed the sad news to them and they are both in shock and very distressed. I would now think they realise that there is a real danger for them to remain in this area."

"Sir, please pass on our deepest sympathies to the family of

Greg and to all of his colleagues"

"Yes, I will. Thank you. There will be a report forwarded in due course. I will leave you now, I have other urgent matters to attend to."

The call was ended.

Gavin walked to the segregated part of the floor where Rajid was sat and took a seat opposite him and relayed the information. Rajid called the team together at his work area and updated everyone. He decided that he would call Superintendent Tinkler and told Penny. He said to his team, "Come on, let's get these bastards, intelligence and planning will win the day. Keep on top of your individual responsibilities and liaison officers, we want and need everything. As soon as its morning in their World, contact them, tell them about Greg, no time to waste, time off is cancelled, we want answers now. Have your break now, have a drink, get together, talk, think aloud, share everything. Twenty minutes or more if you need it. We, we can do it. Gavin if you want, I will contact Santa Monica."

"No Raj, I will leave it for an hour, I think it will be angry over there for a while but I'll get on to it."

They walked away together and Rajid dialled the Tyneside number.

He informed the Superintendent of the circumstances of the murder of Greg Simons and that Josh and Maddison were safe but in a state of shock. He stated his team were even more determined now to get a positive result on this enquiry. Colin wished his team well and thanked him for passing on the sad news.

Colin looked at the clock in his office it was 10:07. He immediately thought about Sarah who would be asleep and made the decision to delay informing the team until she was back in the office. He took his jacket from the stand and told Lauren to hold the office as he was going to HQ to see the Chief. He checked his mobile was fully charged and left the office. He had to be back in the office for 11:30.

Walter was in the IT room and was changing the staffing

schedule for the extra working hours needed over the weekend and possibly longer. He required a minimum of two persons covering the phone tracking at all times. Vinny, Joanne, Ross and Liam agreed to work the extra hours. Joanne would be in before 11:30. There had been no movement on the phone from the location which was believed to be Chapman's apartment.

Billy and Alan had returned to the office and with Lauren they were examining each of the photographs that had been accumulated during the investigation. The vast majority were from the recovered camera of Filipe. Lauren had discarded into a rejection pile any photograph before the time of the canal cruise.

11:14 UK

Colin walked back into the main office, he acknowledged the team and closed the door behind him as he entered his office. Alan said "Sumits up" Billy and Lauren just nodded and continued examining the photographs.

After a couple of minutes his desk phone began to ring. He answered promptly." Detective Superintendent Tinkler."

"Hello boss it's Jimmy"

"Are you two ok?"

"Yes, we're both fine and in the hotel reception waiting to start. There's a marked police car outside, I take it that will be for us. Any updates?"

"Yes, there is, are you on speaker?"

"No boss"

"Greg Simons is the officer looking after Josh in Santa Monica, you may not know that. He was murdered this morning just after leaving a police station. It's not known if he was the target or Josh. The car was shot up and ended up exploding. Not good Jimmy"

"No boss."

"Josh is ok, you can tell Jessica he will be flying back to the UK later today. I believe that the information of the location came from Chapman."

"Yes boss, what a twat"

"You will be asked for the mobile phone from the driver and the DVD from the canal cruise by the local police this morning, they need to be fully interrogated by their analysts as soon as possible. Things are happening fast. I need you and Jessica to stay safe. You will both be in the rear of the command car with the officer running the surveillance. He is a lieutenant known as Jaime and his partner is a sergeant, Arturo. You will play no part other than assist relaying intelligence to NCA, Jessica is the interpreter."

"Yes of course boss."

"I will not be in contact with you today until the operation is stood down and you are in safe accommodation. I will not be here all day as NCA are now the liaison, if needed, the office is being manned 24/7, Sarah is coming in later with Andy. Be safe please."

"Yes boss we will. I have to go the uniform officer is out of the car now"

The call was ended. Colin made a call to Walter to ensure the system was working. Walter verified that it was and a communication channel had been opened with Panama and was waiting to be linked with the command car. He told the Super that he had organised the staff rota for the next few days.

He took his jacket off, hung it on the hanger, opened the door then walked and sat down with his team. Time to have a coffee and a chat, who was going to go out for the lunches?

11:35

Aaqil was on the telephone to the Panama Special Force Office. The Lieutenant, Jaime was confirming that he was in receipt of all the photographs of suspects and known persons, they talked through the intelligence briefing as Jaime confirmed it with the briefing notes. The subject was Chapman, who may be surveillance system aware but he should not have any reason to suspect being observed. Chapman owned a White Rav4 Automatic which was parked in the underground car park of his apartment complex. The team had already planted an electric tag on the vehicle during the night in preparation for the operation. Jaime would make all of operational command decisions and sergeant Arturo would run the surveillance team. Steve and Jessica would be the liaison link with NCA. The team were on their way to their designated positions to relieve the crew who had been watching the location overnight. The operation was starting. It was now 05:45 in Panama City and the city dwellers were starting to move.

Steve was sat with Jessica in the back of the police car when he explained about Greg Simons and the situation with Josh. Jessica was relieved that Josh was safe and managed to keep her thoughts about Chapman to herself and in control. Their bags, collected exhibits and the gathered firearms had been placed in the boot of the car. They were silent, as the car was driven at speed with the warning lights flashing towards the location of the rendezvous with the team, they were to be part of. They were dressed in loose, casual fitting clothes, it was expected to be a long day.

06:24 Panama City.

The officer driving the marked police car switched off the warning lights and turned off the Corredor Norte and then continued to the car park of the Estadio Nacional Rod Carew. They could see a dark grey coloured Toyota Alphard parked near to the stadium and headed towards the vehicle and then stopped adjacent a few metres apart.

Jaime and Arturo alighted from the two rear sliding doors. The two uniformed officers got out of the marked vehicle and opened the rear doors for Steve and Jessica and the officer who had been the front seat passenger made the introductions as they shook hands.

Jaime spoke first in English, "I will first offer my condolences and prayers to the family and friends of officer Greg Simons, we are all one big blue family." There was a slight pause for thought. "Steve have you given the mobile phone and the DVD to the officers?"

"Yes, they have them, I spoke to my boss in England this morning before I was picked up and had them ready."

Jaime signalled to the uniformed officers to go immediately with the exhibits.

Jaime, "We can talk and walk but not too far from the car, we will be in there quite a while I would think. We get good comms here from the city." The sun was coming up from the East and more traffic was heading towards the city.

"I have done many surveillances but this one is different, we have a control in Police Headquarters, there is tracking and intelligence from England and Newcastle. Do you like Shearer, the Toon Army?"

Steve was taken aback and smiled and a little laugh, "Yes of course, do you?"

"Yes, I watch premier league Arturo likes Manchester United, I like Manchester City, Aguero now, but when I was young Shearer was the best. The Liverpool and Newcastle games they were amazing.

Jessica gave a cough to get attention.

Jaime," I apologise Jessica, you do not like football or footballers?"

Smiling she said, "I live a few doors away from Aguero and a few more, Ryan Giggs do you know him?"

Arturo butted in and in a surprised tone, "You know Ryan Giggs?" and they all laughed. It had been a good ice breaker.

They stopped walking and looked at each other and briefly made their own assessment. It all looked and sounded good.

They were all in the same age range mid to late thirties.

Jaime was the smallest and oldest 1.75 metres, slim, short black hair, clean shaven, a cheeky handsome face, intelligent and charming.

Arturo was taller 1.80 metres about the same height as Jessica. He looked more physical but with muscle, which was shown off by the tee shirt he was wearing, short black hair and a well-trimmed beard. He also had a face women might like but appeared more studious.

Jessica was slim but athletic, her long dark hair tied in a pony tail and noticeably attractive even in her olive coloured Panama Canal tee shirt and light green knee length shorts.

Steve was the tallest at 1.85 metres, similar build to Arturo, short neat dark brown hair and clean shaven. In Panama, on surveillance, he would stand out like an elephant in a field full of llamas.

Steve and Jessica would not be leaving the car.

They were introduced to the driver, Juan and communications operator, Barbra. Juan and Barbra would exchange their roles during the operational day.

06:35

Barbra asked for a confirmation communication check from the teams, they were plotted in the specified peripheral position from the Bella Vista apartments, where it was hoped that Chapman was still in his home.

They responded in sequence: -

1:1 position
1:2 visual
2 position
3 position
4 position
5 position
6 position
7 position

Barbra responded, "All complete, 10 in command, log open"

Steve then had a discussion with Jaime and Arturo about

British surveillance methods and was pleased to find they were very similar. Jaime went on to give examples of his previous co-operation with police from other nations, Colombia, Costa Rica, USA and Spain. They were all run under control from Panama with input from the other country, this was with control from London with input from several countries including Panama. It's the same job in the end, follow someone or a group to gather intelligence and act with direction if and when it needs to be but at all times remain invisible.

CHAPTER 27

Saturday 21st May

It's 12:50 in the office in Newcastle, The Super, Walter, Lauren, Billy and Alan are sitting around the briefing desk which is now the lunch table. The Super and Lauren have a mug of coffee. The boss never makes a fuss about his mug as long as it's been cleaned out once that day, Lauren has an ornate rustic brown mug with her police number embossed around which she keeps in her bottom drawer, Billy has an SAFC mug which no one else would touch, Alan is not fussy as long as it's big and clean, Walter's NUFC mug is in his office and has settled for Andy's mug. The lads have got tea.

Billy and Alan had been to the local bakers and brought back four steak-bites, two cheese pasties, a ham and peas-pudding stotty,*(a geordie bread bun)* corned beef and onion stotty, a savoury cheese stotty and a tuna salad in brown seeded bread sandwich. There was also 4 custard slices and a large gingerbread man for dessert. A Geordie feast of local delicacies. Walter passed the A4 plates around, the boss took his steak slice out of the bag, the three lads followed suit. Lauren took the ham and peas-pudding stotty. They started eating their lunch whilst chewing over the facts that they knew and throwing spanners into the works with different scenarios, the boss was just one of the team and he had so much respect from them all, this was team life.

Alan heard an audible tone to indicate he had received an email. He finished his steak-bite, it was still warm and had a sip of his hot tea to clean the pastry flaked from inside his mouth and walked the few steps to his terminal.

"Boss, it's from the cruise company, they've took their time." He paused to read the email then continued," Fuckin hell, that group of Colombians were all with the same travel company and they've sent details of the company and the address in Colombia, but you know that couple that were shot in America with the drugs. Them and two other couples were booked on with the company and started in different places in America, USA I mean. Should I get digging boss?"

Everyone had raised their eyebrows and were looking at the boss, "That's good stuff Alan but we had better forward it to Penny in London. Can you do that now, just cover it that it's just arrived, it should show the time anyway. Then we can have a bit more chat"

Alan sent it on straight away and returned to the table for his cheese pasty whilst the others continued to discuss the latest findings while eating their way towards the waiting sweet desserts.

About the same time in the NCA office as Penny was receiving the email from Alan and inputting the information into the intelligence system, Ayesha received a notification from Fort Lauderdale. There was to be another drugs run possibly being run through Panama in the next few days but it may be a different method. It was from the previous informant 89147. Aaqil had read the intelligence updates on the screen and had already linked the Travel Company to all of the named passengers booked by that company. He then created a number of actions.

Antonio

Research 'Viajes Cattleya' Colombia. Full history, links, offices, etc. Do not make contact with Colombia liaison at this point.

Ayesha

Research the breakdown of those customers on the 'Alisios' cruise who were booked with Viajes Cattleya, directly or indirectly and boarded elsewhere other than in groups and disembarked in USA. Full history times and dates.

Penny

Liaise with Alan to request historic bookings, last three months to start and future bookings from his Cruise Company contact for any Viajes Cattleya customers on a cruise stopping in Central and South America. It is vital that we know of any cruises calling into a Panama port and picking up passengers in the next week, earliest first. There is to be no contact with the travel company. Ask him to link you in with the email, update any legal applications if needed.

The actions are automatically logged on the Operational database.

Alan was just finishing his custard slice when his desk phone started to ring, he took the few steps to his desk and picked up the receiver, "Alan Owens Newcastle Major Crime team, hello."

"Hi Alan, it's Penny from NCA are you ok?"

"I'm champion Penny, how are you?"

"Busy believe it or not. I've input the info you sent on the email and I've been actioned to liaise with you for further information from the cruise company. I'm not standing on your toes but we urgently need more info from them as soon as. It's all on an action form which I've emailed you but I was thinking it might be easier if you have built a rapport or a bit trust with someone to get things done quicker, it is urgent as you can imagine"

"Waye aye, I'll get onto it now. I will ask them to send it straight to you I don't need it and you're in the thick of things, but thanks, it's good to be useful. You will get a copy of my email request, the DPA form as well.

"Thanks Alan."

"No problem, do you speak Spanish, I suppose you do, what does Viajes Cattleya mean?"

"It's the name of the company, basically orchid travel. Cattleya being the official flower of Colombia"

"I thought it meant cattle class, like cheap travel, there you go, thick Mackem" he gave a little chuckle and replaced the phone on the stand. He sat at the desk pulled the keyboard closer and began typing.

Rajid was making a call to Panama, Jaime answered and walked away from the other three. Rajid spoke in Spanish to Jaime, the call was short and he walked back to the group standing outside the vehicle stretching their legs. Barbra had her earpiece in place to hear any communications that would make them active.

Jaime, spoke in Spanish "This is not for the log" Barbra nodded, Jaime continued, "there is information that there is to be another drug transportation very soon from Panama but not the same as last occasion. There will be more information coming later. It is from the same informant so should be correct. If our subject Chapman is involved, we should see some movement. Do not relay that we can keep it for debrief. I will enter it onto my incident log."

Barbra again nodded and said "SI"

Jaime listened as Jessica translated his information to Steve word for word, and said, "Muy bien, bien hecho" (*very good, well done*)

Barbra interrupted, "No hay cambio" (*no change*)

There was more time for chat about football, Panama, beaches, the jungle, wildlife, people, Newcastle, London, Manchester, lots of time to kill. Juan was asleep in the drivers' seat, his head resting on an inflated travel pillow. Arturo placed his earpiece in his right ear and together with Jessica they walked two hundred metres across the car park to the nearest café. They both used the toilet facility whilst they waited for six take away coffees and six tortillas with melted cheese, no fried eggs they're too messy for clean shirts. They walked slowly back to the group at the car, Barbra giving Juan a playful kiss on his cheek to waken him from his dreams. The wait continues. The sun was bright now and the traffic was busy. Yet another "No hay cambio"

It is 08:30 in Caracas and Mike Mather has taken his seat on the short flight to Margarita and is waiting for the acceleration along the runway. He has packed a small forensics case with the shiny aluminium casing and had his trusted shoulder bag packed with the various forms that may be required. He put his head back against the headrest and intended to get some sleep, there was no one occupying the seat next to him, before the aircraft passed through the first light clouds, he was asleep.

Walter is in the IT office watching nothing, no activity, with Joanne when there was an indication on the mobile of Chapman, it was active not for long but confirmed the phone at least was still in the vicinity of his apartment. He looked at the digital clock 14:38. He sent a message to Panama.

Chapman was in his apartment and had been showered and dressed in casual clothing, a white polo shirt with one thick navy-blue stripe down the left of the shirt with a white motorboat motif prominent on his left chest and matched with navy blue dress shorts. He ignored the phone ringing it was the office and he didn't want to answer any questions at this time, not today. He had taken a long weekend off; he would need to use the time. He looked at his black plastic casing water proof divers watch, 08:38.

The pad allocated for use by Steve and Jessica flashed and displayed the message from Walter. Barbra relayed, "posible actividad en la apartmento" *(possible activity in the apartment)*

Walter made a call to the main office and informed the Super who was sat with the others. He listened and thanked him. They were examining the photographs, there were a lot of people visible on the photographs, they were being allocated numbers for reference. The Super looked as if his thoughts were miles away, they thought Panama, they were wrong it was in Heaton, just a few miles away.

"Who is going to pick up Andy and Sarah, what time?"

Alan said, "Sarah wanted picking up at 3 same for Andy"

"From tomorrow can we work two 12-hour shifts, I'm suggesting 6 to 6. It would make sense if you did the morning to evening." The three agreed. "We can have a meeting when they come in"

Lauren, "Boss, do we have any known vehicles, known number plates we should be looking for on the photographs"

"Just contact NCA they have everything now" he said in a sharp tone as he turned and walked into his office and closed the door.

Silence said a thousand words as Lauren, Billy and Alan looked at each other. After a few seconds of deep thought Lauren made a call to NCA. Alan and Billy left the office to collect Sarah and Andy.

At the Estadio Nacional Rod Carew car park, Juan had closed the doors and the dark mirrored windows of the vehicle and started the engine with the air-conditioning on full. He was joined in the front by Barbra who was constantly tapping her fingers on the log book cover, Jessica and Steve had walked to the café and came back with cans of iced tea, cola and water to supplement the large cool box contents which would be kept for when and if they went mobile.

Chapman fastened his blue deck shoes, picked up his private mobile phone and slid it into his right shorts pocket, he checked he had a handkerchief in his left pocket. The wallet was picked up from the top of the drawers in the bedroom and he inspected the contents, flicking through the notes inside, walking to the door he turned the key to open the door and pushed back the brass safety clasp walking through the door he ensured the door was closed and double locked with the key and then walked to the lift.

"1:2 Contact, contact, contact. Chapman is out of the apartments on foot wearing white polo shirt one black stripe, black shorts walking with traffic flow North side towards Perejil."

Barbra made the first entry looking at the clock in the car. 09:12

CHAPTER 28

Saturday 21st May

The surveillance team had sprung into action, cocooning Chapman as he walked in the early morning warmth down the wide avenue. The foot teams had been dropped off in advance and behind his location. 3:2 had taken over from 1:2 and continued updates of his progress, turning left into Via Veneto. 3:2 walked passed the junction and Chapman could not be seen.

"3:2 Chapman lost possibly in Café Flores 20 metres right side of Via Veneto."

Arturo, "3:2 enter café go to pips team hold positions."

3:2 Olga, entered the café, it was small but busy with customers buying their breakfasts, some sitting at the small tables and waiting for service, some eating and chatting whilst drinking their coffees and enjoying their tortillas of eggs and cheese and others were at the counter for take away. Olga saw Chapman, he had taken a chair at a table facing the counter, he had a newspaper. She gave a number of tones on her communications set. She took a seat behind Chapman with a view of the door and could see his reflection in the immaculately clean windows. She took a portfolio out of her carry bag an opened it over the table top hoping to keep customers from sitting next to her.

Arturo interrogated 3:2 "Tones received, Is Chapman in the café?" He received answers in tones. "Yes." "Is he on his own?", "Yes", "Is he making a purchase?" "Yes." "Is it take away?" "No." "Do you have sight of Chapman?" "Yes." "Are you ok?" "Yes." "Can I change Plots?" "Yes"

Barbra updated the log 09:18 Chapman into Café Flores Via Veneto.

Arturo repositioned the surveillance team to cover all directions and maintain the cocoon on Chapman. When he had completed the change, 3:2 gave tones "No cambio"

Steve had made a call to Walter and informed him that

Chapman had left the apartment. Walter confirmed that the mobile was still in the apartment. He suggested that the observer could make a call from their mobile if possible and he would start a search from that location for nearby mobiles. He shared this information within the car which was being slowly driven towards the city centre area. Jaime decided that if it was safe it could be done.

Arturo spoke to 3:2 She returned in tones "Can I talk?" "No change, go ahead." "Is it safe to make a mobile call?" "Yes." "Has Chapman being served?" "Yes" "Has he got a meal at the table?" "Yes." "Phone me now" Olga used her mobile and dialled Arturo.

Steve was informing Walter that the call would be incoming, Jaime told Steve the number of Olga and the exact location, Arturo passed control to Barbra who was completing a cocoon position check from the team as he received the incoming call. Jessica was looking on whilst keeping her finger on the street location of Chapman on her map and listening to the impressive sudden change from the relaxed quite car to a sudden hive of controlled activity. Jaime mobile started to ring, Juan was quietly cursing a driver who had cut him up.

Jaime answered his call. Jessica could hear a series of yes and no and anything else, this was going on as Arturo was in discussion with Olga about a holiday flight to Costa Rica, how was her sister and nephews, is Chapman eating tortillas what had she ordered was there any change. Steve told Arturo Walter had got a signal and location of Olga's mobile and others active nearby. Arturo continued to Olga," if he uses his phone, we may be able to link it near yours. If he uses his mobile to make or receive a call activate yours do you understand? I will see you later back to your control adios."

Barbra, "No cambio"

The car fell silent, momentarily. Jaime, "Not for the log Barbra. That was Headquarters, the post mortem exam of the driver yesterday is completed, he died from loss of blood from a gunshot wound to his upper right thigh which destroyed his artery, also noticeable was the fact he had a broken neck, possibly from the accident impact by his reckless driving." Jessica was translating for Steve and gave a little grimace. "There were no distinguishing marks, they have taken blood for DNA, fingerprints for positive ID. He had a Colombian driving licence in the name of Mario Leonel Higuita, there is nothing criminal known of him in Panama, they are doing more research only on Panama systems. They are passing this to NCA now.

At this exact time, Maria had showered and dried herself and the thick long wavy hair thoroughly, dressed herself in a clean yellow floral T shirt and jeans, her favourite Converse shoes and was sitting at a table in the breakfast lounge of the Hyatt Place Hotel. She had time to kill today and had decided to visit some of the places she knew and spend some cash. There was a large selection of hot and cold food and she would take her time and be selective.

◆ ◆ ◆

In Newcastle, the lads had collected Andy and Sarah and were walking into the office, they had already told them both that the boss was a bit off today, probably worrying about events in Panama and the shift change decision. As they walked passed the boss's door they said, "afternoon boss". The boss replied "Andy team meeting as soon as Walter is here, I'm ringing him now" he told Walter to leave Joanne in control and come to the meeting now.

Walter entered the office and took his seat at the table, the Super came out of his office and asked them all to come into the office, it fell silent. As they all came in the boss asked Andy to close the door. They were all standing in a semi-circle facing the boss who was stood with his back against his desk. "I have some bad news; I've been waiting until we are together to tell you all. In the early hours of this morning, Greg Simons was murdered on his way back to Santa Monica." The reaction didn't take a second, Sarah couldn't control her emotions she shouted "Bastards, bastards, bastards" instantly tears were flowing from her eyes and she was sobbing uncontrollably. Colin took a gentle hold of her shoulders and pulled Sarah in towards his body to comfort her and wrapped his arms around her as her body convulsed with the sobbing, he gave her a handful of tissues, the team gathered closer and formed a group hug. They all had tears in their eyes even Billy was crying despite straining not to, the despair of Sarah was very emotional. Andy disappeared and came back with a cup of water which he gave to Sarah, the boss sat her slowly down in his chair. Slowly they all tried to gather their senses but it was hard to look at Sarah without being upset. Colin indicated for them to leave the office, only Lauren remained, stood next to Sarah rubbing her bowed back. "Bastards, bastards, bastards" Sarah quietly repeated.

"Why didn't you tell is boss?"

"You were asleep Sarah; I didn't want to tell the team without telling you. I've been chewed all day about it Sarah"

Lauren, "We knew something was wrong Boss."

Sarah stood up quickly and tightly hugged Colin, "Thanks boss that means a lot to is. What about Josh and Maddison"

"They're safe under protection"

"Thank God for that I couldn't take any more. Greg, he was a lovely man, he's saved them you know. I'm totally gutted, the bastards. How did he?" she paused "no I don't want to know, not now anyway. Look, I'll be alright just give is a little time."

Colin, "Do you want to have time off, go home with Lauren, it will be for the best, have a couple of days or more if you need it, you're emotionally drained?"

"No boss, no way. I might need an hour but I'm not packing this in no way. I'll be alright."

Colin left Sarah and Lauren in his room as he walked out and sat next to the lads sat quietly around the table. Alan, "You alright boss, that was tough?"

"No, not really Alan. It doesn't get any easier delivering

those messages, rank doesn't help, especially when its someone we care for. Can you ask the girls if they want some tea?"

Billy, wiping his eyes and cheeks, "Tea, Sarah will want a couple of those Moscow Mules. In fact, I could do with a stiff drink, knocked me for six that boss"

Colin, "When this is done, we will have a drink down the quayside and another one when Steve and his lass get back, if she comes up here."

◆ ◆ ◆

Long tones, Olga needed interrogating. Arturo, "Has Chapman met someone?" "No." "Is he on the Mobile?" "Yes." "Have you made a call?" "Yes." he continued as Jessica told Steve who contacted Walter.

Joanne answered and was monitoring Olga's mobile which was shown as active. There were several others that were active in the area at the same time, these numbers were instantly fed into the analysis app. The numbers were constantly changing as calls were ended. As Chapman finished his call Olga closed down her line. It was a start, one of the numbers was used by Chapman, it was now a process of elimination, more calls were needed.

There was series of fast tones, Barbra, "Chapman is moving" she made an entry in the log 09: 49

"5:2 I have sight of café door Chapman is out of the café back towards Via Espania and has stopped at the junction. The stripe is dark-blue and dark blue shorts not black. He has stopped a taxi. He is in back of the taxi, advert for Holiday Inn hotel on the trunk number 278. Off Via Espania."

◆ ◆ ◆

15:50 NCA office London.

Rajid had received the information from Panama with the information of the dead driver and had added the intelligence onto the database. Aaqil had assigned the action to trace and gather any intelligence on the name given, Mario Leonel Higuita, to Antonio who had responsibility for Colombia. The name was recognised immediately by Antonio. He double checked. Mario Leonel Higuita was the founder of the travel company, Viajes Cattleya. He and his wife had run the company for 18 years and then sold it to Grupo Estrella Brilliante 2 years ago. A trawl of internet sites as well as Colombian and Panama accessible sites revealed no further information on him or his wife, Carmen Maria Higuita since the sale of the company.

Antonio took a seat next to Rajid and spoke with concerns on his findings. The finances of the deal were never disclosed, the new company has a registered office in Cali and he was having difficulty establishing the identity of the new owners. The thought process was putting two and two together. Is the company a means of money laundering and accessing export routes for masses of drugs, was Higuita part of the operation, how was he linked to Chapman, is it actually Higuita, where is his wife and family if he has one, if so, do they have an address in Panama? Rajid assigned Penny to assist with the Colombian and Panama enquiries, he would contact Steve with the update information.

◆ ◆ ◆

10:10 Panama City

Chapman had taken the taxi to the Amador Marina and was walking towards the mooring area, the foot units were deployed with a variety of props to suit the environment to maintain observation on Chapman. Juan was positioning the command vehicle to have communication and be hidden from the curious prying eyes whilst Barbra was constantly recording the movements in the log book. In the second row of seats, Arturo was confirming positions for the follow vehicles for when there was further movement from this location and Jaime was updating his laptop and listening to the communication traffic. In the back row of the vehicle Steve and Jessica had their laptop resting on the middle seat showing the current location mapping, they were all wearing ear pieces when the car internal radio system was silent. Barbra was acknowledging unit transmissions, Arturo was giving instructions, Jaime informed Arturo that Chapman owned a boat 'Pasion del Mar', this information was passed to the units. An email was received from Rajid on the laptop used by Steve and Jessica. Jessica spoke in Spanish," Higuita has been identified as a previous owner of Viajes Cattleya, sold it two years ago enquiries continuing."

Steve had emailed a list of all the surveillance team mobile numbers and their crew identity to Walter. These had been entered onto the new app database by Joanne. Arturo gave instruction that the observer if possible, should make a mobile call to him if Chapman was seen to make a call, if this was not possible the next closest member would and identify themselves. Steve had made a call to Walters' office when Chapman had got out of the taxi and was walking towards the jetty's, he was talking to Walter as the commentary was continuing, Jessica was translating the information.

10:13

"2:1 Chapman is boarding a white boat on jetty 3, 5 down left" Barbra updates log, Jaime has an aerial photograph of the marina and places an X on the given location.

"2:1 I cannot see name of boat Chapman is sitting at the wheel and looking at instrument panel and controls. He has started the engines."

"6:1 The boat is 'Pasion del Mar' the boat is still tied up, I'm on the hill overlooking the Marina have excellent vision but I'm not close."

Arturo, "6:1 maintain vision 2:1 remain close but out of sight"

"6:1 Engines are revving must be neutral still tied. He has

phone call 2:1"

"2:1 Yes " within seconds Arturo received the call from 2:1

Steve, "Walter he has a call check 2:1"

"Will do"

"6:1 He has sat at the back of the boat still on call"

Chapman was in conversation with Borja, he described what he was wearing and was given instructions.

"6:1 The call has finished he has placed the mobile on the control panel"

2:1 ended the call.

Steve passed the information to Walter. Joanne had downloaded other numbers which would be checked against the previous numbers and the list was getting smaller.

"6:1 Engines switched off. He has picked up his phone 2:1, "

Steve again relayed the information and Joanne used the app.

"Call ended" it was a very short call

Walter," Joanne got something which is useful for elimination"

10:46

"6:1 Chapman is off the boat and onto jetty towards the buildings."

"2:1 I'm in the café have vision beware taxi arriving. Chapman into back of taxi and away towards the Causeway"

The causeway linked the Island marina to Panama City, the taxi was allowed to travel towards the city unaccompanied where the surveillance team were ahead and waiting. 6:1 maintained observation as it passed into the control of 4:1, another yellow taxi.

Steve closed the line to Walter, the command car listened in silence as the team picked up the taxi and maintained a cocoon, they were in a good position and held their location. Jaime received a mobile call and started to write, he passed a note to Jessica which had a Panamanian mobile phone number and informed her that it was the last number to call Higuita, it had been used on a number of occasions. The full mobile interrogation was being forwarded to NCA. Sarah translated to Steve who opened a call to Walter. Walter did a search on the database and the number had been used and identified when Chapman had made the calls that morning. This had a good probability of being the mobile used by Chapman, Jessica spoke to Jaime and he contacted Panama control and NCA on email. One more call would suffice to request an urgent listening application to assist in the investigation to defeat Serious Crime.

10:54

"4:2 Taxi stopped, Colombia Street and Chapman out and walking into Urraca park."

The other units dropped off numbers for foot surveillance. He was followed towards a central area where there was a small café and play areas, again he was very loosely cocooned with no one making any noticeable interest. He bought a white coffee in a cardboard cup and took a seat on an isolated bench in the shade of a large tree facing the café area.

Arturo", We want pictures of any meetings." The park was quiet, some residents were walking through on their way in to the city, a few parents were playing with the children on the swings and water fountains. The team blended in to the surroundings at a discreet distance whilst being aware of showing themselves.

11:01

"5:2 Chapman has been met by a female, Panamanian, mid twenty's, 1.75 shoulder wavy hair, yellow Tee shirt denim, jeans, blue converse type shoes, recording" 5:2 Stefanie, was thirty metres away with her back to the meeting, she had positioned a small hooded baby pram with a pin sized camera facing the meeting, the images were relayed to the laptop used by Arturo. She was immediately identified from the briefing photographs as one of the two Colombian girls, Susanna and Maria.

This started a quick discussion inside the command car,

Barbra maintained control of the crews, simultaneously recording in the log book all the movements and intelligence gathered. Jaime decided they needed another team for the newly identified woman, according to the information from Josh this was the woman known as Maria. Steve opened the line to Walter, Jaime made contact with headquarters to mobilise the second unit to his control in the city urgently, Arturo was preparing for a two-individual surveillance until this was achieved and gave instructions to the team.

Chapman, "We haven't introduced ourselves, it's maybe for the best but we have to work together to get this shit done then move on."

Maria, "That is true, there is one link, the Colombian who I met last night, he gave me something for you. He is covering himself; I can't give you the location unless I am with you, I am watching you, you are watching me and he will be watching us."

"Do you like boating, can you fish, dive, control a boat?"

"I was born by the Ocean my father had boats, good boats, it's in my blood"

There was no commentary as Barbara was watching the meeting. They were in a discussion, Chapman went to the café and bought two bottles of cola and had a general look around those persons using the park before returning to his seat.

"We will need to go this afternoon, you look good but need to change for the ocean, a bikini, flip-flops and a bag of clothes to change into. Can you sleep on a boat?"

"If I have to, on my own"

"I know what needs to done on shore when we get back, are you involved?"

"I have not been told, I'm a messenger and a tool to make things work"

"I will need help; my last assistant is not answering his calls. I shouldn't have paid him in advance."

"You don't pay me, only the Colombian and I'm paid well."

"We have to push on, I've checked the boat it's ready, when can I pick you up?"

"I will get a taxi to wherever your boat is, is it local?" he nodded," I will be there at one. I will call you Pedro you can call me Carmen" she laughed.

Chapman arranged to meet at the end of jetty three at the marina. They both stood up and deposited the empty cola bottles into the waste bin near to the bench, then without formalities they walked off in different directions.

Arturo had split the team to cover two sides of the park with vehicle cover on both sides.

"2:1 Chapman is out of the park Avenida Balbao and stopping a taxi he is in to the taxi." Three crews were with Chapman.

"6:1 Female on foot walking on Calle 47 towards Avenida Frederico Boyd." Three crews were with Maria.

Stefanie walked to the waste bin and retrieved the two bottles placing them into the pram."5:2 retrieved two cola bottles from the waste bin."

Barbra recorded and marked SH1.exhibit number.

Chapman was watched as he entered his apartment building and an observation was posted on the main doors.

Maria walked into the Hyatt Place Hotel and was followed in by Olga who watched as Maria took the lift to the fifth floor. Olga took a seat in the hotel foyer with a reverse view of the lift exits.

Jaime was organising the local police to do a routine check of the registration book in the Hyatt Place hotel.

❖ ❖ ❖

17:30 London

Aaqil was collating and updating the intelligence that was rapidly coming into the office. It had been disseminated to the other offices involved for progression. He spoke to Radji

"It has been established that Mario Leonel Higuita was

married to Carmen Maria. They had two daughters, Carmen Lucy who would be 32, Gabriella Mariana 28 and a son Leonel Mario 29. They lived in a large property in Buenaventura and ran the Viajes Cattleya from that city. It was unexpectedly sold two years ago. The son was killed in a road accident a short time before the sale of the business. The family left Colombia shortly after that having sold all of their properties. It is believed that the son had run up a significant debt with a cartel in Cali that triggered this move. It is not known where the daughters are. They were all privately educated and attended the local University; I'm seeking photographs from the University and requested passport information from Colombia." He continued," Panama police have interrogated the mobile of Higuita and accessed all the numbers incoming and outgoing. We have a number of contacts from the number we believe to be Chapman's to this phone, notably on the day of the drugs cruise that the girls boarded and the day he attempted to kill Steve Bond and Jessica. There is also another number that links these two phones, this number contacted Chapman earlier today and also on a few occasions yesterday going both ways, Panama are now working on that number. I've sent the numbers to Fort Lauderdale. Panama are applying for listening authorities. They are also checking out their tax, vehicle registrations recordsfor his name which we may get back today. It is believed the woman Chapman met in the park is Maria in the photographs with Josh and Filipe. The cruise company have one ship sailing into Colon tomorrow afternoon it's just a short stop a few hours coming in from Fort Lauderdale and returning to the same place but stopping off in Costa Rica and the Cayman Islands. Awaiting if there are any Viajes Cattleya passengers. Nothing in from Mike Mather as yet."

Rajid returned to his desk and made a call to Superintendent Tinkler, "Good afternoon Sir, it's Rajid just a quick update as of now."

17:42 Newcastle

Colin shouted, "Someone put the kettle on meeting in five minutes. Sarah"

Sarah responded and walked into the boss's office and took a seat as he had indicated.

"Sarah, I'm concerned about you, you have had an emotional day, are you certain that you want to stay on in the office, I can get someone else just change a shift around."

"No boss, I'm fine now, thanks for waiting for me today it must have been hard."

"If it was hard for me, a rough tough polis, it was sure tough for you." He paused." Anyway, if you are staying I'm not taking the responsibility off you about the liaison with NCA , or anywhere else for that matter

"Thanks boss, I'll not let you down."

"Never in question. This is our need to know just us two. They have identified the guy who tried to kill Jimmy and Jessica a guy called Mario Leonel Higuita, it's all in my book which you have access to in the filing cabinet so don't worry about remembering names. He used to own the travel company in Colombia that was used to book the drug couriers on to the cruises, and, he is linked to Chapman by mobile phone tracking analysis. Alan has forwarded info to NCA about the cruise going into and leaving Colon tomorrow with the passenger's details including some from the same travel company. NCA are working on that. Jimmy is in a command car with Jessica doing a surveillance on Chapman and they're certain he has met up with Maria in Panama City, it is still in progress"

Sarah quietly, "Bloody hell boss"

"The info is that another drugs run is happening soon, possibly today or tomorrow, so the Panama surveillance teams are staying live 24/7. Walter and his team have done a cracking job they're in direct touch with Jimmy, they're also working 24/7. I don't think there should be anything NCA should need from us but if they do, I'm sure you and Andy will cope. Main thing is when I go home anything that comes in, that I should know about, just ring me, my mobile will be at my bedside. Any questions?"

"Anything new about Greg or Josh and Maddison?"

"Nothing, they are still at Oxnard under police protection and will be taken to LA airport this afternoon for the flight to Heathrow, I haven't had an update."

"Can I call Oxnard and speak to them?"

"If you want to, Oxnard may not allow it, they are in control and I would imagine quite twitchy, you can try."

They walked in to the office together the rest of his team were at the briefing table with drinks in place and took a seat.

The boss kept it short and thanked them all for their efforts on a really tough day. He passed the thanks from Rajid for the prompt enquiry from the Cruise company which was now been acted upon. He did say actions were currently underway in several different places in The Americas with hundreds of officers, which all started from here in Newcastle, he was proud of what they had achieved. Josh should be flying home soon with Maddison. Jimmy and Jessica were safe and would be staying in Panama until the end of the enquiry as witnesses to their attempted murder. Everyone was to go home have a good night and be back bright and early tomorrow. Do not bring any more milk and bread on a light note. They finished their drinks and all gave Sarah a hug before leaving and making their way home.

12:10 Panama

Police officer Paco Mendez from the tourist police entered the Hyatt Place Hotel and was greeted by the reception staff who knew him well, he was a regular visitor. One of the staff ordered a coffee for him and they entered the office behind the reception desk. They had the usual chat about strange guests, some men trying to bring the street girls into the rooms, a couple of the local beggars were pestering the guests near to the doors and other routine hotel business. Paco finished his coffee and asked to examine the guests register for the last few days, he visited the reception with the senior receptionist, Eduardo. Looking down the list, arriving last night 21:10 Gabriella Mariana Higuita: Colombian National: full passport details: room 508. He asked Eduardo for a sheet of paper and randomly wrote down the details of a number of residents including Higuita as would be the normal visit routine. Eduardo was certain the lists got thrown in the bin when Paco got back to the office. Once outside of the hotel Paco made a call.

Jaime answered the call, "No, Si, Madre Mia!" He wrote down the full details and thanked Paco telling him to keep the list as an exhibit. He told the crew in the command car, Jessica translated for Steve who said, "No, bloody hell." Jaime was sending the email to NCA and Panama Headquarters. Arturo informed the teams the female subject was to be identified as Higuita.

CHAPTER 29

Saturday 21st May

    10:32 Oxnard Police Headquarters
    Josh and Maddison had showered and were sat in the comfortable chairs of the welfare room when there was a knock on the door, a uniformed officer entered informing them he was from the Intelligence Department. He showed Josh the image of Chapman and the female in conversation on the park bench. Josh identified the female as the one he met in Panama who used the name of Maria. The officer asked if they would take a call from Sarah in Newcastle, Maddison immediately agreed. The officer then left the room.

◆ ◆ ◆

    12:33 Panama City
    The tag was activated on the white Toyota Rav 4.
    Barbra, "Activacion en el auto." *(Activity at the car)*
    "3:2 White known Rav out of car park Chapman driving."
    The three-car team followed down the wide one-way system towards the city centre passing the junction of the Hyatt Place hotel.
    12:35
        6:2 had taken over from 3:2 to simplify the shortened surveillance teams and used the same seat as Olga. She gave lots of tones on her handset. Barbra," Attention Higuita is active in foyer."
        "6:2 She is wearing the same clothes and pulling a small black travel case, out of the hotel. She is approaching a taxi: into taxi 231 and off"

The taxi took the same route down the wide Via Espania towards the city.

Chapman was followed and drove across the causeway towards the Marina, Aaron in 2:1 headed for the observation point used on the previous occasion and parked up on the high ground.

"2:1 has observation he is slowly driving towards jetty 3 and stopped. He is out of the car having a look around the area. He is lifting the rear door, he has removed two large black holdalls, they do not look heavy, recording, wearing the same clothes, closing the rear door carrying the bags towards the boat, he is on the boat, gone down into galley."

"5:2 The taxi is heading towards the causeway 2:1 you take the observation"

"2:1 I have the taxi crossing; Chapman is back on deck and returning to his car. He has lifted the rear door, the taxi is approaching the jetty, Chapman has pulled the door down. Taxi stopped next to Chapman and Higuita out of taxi, they kissed each other on both cheeks in greeting. She has the black travel case from the taxi driver who has been paid by Chapman. The taxi has gone and Chapman lifts the rear door. He has taken two more black holdalls from the car and a small white travel case. Door closed walking to the boat: onto the boat the bags down into galley. He is off the boat back towards and into his car. He is parking the car in the shaded car park opposite the jetty walking back to the boat. Higuita on the deck."

Chapman, "You are on time, that's good. What do you think of the boat?"

"Very nice, my father has something similar" she lied.

"You can get changed downstairs while I warm up the engines and put out a couple of rods, look the part you know"

It took her five minutes to change into her white bikini, tie her wavy hair back and quickly inspect the inside of the cabin and galley. She returned to the deck and stretched out on the white leather seating in the shade of the hard roof, it was so comfortable. Chapman handed her a glass of cold sparkling wine from the fridge on the deck. He loosened the mooring ropes and wrapped them neatly on to the stainless steel boat cleats. He took his seat at the helm with all the controls clearly visible in front of him, slowly manoeuvred away from the mooring into the corridor that led to the great Pacific Ocean.

Juan had driven the command vehicle to the location of 2:1 on the high ground of Amador Island, they watched as 'Pasion Del Mar' slowly accelerated away from the mainland. Jaime was in contact with Panama Marine Section, he gave the approximate position of the boat and its heading, unsurprisingly there was a lot of small boat traffic on this wonderful weekend but this one was travelling at a faster speed than others and it was now identified on radar. Jaime, "Well, we know where the boat is, no eyes or ears, just hope they come back." Arturo stood the team down but to remain in contact no more than 20 minutes from the Marina.

19:24 London

Ayesha received an email from Fort Lauderdale identifying the mobile number of Mario Leonel Higuita as the same as used on two occasions by the informant 89147. It was not used by the informant purporting to be 89147 earlier that morning, they gave the number that was used. Ayesha forwarded the information to Walter in Newcastle and to Jaime and updated the database. Walter added the phone to a growing list that was being followed, Jaime requested an application for listening to this mobile.

◆ ◆ ◆

14:50 Porlamar

Mike Mather had visited the Venezuela National Police office on Margarita Island and had requested their help in solving the murder of Filipe.

He requested that a check be made on all females entering

Porlamar Airport on Sunday 15th May and leaving on Monday 16th May.

Venezuela National Security had enforced electronic fingerprinting and a photograph of every person entering through Porlamar airport in an effort to reduce the major drug trafficking from the Island. The senior officer liaison accepted the request and explained it might take a few hours. He was to be assisted and monitored by a uniformed officer when he visited and made enquiries at Hotel Colinas del Sol.

He had now arrived at the hotel in the marked police car. They entered the hotel and the officer explained what was needed, the receptionist accepted and stood back from the desk and made a call to the hotel manager. On examining the registrations book there were very few listed, not many would venture to this beautiful island that was now home to robbery, drugs and murders. One room was noticeable 103, a ground floor room booked and paid for by a company, Viajes Cattleya. No one had signed in for the room. The officer requested the key for the room. The room had not been used since, as any clients that did visit, preferred to be at a higher level, it was believed to be safer from robberies. At this time, they were joined by the manager, a small man in his fifties, immaculately groomed and wearing a dark suit. The officer held a short discussion with the manager assuring him this was not to be recorded against the hotel records. The three then walked along the ground floor to the room.

The room was on the ground level with a pathway that ran from the roadway to the central reception area. Other paths led from this pathway towards the dining area, the swimming pool and bars. There was low level lighting along the path which would be used during the hours of darkness. The manager opened the door and stood to one side as did the police officer, Mike looked from outside the door, a highly polished tiled floor, he surveyed the room from the doorway and believed this was the room where Filipe was murdered. He opened his forensic case; he slipped plastic coverings over his shoes and took out his camera. He started taking photographs of the exterior approaches to the room and the door number, standing in the doorway he took photographs of the internal layout of the room, then switching to video mode made a sweep of the room recording everything. Slowly moving in to the room towards the bed and bedside cabinets, taking photographs from all angles. He switched to video mode and placed the camera on the bed side drawers facing down the bed towards a set of drawers and pressed record. He inspected the bathroom which was cleaned thoroughly, even the traps in the sink and shower were clean of any debris. He removed the bedding, pillows and inspected the mattress, nothing, he pulled the mattress away from the headboard and made a close inspection for hair samples nothing. As he did, he saw some marks on the headboard, a Victorian style headboard with brass rails, spindles and two cross bars. The marks were just below pillow height; they were fingerprints. Mike took his fingerprint dusting powder and brush and lightly covered the area; they were good marks he photographed the images and lifted the marks identifying each one in location. Mike spoke to the officer who thanked the manager for his assistance and asked is there any CCTV coverage of this room, "Yes possibly". The manager walked in the direction of the reception area, whilst Mike carefully placed the samples and equipment in to the exhibits case, they then followed the managers route.

Despite the hotel being very quiet, it had recently had a facelift and had been modernised, awaiting the rush of tourists from Canada, USA and Europe, if and whenever that would happen. They went into the reception office which housed the bank of four small monitors and CCTV computerised system. Camera 8 would record the area of the ground floor pathway, the manager selected that camera recording and commenced from12:00 on Sunday 15th May, it was on fast forward mode. Mike scribbled some notes.

16:39 male in b/ cap carrying a large black holdall into room, face not seen path from road

16:53 same male leaves the room no bag to road
20:28 female dark t shirt short denim jeans wide brimmed hat long straight hair enters room path from road
20:31 same female leaves room to road
01:34 female wearing hat long hair to room with male no faces.
02:28 2 males white coats/ hats pushing trolley down path from road enter room
02:30 2 males out pushing lumpy trolley to road
02:32 female in hat dark t shirt out towards road

The officer asked for a copy of the recording to be down loaded onto a memory stick. While they were waiting, they had a cold bottle of cola courtesy of the worried manager. Steve made a call to NCA, Antonio answered, he wrote down the intelligence and would await the arrival of the CCTV download and hopefully Photographs and fingerprints from the airport. It only took ten minutes for the download and exhibit to be signed. Steve asked for a bottle of water used by the guests and was given a large bottle of Polar, he asked the manager to sign the exhibit label and attached it to the bottle, they left the hotel thanking the manager for his assistance and reminding him to not use the room until further notice.

◆ ◆ ◆

14:00 Panama

'Pasión Del Mar' was still cruising in the Pacific towards the Pearl Islands and was approaching Sabogo Island. Maria was at the controls while Chapman set up four large fishing rods and placed them in secure rod holders at the stern just above the swim platform, the ocean was flat calm with barely a ripple on the surface, the cruising speed was smooth, they were not drawing attention other than the quality of the boat and the lady behind the controls which is what they wanted people to see. Chapman had stocked the livewells with frozen bait which was rapidly defrosting, some nice sized mackerel to entice the tuna when they stopped at the fishing point. He joined Maria in a seat opposite the helm and opened two near frozen bottles of Balboa beer which he placed in the neoprene cooler holders and passed one to Maria. For a short time, they forgot the reason for being out on the Ocean and were enjoying themselves and getting friendly.

The surveillance team had been stood down and were relaxing or sleeping where they could find shade, some in the woods some on the cliff tops below the trees. The Command team had taken a break at Playa Veracruz, Jaime, Arturo, Juan and Barbra had their ear pieces in as the six entered the La Casa Bonita restaurant. They ordered Ceviche, salad and tacos; it was going to be a long day. They were sat inside in the airconditioned room when Jaime's' mobile alerted him, he walked away from the table. Headquarters had traced an address for Higuita and two vehicles, a car and a coach, they were being chased up now for further observation sightings. Jaime made a note and returned to the table.

◆ ◆ ◆

20:00 Newcastle

Sarah made a telephone call to Oxnard Police Headquarters and was put through to the extension in the welfare room. An officer answered the call and asked Josh to take the phone.

"Hello, Josh speaking."

"Hi Josh, It's Sarah. Are you both ok, I'm worried about you?"

"Yes, we are Sarah, I'll admit we are badly shaken after what happened to Greg."

"We all were, I only ever spoke to him on the phone but he was always pleasant and sounded like a lovely man."

"Greg actually told Maddison and I that he wanted to meet you, he thought you were great and didn't understand you at times. It was more or less the last thing he said to us and hoped he could come to England to meet you"

Sarah was fighting back the tears again, "That would have been great." There was a pause," When are you getting your flight?"

"I've been told we should be leaving here under heavy protection very soon, no departure procedures just driven to the plane and board together. Maddison would like to speak to you."

"Hi Sarah, I hope you are ok, I know it would have hurt"

"I cannot tell a lie Maddison, I've cried buckets"

"That was one of the things Greg said he liked about you, when he didn't understand what you were saying"

"I must tell you this Maddison, that telephone stuff you sent over that Walter is using is amazing, you should patent it, it's cracking. With your help we're going to get these bastards, excuse my French, we will, we're pulling out all the stops. When you get over here, you'll love it, get Josh to bring you up to the toon and we'll have a blast together. Look I'll let you go, I've got things to do, have a safe journey and I'll see you here sometime soon."

The call was ended and Sarah burst into tears and headed towards the ladies' rest room.

20:12 London

Penny received an email with attachments from the Cruise company. The 'Western Horizon' would be stopping in Colon for 3 hours on Sunday afternoon, it was only a service stop to allow some passengers to join the cruise and others to disembark. It would then sail to Costa Rica, Grand Cayman and end at Fort Lauderdale. There were four couples booked by Viajes Cattleya from Fort Lauderdale for the whole cruise, three couples would be joining the cruise in Colon. The full intelligence report was input into the operational database.

♦ ♦ ♦

14:38 Panama

Marie had pushed the control lever into neutral on the boat as Chapman was dropping four fishing lines, baited with bloodied mackerel, from the stern of the boat, they watched as the lines sank with the weights pulling the lines down. She moved the lever gently pushed forward to go slow and drag the baited hooks. They were only five hundred metres off Mogo Mogo island, Maria preferred the shade from the hard top at the helm rather than the scorching heat at the stern or swim deck where Chapman was constantly tugging at the rods. Maria was getting cold drinks from the deck fridge when the sound of a large reel spinning, jumped them both into action, Chapman took hold of the rod in the boats holder and planted it into the holder in his rod belt and started to control the rod pulling hard on the rod and winding in the reel, Maria started to reel in the other lines to prevent a tangle. It felt heavy, a good fighting fish, Maria sat in comfort at the helm and kept the boat straight and slow and shouted encouragement to Chapman as he slowly reeled the fish closer to the boat, 35 minutes had passed when they saw it in the clear water below the boat, a beauty a large yellow fin tuna. Maria got the 1.5 metre gaff from its holder on the hard top and took it to the stern, Chapman was tiring but pulled it alongside the boat level with the swimming deck, he put the rod into the boat rod holder, Marie took hold of the rod and kept the line taught as it swam alongside the boat, Chapman got onto the swim deck and in one move spiked the gaff into the fish through the gill and pulled it onto the swimming platform and almost fell off himself, then strapped the fish down with a tie down heavy nylon ratchet strap. They thought it would weigh near 130 kilos. Maria was ecstatic, clapping, and gave Chapman a high five and an ice-cold beer in a holder and got one for herself, they both fell in to the comfort of the cool leather chairs on either side of the deck. A few of the people on the boats nearby who had watched the tussle, came closer to have a look at the fish on the back of the boat, they waved at each other as they passed, what a lovely couple, or father and daughter. After they finished their beer, Chapman set the co-ordinates for San Miguel on the Isla del Rey, they would get a smooth mooring for the night and free food and drink in return for the Tuna fastened to the stern of the boat. He made a call to a contact on the island to have a vehicle collection for the tuna ready.

❖ ❖ ❖

15:04

The detective had examined the exterior of the house on Calle Ponciana Drive, a street of large houses with extra land space and swimming pools. He could see the car that was registered to Higuita but he could see no signs of activity in the house or the grounds. He rang the doorbell, there was no reply and as he stood a neighbour walked by, "You looking for Leo?"

"Yes, him or his wife, family. I'm from immigration just routine yearly check on their Padron"

"His wife died last year after a short illness, he's probably driving his bus, he does tourist trips. He's only been here two years and he's doing tourist trips. Nice guy, quiet,"

"Is there anyone else live there now?"

"No, his daughter has been a few times, a few weeks ago she was here, she pops in pops out, never stays long, Gabriella."

"Ok, I'll call back next week sometime or the week after, not urgent, Thank you."

"Shall I tell him you called?"

"Yes, if you see him."

The officer returned to his car and made a call.

Jaime and the command car team had returned to the command car and had parked in a quiet wooded area protected from the mid-day Sun by the large trees, Juan and Barbra were sat on the grass chatting, Steve had sat in the drivers chair as there was more room, Jessica was stretched across the seats in the back, Arturo was having a sleep with his head on Juan's pillow and Jaime was sat opposite him chatting to Steve when his mobile rang. He took the call and listened, again writing the information into his incident book.

As this was happening Steve took a call from Walter, there had been an activation on the phone believed to belong to Chapman in the Pacific. There was a discussion about the two incidents. Jaime contacted headquarters for any information from the call, asking if it had been listened to, he would receive a reply shortly. Jaime decided to obtain a warrant to enter and search the address of Higuita and to secure an observation post on the premises. He set actions in motion for the warrant and a covert method of entry so as not to cause any damage or knowledge the house had been searched.

Jaime took another call from headquarters; the listening order had been approved and one call had been made from Chapman's mobile. He listened to the officer reading the conversation which had been conducted in Spanish. He made the entry into the incident book. "Chapman has caught a large Tuna and has made a call to a restaurant in San Miguel on Isla del Rey to have a vehicle ready for collection in about 40 minutes at the mooring and booked a table for two at 9 tonight. He is not coming back tonight then." He gave Arturo a shove in his ribs and woke him abruptly. "Stand down the surveillance team but they should be ready to respond to a call, cancel the other team likewise be ready for a call, set them both up in city hotels, no going home, only moderate drinking, keep receipts. Provisional start at 0700." Arturo gave the instructions.

Jaime made a call and booked six rooms at Dreams Hotel in Playa Bonita just a short drive from their present location.

◆ ◆ ◆

15:46
Chapman was at the helm when he guided 'Pasion del Mar'

into the vacant mooring in San Miguel harbour. The three-restaurant staff were waiting and started to clap when they saw the Tuna on the Swimming board at the stern. They reversed the converted Golf buggy with a flat back to the edge of the jetty and then jumped onto the boat, it took all of them including Chapman to manhandle the fish onto the flat back board. It was agreed that it would be a 50/50 share of the meat and they would seal the meat for Chapman in large steaks or kilo pieces per pack for refrigeration and tonight's bill was on the restaurant. That was the usual deal but this was his biggest catch. As they drove off Chapman took the hose from the jetty and washed the blood and debris from the washboard, attracting the local seabirds. Now they just had to wait further instructions, time to relax on the nearby beach and snooze in the cabin.

As Juan was driving towards the hotel Jaime took another call. Unit 6, on Calle Alemania had been checked out and it was locked up. A brown coloured luxury coach, 53 seats possibly, could be seen inside and also a similar coloured luxury mini bus possibly 15 or 20 seats. He asked for a warrant to search be obtained and an entry made with no damage. He entered the details into his incident book.

◆ ◆ ◆

16:30 Margarita

Mike Mather had returned to the Police headquarters on the Island. The liaison officer had a list of females who had entered and left the Island on the dates specified. There were only 7 females who had entered and left the following day, these were shown individually on cards with fingerprint recordings and facial photograph. Looking through the cards one was noticed straight away,

Susanna Piqueta Cuadrado. This female looked similar to the females on the cruise with Filipe but with straight hair. He took out the fingerprint marks he had recovered from the room and on close examination they looked very similar to the fingerprint recording on the card of her left index finger. He made a call to NCA

❖ ❖ ❖

21:39 London

Antonio took the call from Mike and entered the information into the database. "Are you saying this female is Susanna?"

"No, it's recorded as Susanna Cuadrado who has straight hair but I think it looks more like Maria who has wavy hair but the fingerprints should prove it."

"So, do you think the Maria currently in Panama is the murderer of Filipe?"

"Possibly, I'm sending the images of the registration card with the photo and the fingerprints together with the marks I recovered from the room and you can check them out."

The call ended; Mike forwarded the images to NCA.

Aaqil updated the intelligence log and forwarded it to all of the agencies.

Jaime read the update and asked Arturo to get Stefanie to take the coke bottles for fingerprint examination straight away.

CHAPTER 30

Saturday 21st May 16:30 Panama

Steve and Jessica had entered their rooms at the Dreams hotel and made an inspection of the room and the views from the balcony. They were in adjacent rooms and looked down towards the pool and relaxation areas, they saw Juan had already dropped his bag off, changed into swimwear and was diving into the pool, it seemed a good idea. They agreed to get changed and Steve would knock when he was leaving. In ten minutes, they were all sitting in large square wicker chairs with thick cream cushions around a wicker table with a gleaming glass top, they were dressed in swim attire and tee shirts and had a mixture of cold drinks and coffee. Jaime did a run through of the intelligence known to date including the fingerprint similarities found in Margarita. Steve asked if Newcastle were aware of the development in the murder investigation. Jaime said he believed so.

Steve made a call and Sarah answered, "Hi Sarah it's Jimmy" this comment made Arturo and Jaime look at him, Jessica explained the reason and they laughed while Steve continued his call "How are you?"

"A bit shitty to be honest, I've had better days but hearing you is cheering me up, how's the holiday?"

"It's different, I can tell you that, but I'm in a cracking hotel with some lovely people, its red hot the sun is shining, what more can I ask for?"

"Are you on speaker?"

"No, why?"

"Well you want a bucket of ice-cold beer and a good shag, is Jessica with you?" Sarah laughed, it felt good but wrong to laugh in the day she was having.

"It's good to hear you laughing Sarah, are you up to date with everything?"

"I don't know, I'm the liaison officer for the office but it only comes through every now and again, there's only me and the boss that get told stuff and we cannot tell anyone unless they clear it. Is there something good like?

"I'm hoping so, who's there now?"

"Just Andy and me, we haven't got much to do, just here in case we are needed, looking through some photo's that Filipe took, it looks a fab place over there mind"

"Yes, it's a nice place and despite the murders and drugs and other stuff the people I have met are good people. Who is in Walters place?"

"Matty and Vinny have started now, they know about the app and everything Walter made sure before he left."

Steve ended the call and returned to the table.

◆ ◆ ◆

15:10 Los Angeles

Josh and Maddison were sat in their seats adjacent to each other in first class on the American Airlines Boeing 777. The doors were now closed and the crew were preparing for taxiing to the runway. Josh felt the nudge as the plane was slowly pushed backwards away from the terminal, a feeling of relief overcame him as he hid his face, looking out of the window onto the tarmac, the tears started to roll from his eyes. His thoughts were with Filipe and Greg. Maddison was silent and deep in thought, lots of thoughts, her life had been turned upside down and inside out and she was flying away from her family and home country, the plane trundled along the taxi route and made a turn onto the runway and stopped. They hadn't looked at each other since the first push from the terminal, the four engines roared as the thrust accelerated the plane along the runway, they looked at each other and looked forward to a new life, possibly together

◆ ◆ ◆

17:40 Panama

Specialist officers from the National Police climbed into the garden of Higuita's home from the cover of the woodland at the rear of the house. The property was not overlooked at the rear as they made their way to the building. They checked the rear doors and found the door into the garage was not locked and entered. There were no vehicles in the garage. It was clean and neat with tools in storage cupboards and shelves, a large upright cupboard contained fishing rods of different sizes and fishing tackle. There were two large chest freezers, these contained a large quantity of what looked like large Tuna steaks. The house alarm was linked to the police control room and had been disabled. One of the officers took five minutes to open the lock on the door linking into the house, they placed protective plastic covering on their boots before moving into the living area and moved from the hall into the kitchen. It was modern and very clean, the cupboards were full of pots, plates, bowls but very little food was found in the cupboards or the fridge freezer. Moving into the living room, the furniture was large, looked new and expensive, a large family photograph inside a gold coloured frame was hanging in the middle of the wall, Higuita and his wife were sitting on chairs together holding hands and smiling, standing behind them from left to right was their daughter Carmen, son Leonel and daughter Gabriella it was a professional posed photograph. The officer in charge took a photograph with his mobile and sent the image to Jaime. They continued the search without leaving a trace they had been there and left the property as they had found it.

Jaime was still sat at the table when the image arrived, he made an entry into the incident book and passed the mobile to Steve. "That's Maria" Jaime sent the image to NCA.

No sooner had he sent the image to NCA, he received a call from the forensic department. They had lifted the images from the coke bottles in the park, they were good quality images and had been forwarded onto NCA.

00:15 London

Rajid had sent Gavin, Penny and Ayesha home and was running the office with Antonio and Aaqil. They sat together in the office, Rajid had relaxed the rules and they had a drink at the desk, he asked Aaqil to summarise what they knew.

"Mike Mather has done some brilliant investigation work in Margarita, it's worth a mention in the report," Rajid nodded, "Originally he found the room used by Filipe and recovered the camera from where we got the photographs of the two girls. He has used his contacts to get the photograph and fingerprints from Porlamar airport of the female, and, unexpectedly found a fingerprint mark on the bedframe in the room which has been identified as the murder scene. Mike is liaising with the Venezuelan Police re the offence in their territory. We have also got fingerprints from a coke bottle in Panama City believed to be from the same female. I'm not an expert but we have all had a look and there are a lot of similarities in the marks, from the room, the airport and the bottle. We should have that confirmed within the next half hour they're being examined now. If it is proven, it appears that the murderer is Gabriella Mariana Higuita otherwise known as Maria. We now know that she is the daughter of Mario Leonel Higuita, who attempted to kill Steve Bond and Jessica O'Brien. Father and daughter were connected in the drug transfer from the coach tour to the Cruise ship, there is a connection with Martin Chapman in the circumstances of the attempted murder but also linked by mobile phone calls to the father. It is believed that the father was the informant paid by Fort Lauderdale for the information on the drug transfers but since his death another call has been made using the code number by a female which we believe to be Maria. There is no link between Martin Chapman and Maria until they met in the park earlier today and are now on the Pearl Islands. All of the phone numbers that are currently known are subject to listening authorities and Newcastle are tracking any signals. The house of Leonel Higuita has been searched, there is nothing found, that has been seized. The family photo which we have seen includes Maria, also a safe located in the wardrobe in the main bedroom which wasn't opened, nothing in his car. The premises that is used for the coaches is being searched now, we should know if there is anything significant found shortly. It should be very interesting when they return to Panama City, if they return, they have about 20 hours to meet up with the couples going on the cruise from Colon booked with Viajes Cattleya."

Antonio," From an evidence point, if it is her fingerprint, we can prove she has been in the murder room but not the murderer. We know she is on the island but nothing else other than she arrived and left. It would be difficult to prove beyond doubt that the woman in the hat was Maria. We don't know if she has been in contact with her father or if she knows he is dead. From what we know Chapman believes that Steve Bond and Jessica are dead, there is no contact from him to Higuita after the time the murder was supposed to have happened just unanswered calls. He has told lies to Newcastle on the basis that he believes Bond to be dead but he has not been in touch with his office or Newcastle to establish the fact, he is not aware of the recent developments in Margarita, the photographs of Maria, he probably does not know she is the same person or daughter of Higuita, on that, we don't know if Maria knows if Chapman knew her father. There are still a lot of missing links."

Rajid, "We are awaiting results of the property search and enquiries of the Pasion Del Mar ownership. There has to be some communication for the delivery of the cocaine to the cruise ship. I believe we are on top of the situation but their actions will dictate what course of action Jaime and Panama police will take. There is nothing, no intelligence on persons responsible for the murder of Greg Simons other than we knew there was a threat to Josh, who is now safe. It has been excellent work; I will contact Sarah later with an update for the Super. It's been a long day if we can cover the phones while one or two get some sleep over the next few hours it might help until the others come in."

CHAPTER 31

Saturday 21st May 19:10 Pearl Islands

Chapman and Maria had been relaxing on a beach and swimming in the warm tropical sea just a few hundred metres from the marina, they were just friends enjoying a day at the beach. As they were walking back towards the boat, Chapman looked at Maria, "Why are you here?"

"I have been told to come here"

"But why, I have never met anyone involved, it's the way they do it?"

"I don't ask questions it is not wise to ask questions. I just do as I'm told"

"Have you been sent to kill me?"

"Why do you say that, do you not think they would send a man, not a woman to do a man's work?"

"So why?"

"I will get a call, or you will get a call, I have something to tell you. If something goes wrong, we both get killed, if not we get very well paid"

"How did you get involved in this?"

"Me, not my choice, my brother was involved and fucked up, not his fault he owed a lot of dollars. They killed him and passed the debt to me, the more I work the less I owe. You?"

"I was in Colombia and I got involved, I was set up really, compromised, I did something I shouldn't have done. I left and came here to retire and fish, buy a little boat, they knew I was here they made me an offer, I had to accept."

"A little boat, that is not a little boat"

"It was part of the deal, set up. They took the boat off someone for his debts and now I work to pay off my debts. I suppose we are all used."

"Have you met anyone at all?"

"No, just a call, do this, tell me this, be there at this time, even when I get cash it is just go there. That is why I'm worried, you will kill me."

"I couldn't kill any person, unless they were killing me, my family. Will you kill me?"

"No, we should not ask such questions, I do what I have to do, and leave it somewhere, someone takes it and leaves it somewhere, no one meets anyone."

"Where is the man who takes it from you?"

"I don't know. He had a job to do, I believe it was done and he has gone. In a cell, dead or just disappeared."

"So, what happens now?"

"We do as we are told and enjoy life while we can"

"If I get a message to kill you, I will let you know."

Maria gave a little laugh and Chapman swung a playful slap over her head as they continued to the boat to get showered and changed. Before going to the restaurant.

◆ ◆ ◆

20:00 Panama City

The enterprise units around Unit 6 had been vacated and the area was quiet as the special unit approached the front of the premises. They parked their van across the front of the office door blocking any view from people passing by the unit. They were dressed in industrial clothing suitable for the area. It did not take long for the locksmith to bump the top lock, the larger mortice lock took a little longer, then covered by the van they opened the door and stepped inside. The brown coach was parked directly behind the electric up and over door there was a smaller coach parked immediately next to it. The small office was made from UPVC and glass, inside was a small desk with a computer set up on top, it was switched off, a printer on a set of drawers, one four drawer filing cabinet and a key board on the side wall. The keys for both coaches and a car were on the key board, they were not needed, the doors were open on the coaches and there was no car found. The search started from the front, the office. There were a few leaflets from tourist spots and hotels in the drawers of the desk, a box full of pens, ruler, a few pencils a mobile phone charger. Under the desk there was a safe built in to the floor under the carpet. The filing cabinet was neat with envelopes for each vehicle, insurance, maintenance, fuel receipts, an envelope for the building, the same taxes, insurance business receipts. The printer was switched off and the drawers below contained reams of paper. Nothing out of order. The coaches were examined both had been cleaned no litter, debris and ready for use, the storage cabins were empty an empty case trolley was positioned next to the coach.

There was a room the width of the building with the door situated behind the large coach, again it was double locked. The locksmith did his work and they entered and put the lights on. There was shelving three racks high filled with new or nearly new suitcases different colours and styles about thirty of them. A photograph was taken from the doorway. One suitcase from the middle row, a random selection taken from the middle rack was opened, it was empty, an officer felt inside the case, a photograph was taken, the material was unzipped open there were 20 patterned oblong blocks moulded into the base of the case, a photograph was taken. Another random selection from the rack, the same appearance and moulding inside, built specifically to fit a kilo block of cocaine. Two large metal cabinets, wardrobe size were opened, each had three shelves and they were filled with vacuum packed clothing, male and female. A solid bench along a part of the wall which was believed to be the packing area was next to two large chest freezers, the same as seen in the house. These had locks which were opened by the locksmith after a short wait. Opening the freezers, it looked full of frozen Tuna meat, after removing the top three layers the black wrapped packages could be seen. There were several photographs taken before the Tuna meat was put back in to position, the freezer doors closed and locked. The IT member attached a camera inside the ventilation cover which would record any activity inside the room. The doors were closed and items put back onto shelving. The door was locked as they retraced their steps to the office, a camera was fitted inside the office fire alarm. They left by the front door in to the side door of the van still unseen, the doors were locked, no one would know they had been. They drove off, as they were travelling, the leader sent photographs from his phone direct to Jaime. The photographs taken by camera would be downloaded and sent to NCA and listed as exhibits.

❖ ❖ ❖

20:15 Pearl Islands

Chapman had emptied the black bags of fishing tackle and diving equipment that he had brought on board, they had taken their turn to use the head and to shower away the sand from the beach. Maria was sitting in the leather chair on the deck, listening to the sound of the ocean gently lapping against the hull of the boat, looking up to the dark clear sky. They were both wearing clean clothing, Chapman was wearing a similar shirt but black with a white stripe and black shorts and Maria a turquoise Tee shirt and white shorts. They both picked up their mobile phones and switched them on. Chapman picked up the folded black canvas bags and they left the boat to walk the short distance to La Tortuga restaurant they would be a little early.

These two phones immediately registered in Newcastle. Matty contacted Steve and confirmed that these two known phones were very close together on Isla del Rey.

Chapman and Maria were greeted by the owner at the door of La Tortuga who took the bags from him. He directed them to a table overlooking the bay, Chapman regularly would bring female friends to the restaurant but this one was different, younger and very attractive. The couple were well attended too by the few staff that were there but they were given plenty of space. They did not talk any more about the earlier conversation they had and were enjoying the evening together.

At the same time Steve, Jessica, Arturo and Jaime were sat together at a table in the hotel restaurant. Steve passed the information about the phones being activated and Jaime shared the images of the search at the Coach Unit. As much preparation had been done as could be, it was now waiting time again. They enjoyed each other's company and had an excellent meal together, an alcohol-free night.

21:30

Maria's mobile rang, she stood up and walked out of the restaurant, she listened and would only answer "Si". The call lasted twenty seconds and she returned to the table and spoke to Chapman. They had finished their meal and told the staff they were leaving and asked if everything was prepared. The owner approached and informed him the buggy would be at the boat ten minutes after they would get there. They thanked him for a wonderful evening and started on the downhill walk to the marina.

"So, do you have to kill me?"

"No, not yet," she paused smiled and shook her head," I have the co-ordinates to give you we have to be at the point at 01:30. I don't know how far we have to go"

"I'll have a look at the charts when we get back and set the navigation system."

They started to walk quicker.

Jaime received a call from Headquarters listening room. They would relay the call as it was spoken, Jaime took out the incident book and wrote down what was said.

"You can give the envelope to him now you must be there at 01:30"

"Si"

"You can handle the boat and weight"

"Si"

"You know what to do"
"Si"
"No mistakes. Turn your phone on at 07:00"
"Si"

Jaime finished the call and made contact with the marine section and gave them advance warning that there will be movement which needs monitoring.

Chapman assisted Maria on to the deck, it wasn't required but it was polite, she went down the steps into the cabin area and retrieved the small envelope from her bag and handed it to Chapman. He opened the envelope and read the co-ordinates for the location, he studied the charts and it was a possibly two-hour steady cruise to get there to the South of the Island of San Jose, towards Colombia but the ocean was flat calm and there was good moonlight. He started to configure the numbers into the navigation system as the buggy turned up at the rear of the boat. The staff from the restaurant lifted the four black bags full of packed Tuna meat onto the swimming platform, they waved as they drove away.

They both lifted the bags on board, Maria passed them down the steps towards the galley where Chapman emptied the meat into the large freezer unit. They were both busy, Chapman was placing the rods into the boat holders, Maria was clearing the galley and the area of the aft stowage freezer and lockers. They planned to leave at 22:30, in half an hour, Maria went down into the cabin and lay on the leather sofa and quickly fell asleep, while Chapman checked the charts and co-ordinates, ensured there was plenty of fuel to make the journey and then waited.

◆ ◆ ◆

Sunday 22nd May 04:00 Newcastle
The phone rang on Sarah's desk, she was sat with her head

down on her arm, resting her eyes, she sat bolt upright and gave her head a shake and answered, "Hiya, it's Sarah speaking"

"Good morning, well nearly, Sarah are you wide awake?"

"Waye aye Raji, are you ok, have you got something for us?"

"Yes Sarah, quite good as well"

"Oh, do tell"

"On the murder enquiry in Margarita, Mike Mather has done an excellent job, he has identified the room where the murder took place and has recovered some CCTV footage of the person responsible, but we cannot identify them from the images not good enough but it gives the time frame, and, he recovered a fingerprint from the bed frame"

"Bloody hell Raji that's brilliant."

"There's more, everyone who enters Margarita Island airport in Porlamar has to have their fingerprints and photographs taken"

"You don't say, come on tell us"

"The fingerprints have been identified to a woman who we believe to be known as Maria"

"Bingo, not Susanna?"

"No, definitely Maria, and we have confirmed that by getting a finger print off a coke bottle by one of the surveillance team."

"Raji excuse my French, but that's just fucking amazing, cushty lush."

Rajid, was laughing.

"There is a bit more, the guy who tried to kill Steve, Higuita, he is Maria's father"

"No way, that's freaky. I've been scribbling when you've been talking, I will write it down for the boss for when he comes in. Amazing, the boss will be dead chuffed."

"I will send up the electric record for him to see the info but I thought I should keep you in the loop"

"Thanks Raji, that's made my day already, I cannot wait to see the boss."

"You sound happy Sarah; you have certainly pepped up my

morning that's for sure"

At 22:30 in Panama as Jaime, Arturo, Steve and Jessica were heading for their bedrooms, Chapman slipped the ropes from the mooring and tied them neatly around the cleats and slowly moved away from the harbour, the boat lights were illuminated but were not needed as the moon was so bright on the flat calm ocean. Maria remained asleep in the cabin as Chapman slowly pushed the throttle gently forward to increase the speed as soon as he was clear of the boats and yachts moored for the night.

06:00 Newcastle
Andy had a very quiet night just keeping Sarah company really but he had something to do now, the kettle was on and the sliced bread was primed to drop into the toaster. Sarah had been to the bathroom and spruced herself somewhat, she was feeling surprisingly bright and awake and certainly in a better mood than the last time she saw the boss. The boss came in through the back door, up the stairs from the car park he greeted Andy and Sarah.

Sarah, "Boss, my office now" the three of them laughed as the boss followed Sarah into the room and closed the door.

Boss "Can I take my seat, I'm hoping you have something good to tell me, have you told Andy?"

"I have not, anyway." Sarah went on to give the boss the full intelligence update from Raji.

"That's excellent, I am going to make the decision to brief everyone this morning up to date, keep it quiet though. What did you say to Raji?"

"I just told him it was excellent news, well done."

"I bet you did."

An hour later during the team breakfast of toast and croissants, Superintendent Tinkler informed his team of the recent update and thanked them again for their efforts. There was a good feeling in the room, no back slaps, not yet, the job wasn't finished.

◆ ◆ ◆

Sunday 22nd May Panama

It was just after midnight when Chapman pulled back the throttle and slowed to a crawl, the distant light of San Jose Island was flashing in the distance to the north, he had made good time and was close to the designated spot, they would be on time, they always were. The boat stopping had woken Maria and after a quick visit to the head and a wash of her face she climbed up onto the flybridge. Chapman was at the back fixing up two rods that were prepared for fishing, he attached a couple of bright lures and dropped them into the depths before applying the brake and let them drag along on the current. They decided to have a coffee, Maria went down into the galley and made two large mugs of coffee, it took a few minutes for the water to boil, she placed the lids on the mugs and took them upstairs. They sat on opposite sides at the stern of the boat, it was still very warm, clear and calm, there were several tugs on the fishing lines, possible nibbles they just sat in the silence, waiting. They did take three decent fish, a couple of King Mackerel and a large Redfish, Maria had reeled in one of the Mackerel, they were all brought onto the swimming board and Chapman had removed the hooks and released them back into the Ocean.

01:20

Chapman reeled the lines in and took the rods down from the holders, they were stowed away down the steps in the aft stowage locker. Maria was watching the radar intently, nothing could be seen moving within twenty kilometres of their position, Chapman was holding exactly on the coordinates he had been given and allowing for the drift of the ocean and making slight adjustments. "They're here" he told Maria, she was looking but couldn't see anything and then she saw a slight ripple in the water coming alongside the boat, "Come and take the wheel, keep the same speed, straight"

It came closer, it was about the same length as the boat but only the top visible above the surface, it raised up a little more as it came alongside. A submarine, the same colour as the Ocean, it looked like a long canoe and where the seat should be was a square slightly raised doorway. Chapman stepped onto the submarine, it was only two metres wide holding onto the boat with one hand he knocked on the hatch door, "Don't look when they come out it is not very pleasant." The hatch opened and three men, quite small in height climbed out onto the deck of the vessel. They were only wearing briefs, they all immediately pissed into the ocean, the first valuable package was pushed up through the hatch, Chapman grabbed it and lifted it over the gunwale and dropped it onto the deck, another nine packages followed. As this was happening the three crew had jumped into the ocean and climbed back onto the fibreglass surface of the submarine, the last crew member climbed out of the hatch onto the deck and immediately squatted down, holding on to the top of the doorway emptied his bowels down the side of the submarine, he then jumped into the cleaner water against the drift. Once cooled, a matter of a minute, they had climbed down into the cramped and stinking belly of the submarine, Chapman closed the hatch and heard the revolving lock click in to place, he jumped back on to the swimming platform as the submarine slowly moved away and disappeared from view.

Maria "I have heard of the submarines they are supposedly built near my home city but in the jungle, it looks so fragile"

"They are only built for two maybe three trips, they can go up to Canada then when the delivery is done, they sink them before they fall apart, no head, no galley. Increase the speed back towards San Miguel I'll take these down." Maria maintained the course as Chapman took the ten kilo packages down into the galley, he was careful not to split any of the internal kilo block packaging and leave powder or residue in the boat. He removed the Tuna meat from the freezer and placed the blocks in the bottom of the freezer and placed a false metal floor over the top and then placed the Tuna on top of the contraband. There was too much Tuna meat to fit in the freezer he discarded most of it over the gunwales into the ocean, he did keep a small amount of the excess to use as bait. The external packaging was folded and weighted with a couple of heavy fishing weights and dropped overboard. The galley was cleaned thoroughly and when he returned to the deck, he used the hose to wash the deck and the swimming platform. He had made two more mugs of coffee and took a seat adjacent to Maria at the helm and placed her mug in a holder. Chapman checked the charts and fixed new co-ordinates in to the navigation system, a small, uninhabited, well protected cove a few kilometres from San Miguel, they would spend the rest of the night there.

It was 03:50 when Chapman dropped the anchor in the middle of the bay, a wide square shaped bay surrounded by jungle four hundred metres from the shore, the ocean was still calm, the distant calls of some of the birds could be heard, it was a tranquil place for a few hours' sleep, Maria went down into the cabin and Chapman lay out full length beneath the stars on the large double seating on the rear deck and went into a deep sleep.

Just as the Sun was starting to emerge in the East, Maria gave Chapman a little nudge, "Time to wake up, cup of coffee"

He slowly prised his eyes open looking straight up to the sky which was getting slowly brighter, "Coffee would be nice". He sat up and turned towards the helm and saw Maria standing two metres away holding his AB Wood Mahogany spear gun which was armed, the double barbed spear pointing at the middle of his chest. "I guess I'm not going to get a coffee."

"No, this is a beautiful place you should remember this place, not for long though."

"Why are you doing this, I thought we were friends, we have helped each other, why have they told you to do this?"

"I do as I'm told"

"Why for God's sake?"

"This boat was, is, my father's boat and you paid nothing for it, it's worth $300,000"
"They took the boat, not me"
"The boat was to pay for my mothers' healthcare, his insurance, she died because he couldn't pay for her healthcare"
"But that had nothing to do with me, nothing, I didn't know, I've just done as I was told same as you."
"I think my father is dead, I cannot contact him"
"I don't know him; I don't know anyone."
"My father drives coaches and cars, you may know him"
"I've never met him, I spoke to him, you can have the boat, I'm finished this is my last time for them, I'll go back to England, please don't do this, we have been friends, I don't know who you are, you don't know me"
"Could you swim to the shore, the beach?"
"Yes, yes, you have the boat."
She indicated for him to stand and walk to the stern "Climb down onto the swimming board." He climbed down, "Where is your wallet, I will seal it in a bag and throw it to you when you are in the Ocean." He took his wallet out of his hip pocket and placed it onto the aft gunwale. As he stepped back, she released the spear into the right of his chest, the barb protruded at least fifteen centimetres out his back. He had instantly grabbed a cleat on the stern with his right hand, his knees were buckling as blood ran down from the wounds in his chest and back, he was looking in to her face as she was placing another spear in position, She closed on him, "I did not want to damage the leather or the boat." She had seen that look in a young Englishman's face not too long ago, "Why". The second spear powered through the centre of his chest cracking bones as it passed through, he collapsed onto the swimming board, his last defiant message was to smear his blood along the stern of the boat just below the name 'Pasion del Mar.'
She cut the lines to the spears and collected her coffee from the galley, she sat on the deck and watched the sunrise illuminating the cove, it truly was a beautiful place. After finishing her

coffee, she again checked the radar screen and there was nothing moving within ten kilometres, the small fishing fleet from San Miguel would be leaving soon. Climbing down onto the swimming deck she ensured that Chapman was dead, no need for a plastic blanket here, it took some effort to push, then pull the spears through his dead body. She fastened two diving belts around him and pushed him over the edge and watched as he rapidly sank into the deep ocean around the island. The hose was pulled out and it was used to remove any sign of blood from the stern and swimming platform.

It was now time to head back to Panama City, the co-ordinates were set and the throttle pushed forward to a gentle cruising pace it would take two hours to get back to the marina.

CHAPTER 32

Sunday 22nd May

O5:55, Steve was showered, dressed and ready to start the day as he stepped out of his room carrying his overnight bag. He knocked on the door next to his, in a matter of seconds the door opened and Jessica walked through the door carrying her overnight bag and they walked down to the dining room together.

As they entered, they could see Jaime at the fresh fruit counter, scooping up mango, pineapple and banana pieces and some yoghurt, they were early and Jaime was the only person to have taken a seat in the dining room. They dropped their bags near to the entrance and joined him at the table, the waiter was there immediately, they all ordered coffee. They made their way to the self-service breakfast area and got an assortment of fruit and cereal and returned, Arturo had joined them. Jaime explained that there had been movement of the 'Pasion del Mar' during the night from San Miguel, there was no meet up with any other boat, it eventually stopped in a cove off the Isla del Rey for a few hours and it was now on a course to return to the Marina. Arturo made a call to Barbra for her to get the teams in place as soon as possible. There had been no activity on any of the cameras at the house or unit. Juan would be picking them up at 06:30.

Twenty minutes later Maria slowed the progress towards the marina and went down to the cabin, there was only 5 kilometres left on her journey. She prepared a mug of coffee and collected the 'Colombia' phone from her travel bag, switched it on and waited as a signal was verified. Collecting a pen and paper, the coffee and the mobile she returned to the deck aft seats and took a long look at the wonderful world around her; the ocean had an early morning ripple of a wave which made a calming sound as it hit the hull. Maria enjoyed her coffee while viewing the horizon in peace. There were a few small boats moving between the islands and the mainland and four or five, she never counted, large ships waiting in the harbour for their turn to proceed through the canal. She waited.

Walter was back in the office when he saw the indication that one of the mobiles being monitored had been activated, it was located not far off shore from Panama City, he contacted Steve.

The two surveillance teams were in position, Arturo had the lead and the other team were nearby as a back-up if required. Juan was again in the driving seat; Barbra was the communications lead sat in the front passenger seat. Jaime and Arturo were sat in the second row with an array of tablets, mobile phones and radio's, Steve and Jessica were seated in the back row with the cool box between them, which had been replenished by Juan. The windows were closed and the air-conditioning was already blasting out cold air. Steve took a call from Walter warning that a mobile used by Maria had been activated about 5K out from Panama City, this message was passed directly to Jaime who contacted the listening office. The car was quiet, waiting, everyone was waiting.

The mobile vibrated, Maria picked up the pen and put the paper into position on a bench behind the helm seat, she had turned the seat and was in the shade of the hard top.
"Has your journey been a success?"
"Si"
"You can carry your catch by yourself?"
"Si"
"Your new friend will help?"
"No"
"Outside same restaurant at 12, Emilio will be waiting."
"Si"
The call was ended. Maria clicked the brake on the chair and swung around to face the controls and the wheel pushing the throttle slowly forward and picking up a steady cruising speed

so as not to draw any more attention.

It took the time to dial Jaime's number and his phone was ringing. The wording was read slowly and deliberately by the officer in the listening office, Jaime thanked him and ended the call, he then relayed the call to those in the command car. "Is Chapman there or not we shall soon find out." His mobile rang it was the marine section, the boat was approaching the marina.

Barbra, "Be aware the Pasion del Mar is approaching the Marina."

There was a ten-minute wait, it felt like an hour, before the boat was definitely identified by Aaron who was in the position on the hill overlooking the marina and the entrance.

08:09

"2:1 Attention, attention, Pasion del Mar is entering the channel towards the marina moorings."

Barbra wrote her first entry into the log for intelligence of the day by the team.

"2:1 It is moving slowly, passing other traffic towards jetty 3"

"2:1 only one person can be seen at the wheel"

"2:1 it has turned into jetty 3 the female Higuita is at the controls"

"2:1 slowly reversing toward mooring spot, still only Higuita seen"

"2:1 She is out of cabin to rear of boat and is securing the mooring ropes, the engines have been switched off"

Jessica, "Where is Chapman

Arturo, "Aaron would say if he sees him"

"2;1 She has gone downstairs out of view"

The marina and the jetties were starting to get busy on another beautiful Panama day, everyone was busy loading fishing tackle, cool boxes and busy with their own needs to bother looking at anyone else.

Maria was out of view for twenty minutes, when she emerged Aaron could see her hair was wet and she had changed.

08:56

"2:1 Higuita back up onto deck, may have had a shower, her hair looks wet hanging loose, wearing navy blue tee shirt white shorts. She is stepping onto the jetty. Walking towards the Rav car, Chapman's car, repeat Chapman's car. She is reversing the car up the jetty towards the boat, I am recording this, parked the car rear towards the boat and raised the tailgate, stepping onto the boat and down the steps."

"2:1 carrying a black holdall in each hand look heavy from the boat and into the back of the Rav. Back onto boat, recording, returning two more identical bags into back of Rav, back onto boat, returning two more bags. She is talking to a female from the boat moored to left of Pasion del Mar. She is opening the bag and has taken out four red coloured packages and given them to the female who is walking away waving. She has placed the bags into the Rav. Back onto boat again returning two identical bags into the Rav and back onto boat, two more bags the same, from the boat into the car, she has lowered the tailgate and back onto boat."

Barbra "That is ten bags confirm.

"2:1 Yes, confirm" a few minutes passed.

"2;1 Back into cabin where the wheel is appears to be locking doors, clearing a few items, she has the black travel case, off the boat to the Rav places case onto rear passenger seat and into driver's seat, Attention, attention the vehicle is mobile and away from the jetty towards the causeway."

Arturo, "Keep close but loose we have the tracker but move in on stops"

Jaime had made plans for the vehicle to followed if possible, by the city CCTV system and had placed one of his operatives in the control room.

"5:1 vehicle onto Avenida Amador towards city"

"5:1 vehicle onto Avenida 4 de Julio towards bridge"

"4:1 vehicle onto Carretera Interamicana "

Jaime told those inside the command car she was heading

towards her father's house, Jessica translated for Steve, Jaime contacted the officers observing the newly installed covert cameras

"4:1 off the Carretera onto Calle Bruja"

"7 now on Boulevard Andrews turning left, turning left "

Arturo, "let the vehicle run no entry, no entry, plot will be given for exit." He waited until the vehicle had been spotted by the cameras, he was viewing the recording with Jaime on one of the pads. "The vehicle has stopped outside her father's house in Calle Poinciana Drive, she is out of the vehicle and opening the gates to the grounds of the house. The vehicle is driven through the gates and stopped, the gate is closing she is out of the car towards the door and into the house."

08:41

Jaime was watching the screen as Arturo plotted the team positions for when she left. Jaime lifted the screen to enable Steve and Jessica to watch, she was seen to enter the living room and walk out of sight into the kitchen area, returning with an open bottle of cola and some keys. She put these down on a coffee table in the Livingroom and walked out of sight again, she was not visible for eight minutes when she returned and picked up the bottle of coke and walked out again.

While she was not visible, they were theorising what may have happened to Chapman, they believed he had been killed and probably by Maria but again there was no body, no witnesses. They have been on the boat and other places together so any DNA and fingerprints found could be explained.

Maria emerged with a suitcase, bright red in colour, it was on wheels. She left the case and walked in to the kitchen with the empty bottle and returned immediately to the living room, she stopped and was looking at the family photograph for a short time and blew several kisses towards her family. She picked up the keys from the table and pulled the case towards the house door, she locked the door behind her and lifted the case into the rear passenger seat of the Rav.

09:32

Arturo" Attention, attention Higuita has picked up a red suitcase placed it onto the back seats of the Rav and is into the car, the engine is started and moving. The gates are opening, driving through the gates and back on return route towards Boulevard Andrews"

"2:2 at junction, vehicle towards junction turn right, turn right reverse route towards Carretera Interamericana"

"1:1 continuing along Calle Bruja towards Carretera Interamericana."

"1:1 on to Carretera Interamericana towards the city"

Maria continued towards the city and then turning onto Calle Diablo in the direction of the bus storage unit and the ports, as she approached Calle Allemania, Arturo told the surveillance to stop back. Jaime contacted the camera observers.

09:48

The car was parked with the tailgate door next to the pedestrian door, Maria got out of the car and opened the door to the unit and lifted the tailgate. She entered the unit and put on a pair of blue rubber gloves, then returned and lifted the ten bags out of the car and put them inside the unit then closed the tailgate and locked the car and closed the unit door behind her. She collected a case trolley and placed the ten bags onto the trolley and pushed them into the room at the back of the unit. Jaime had lifted the tablet for Steve and Jessica to see the images.

Maria unlocked and opened the two large freezer storage boxes, then took two suitcases from the shelving and placed them on the long bench and opened them both with the moulded blocks on the bottom. She was seen to pick up several black blocks from the freezer and position them inside the cases, when the mouldings were full, they were strapped down with strong adhesive tape, she then placed a hard plastic false bottom that pushed down and clipped into place then fastened the zip under the frame of the case concealing the contraband. The clothing was taken from the cabinets and the vacuum-packed bags were opened and spread on top of the base material. The cases were closed and placed onto the floor. She repeated this five times, ten cases in all. She then opened the black holdall bags and replenished the stock in the freezer cabinets, there was insufficient room for all the tuna which was starting to defrost, she filled two holdalls with the excess tuna.

The cases were loaded onto the case trolley and she pulled them into the area of the coach, she loaded the cases into the storage unit of the coach and closed the door. The holdalls full of tuna were collected and dropped near to the exit door. Maria returned to the room, tidied the room and locked all of the doors.

Arturo had positioned Alejandro in a covert observation point to observe Maria as she left the building. Maria locked the doors behind her and placed the two holdalls of tuna in the rear of the vehicle.

10:42

"7 Attention, attention, Higuita is out of the unit, tailgate up two black bags into rear of vehicle, tailgate down the vehicle is driven away along Calle Alemania away from port towards city"

The officer monitoring the tagged vehicle noticed a stop and informed Barbra, it was a brief stop on Calle Alemania, 400 metres from the unit. Arturo assigned team 3 to investigate the area. The surveillance headed towards the city.

"3:2 two bags containing tuna recovered from waste bin on Calle Alemania, photographs taken."

Maria continued on Avenida Omar Torrijos Herrera turning onto Avenida 3 S, at this time she was being monitored by the city CCTV system who was giving commentary on her movements, the traffic was light and easy flowing. She drove into Calle 45 E and stopped near to the junction with Calle 47. The camera operator zoomed into the parked car.

"CCTV relaying a male mid-thirties white shirt dark trousers has entered the car. They are in discussion, the car is now continuing on Calle 45E onto Balboa Avenida, turning into the

Hilton Panama hotel underground car park, lost vision."

Arturo," Units deploy cover all exits from the hotel, CCTV continue coverage on exit from car park, Barbra will plot vehicles."

Jaime requested an immediate inspection of the hotel registration book and for a still photograph of the male inside the car. Juan was finding a quiet location to park the command car whilst Barbara was plotting foot and vehicle positions.

Jaime, "We are going to have to make a decision, we have evidence for a charge of murder on Margarita of the English citizen. The boat is presently being observed and will be forensically examined as soon as it is deemed safe to do so, for links with what we believe to be the murder of our ex colleague Martin Chapman, in Panama. We also have Maria collecting and packaging vast amounts of what we believe to be cocaine. Is there any benefit to let this run any further, will we gain much more.?"

Steve, "There is the possibility we could get linked to the organiser, the man on the phone. It sounds like he has ordered a murder but would be hard to prove or even identify him. The Fort Lauderdale cops would like it to run and probably take another syndicate out over there, it's causing them headaches and the cartel must be hurting"

Jaime, "I do not like, not having control over the subject, where is she, who is she with. If she comes out and heads back to the bus lock up, I'll let it run, anything else, take down"

"I agree"

"You don't need to; I've made the decision"

"Sorry Jaime, yes boss." They shook hands.

Jaime sent an update to NCA.

CHAPTER 33

Sunday 22nd May

Maria parked the car then placed the red case into the boot of the vehicle and closed the tailgate. "I was told you were going to give me something" Emilio" No, you were told I would be waiting, now he is waiting, please to the lift"

Maria took a small dark blue clasp bag off the back seat and closed the car. She had to give the bag to Emilio for inspection, "No guns or knives, just condoms, gel, book and a pen, what I expect to need." Emilio had a look inside and gave the bag back to her smiling.

Borja had the penthouse suite with a long view over the Pacific towards the Pearl Islands, they arrived at the door and Emilio inserted the card, opened the door and directed her into the suite. He closed the door behind her. Borja was sitting in a high white leather swing chair near to the full-length window, he was wearing the quality white towelling robe supplied by the hotel. He beckoned Maria over, "Please sit, feel comfortable, is the room too cold or hot, you let me know."

Marie took a seat facing him and wanted to speak but knew better, she waited.

"Do you want a cold drink, not alcohol you still have some work to do?"

"No, I'm ok thank you"

"We have time for a little talk, what did you think of our police friend?"

Maria was not expecting this question and was concerned, "Who would that be?"

"He never told you? Your friend on the boat was an English policeman, he was good but he had served his purpose. Was he good to you? Did you kill him as you were told?"

"No, he never said, I didn't know" looking quite shocked."

Yes, I did. He was friendly and trusting, I did it when he fell asleep on the back of the boat."

"Did it take long?"

"I don't know he never woke up, should it take long I don't think I could have handled him he was a big man?"

"No, it was a strong dose to kill instantly or very quickly, I didn't want you to be harmed."

"Thank you, I suppose"

"I think your father is dead, he was supposed to kill another two English police. I haven't had contact from him, but I'm told the police are dead, so maybe they all died, or he has left my group of friends."

"I think he's dead I have had no contact. Is the boat mine now?"

"I like the way you think, enough talking. I was bad to you last time; I want to be good to you this time. Please use the bathroom and prepare, there is some nice underwear for you, please it would look good for me." He signalled for her to go to the bathroom.

She walked into the bathroom and examined the underwear, top quality, well worth keeping, Carine Gilson black soft lace triangle bra and matching briefs. She put her bag on the marble top next to the sink, she kicked her converse shoes off and took off her clothing, folding the shorts and tee shirt and placing them on the seat. She opened the bag and took out the gel, applying it inside her vagina, she took out the black fountain pen, it was 13 centimetres in length and 12 millimetres wide and inserted the pen inside her vagina, it was not uncomfortable and easy to extract with a pelvic thrust, she removed it three times to be certain she could do it easily. She dressed in the underwear, it had a soft gentle feeling on her skin, tied her hair back and fastened with a hair grip then applied a small amount of red lipstick and stood back. Looking in the mirror she said to herself, "dressed to kill".

Maria walked into the master bedroom, Borja was lying naked on top of the super king size bed which was covered in pillows and cushions, top quality luxury. He was facing her, half aroused, she paraded herself at him and stayed at the bottom of the bed, rubbing her hands over her breasts and through her hair. She showed the condom packet to him and he beckoned her to come to him, she opened the packet and threw it away, holding the unfurled condom she was on the bed on her hands and knees crawling up towards him, he was fully excited, Maria was calm and enjoying the toying. She placed the condom on his erection and slowly started rolling it down the shaft, she put her right hand between her legs which he thought was part of the show, she removed the pen and positioned it below his testicles, the top was twisted exposing the short needle, she started to slowly masturbate Borja with her left hand. She pushed the needle into his skin and pushed down on the container forcing the fluid to empty into his body, he made a shout, Maria grabbed a pillow and put it over his face while keeping the pressure on the pen. He was right what he said, it didn't take long, a few seconds. When he had stopped moving, she stood up at the end of the bed, "Dying for a fuck were you?"

She collected some tissue and a wet wipe from the bathroom and returned to the dead body, lifting up his testicles she looked for the injection site, there was a small dot of blood which had stopped bleeding, she cleaned the area and left the tissue on the site for any residue for a couple of minutes, there was nothing visible to the naked eye, these were flushed down the toilet. She opened the sliding doors to the balcony, taking the pen apart into small pieces she dropped them over the side of the building and returned inside. Returning to the body she gave him kiss marks in lipstick in various parts of his groin, chest, and neck. Pulling her hair out of the grip in parts, she opened the door and shouted for Emilio loudly. The door adjacent opened very quickly, he looked at Maria and without saying anything ran into the suite and saw Borja dead, lying spread-eagled on the bed, "Fuck, fuck, fuck, fuck"

Maria, "For fuck sake, stop saying fuck, what are we going to do?"

"What have you done, what have you done, we are dead?"

"I did what I was told, I fucked him like he wanted, everything he said, I was still fucking him, he started to go soft, I looked and he was dead."

"I will contact Manolo; you get dressed stay here." He ran out of the door, she was stifling her laughter as she again ensured his body was clean before walking back into the bathroom and dressing, she still wore the underwear.

She took the seat in the window that Borja had been sitting on and was gazing out onto the Ocean, she wanted to be back out there, a picture of Chapman flickered in her mind, briefly.

The room door opened quickly and was just as quickly closed, Emilio walked directly to Maria. "Manolo is not happy; he wants photographs of what happened"

"You want me to strip off and get on the bed with him?" Maria said incredulously

"No, no stupid. You take the condom off and point it down." Pointing at the limp penis," It will look like he has had a heart attack."

"He has had a fucking heart attack idiot"

"Don't fucking call me an idiot, Manolo does not want his wife and family to know that he died fucking a whore, no, no, he does not want them to know he died when, he was fucking. Just take the condom off, point it down." Maria did as she was told.

"Manolo says you have to do what Borja told you"

"I did, he fucking died"

"No stupid, what to do with the cocaine."

"He did not tell me anything, just to fuck him, he would have something written down names and hotels"

They started looking in drawers in the bedroom, the first drawer Maria checked the bed side drawer next to his head, she found a folded sheet of paper with a list of names, hotels and times. She looked at the bedside clock," I have to go I have no time. What will you do?"

"I have to contact the police"

"No, no you can't do that, not Borja, they will know him."

"It has to be recorded as natural or the other cartels may take advantage, that's what Manolo has said. I am doing what Manolo tells me, I suggest you do the same. Go"

Maria left the suite and took the lift to the basement; she now had a big problem. She opened the car door, which activated the tag.

Barbra, "Attention, attention the car has been activated"

Maria took her mobile phone out from the black travel bag, switched it on and pressed the known numbers.

The DEA desk officer in Fort Lauderdale answered the call.

"This is 89147"

"Please wait for verification" it took as long as it took the record the numbers on the keyboard. "Hi, have you some more intelligence since your last call?"

"Do you have any cash figures that I asked for?"

"Yes, they are looking 10G a K and 10G an arrest, interested?"

"Is your pen ready write this down?" Maria read from the list the names of the passengers who would be carrying the cases. "I will be in contact for the payment and closed the phone."

A thought jumped into her head, using her Colombia phone she rang Borja's number. Emilio answered, "Have you contacted the police yet?"

"No, I'm still busy. Why"

"Call him again, please listen, they will find my DNA it will be all over him, we were quite active, you can imagine. It would not look good, I'm too far away to do anything, please call him. We could use the boat."

"Ok, I will only ask once it might be better"

Maria switched her mobile off and put it into the drivers doorwell. She started the engine and started praying.

12:17

Barbra, "Attention, attention, the car is active and moving"

Jaime's mobile rang, he took his earpiece out to concentrate on the call and wrote down precisely what was recorded. The surveillance team had picked up the Rav and with the aid of the city CCTV and the tracker they were back in control.

Jaime turned to Arturo, Steve and Jessica and gave the details of the call word for word.

Arturo, "She is one killing machine and an excellent informant."

Steve took a call from Walter with the information from the two mobiles in the same locality.

Jaime had the start of a headache and the surveillance commentary kept coming in to the command car. No one said it would be easy. Get 7 ahead to the bus unit and concealed I want good imagery. Barbra responded immediately. The command car went quiet, deep in thought, while the commentary continued.

CHAPTER 34

Sunday 22nd May

7, Alejandro had ridden his Suzuki motorbike at speed passing the heavier traffic flow to gather some distance ahead of the Rav, he had concealed himself behind a wooden fence and was hidden by some large industrial skips and overhanging trees. He had an excellent view at the front of the bus unit in Calle Alemania, he waited.

Jaime received the image of the male getting into the car with Maria. He had been identified by their intelligence as Emilio Sanchez Martinez, a member of the MMV cartel and constant travel associate (*Body Guard*) of Borja Sanchez." Madre Mia"

The phone rang, Maria picked up, "Si"

"He says yes, he will stay here until you get back, you come straight here. I'm arranging here"

"Si,si, si. Gracias"

She could relax and started a smile, another productive day. She was on Avenida Omar Torreijos Terrera, approaching the junction for Calle Alemania.

Barbra,"7 Higuita is approaching your location".

As she drove into Calle Allemania, Arturo" All units take positions from last occasion to you 7"

Steve took a call from Walter informing him there had been calls between the two mobiles in differing locations which tied up with the surveillance position.

Jaime took a call from the listening post officer who repeated the call verbatim and slowly. Jaime wrote it down at his speed.

"7 the Rav is at the unit, stopped but engine running, she is opening the small door and entered the unit."

Jaime took a call from the camera observer, he watched as she collected the keys for the big coach from the office, and appeared to switch the computer and printer on, she then pressed the control of the automatic large door which began to open, he was on an open line to Jaime, who relayed to Barbara for the log.

"7 the large coach is slowly moving out of the unit and stopped, the engine is running, she is into the Rav and has driven the Rav into the unit"

Jaime repeated the camera observer." She has stopped the engine is out of the car, she has a mobile and some paper in her left hand. She is lifting the tail gate and opening a red case. She has taken a brown garment from the case; she is taking off her tee shirt and wearing the brown blouse buttons fastened. The tee shirt thrown into case and pulled down, tail gate down walking to office. Collected a brown clip board and placed the paper onto the board, reading from the board. She is using the computer keyboard. Something is being printed, she has attached the printed sheet onto the clipboard, switching the computer off and leaving the office pressing door control which is lowering the large door, back to door"

12:42

"7 out of the door, locking door. Pulling hair into pony tail, confirming brown buttoned blouse large sunglasses white shorts. She is opening the luggage compartment driver's side, there are cases inside she is pulling a case towards her, tearing off piece of rectangle paper from the sheet on the board and attaching the paper into i.d. pocket." 7 continued commentating as she did this to all of the ten cases. " Into coach adjusting mirrors, instruments, door closing and attention, attention bus Prevost make, brown, Tours de Leo on back moving away from unit"

Jaime to the command car," Another conversation, would appear that she has to go back to the hotel and clear away, possibly, probably Borja with the help of Emilio Martinez, after this bus business, I need to think." He paused for a few seconds, " Arturo get the other team to plot on the hotel, chase up the reception enquiry, get someone to get a copy of this photo" he was showing Emilio in the front of the car," issue to all their crews, I want the hotel CCTV monitoring now. Barbra you're the surveillance command" She nodded whilst listening to the commentary.

He turned to Steve, "We hadn't planned for this, but we are prepared, I have an email from NCA saying Fort Lauderdale want the drug couriers to run, the informant we now know is Higuita. So that is straight forward, she drops the couriers off and drives away, we arrest her here for the drugs here. There is strong evidence that she murdered the English man from Newcastle in Margarita, we could arrest her on suspicion of that murder for Venezuela Police. There is a high possibility that Chapman was murdered by her but there is no evidence and no body, she is linked with a conspiracy to murder in Santa Monica of the American officer, now a Colombian cartel leader is believed dead in a bedroom of the Hilton, who she has recently visited and has her DNA all over him and is planning to dispose of his body if I am hearing it right. When do I say, that's enough or do I let her kill more bad guys?"

Steve, "You and your team have her under control boss," Jaime smiled at Steve, "If I may say"

"Si, Si"

"Why not let it run and pick her up ideally, when, if, Emilio and her, possibly others are loading the body on to the boat, all suspicion of murder, drugs running, good result and a big hit on the cartel." Steve stopped as Jaime mobile was ringing.

He took the call, listened and wrote into the incident log. "That was Paco Mendez the tourist police officer, good guy. The Penthouse has been hired by Cattleya group, a frequent visitor and also the adjoining smaller room for protection personnel. The occupier only uses the room and never ventures into the other areas of the hotel, he has room service and he is generous in tips from his attendants. The manager believes he is a big criminal from Colombia but it is a regular and excellent income. There is no trouble. I've asked Paco to monitor the CCTV which he has fixed up on the on the floor and the lift."

Arturo," The first teams are on point at the hotel covering the exits, one in the reception area. They have print outs."

Jessica, "Do the cartel know she has a surplus of cocaine in the freezers, why ask to collect more? Would his visits to the Hilton coincide with the drug cruises?"

Jaime," You should be an intelligence officer, good thoughts, starting her own business, getting rid of opposition. I'll get you a job here, it's not always this exciting or difficult"

Jessica, "I might take you up on that" they both smiled at each other, Steve had a look of concern, then she gave him a smile.

Jaime, "It's up to us now, let's do it."

The bus was being driven back towards the city and had turned onto the Allbrook Mall service road.

"6:2 Halt, halt outside of Albrook Wyndam Hotel, there are people waiting with cases."

"5:1 Higuita out of bus with clipboard and talking to people outside of the hotel, checking documents there are six people, three male three female, possibly couples. She is opening the nearside luggage doors, the people are boarding the coach, there are twelve cases placed into luggage space. She has closed the door down and is getting into the coach. Attention, attention the coach is driven away from the hotel"

"1:1 Coach turning into Calle Curundu towards city." The surveillance continued.

The coach stopped and picked up 14 passengers and cases at the Hotel Crowne Plaza and then onto the Hotel Panama Marriott where a further 18 passengers got on to the coach and their cases placed in the luggage storage.

13:30

The coach was travelling on the Corredor Norte in the direction of Colon, the following surveillance convoy were spread out along the motorway. The command team took the opportunity to have a cold drink and a snack, taco, crisps, a sandwich as they travelled easily at the back of the convoy. Barbra was maintaining the communications and the log periodically with locations as they passed. Arturo was contacting each team individually by mobile calls and praising their work so far and giving them encouragement. Jaime was enjoying the relative quiet, he hadn't had a call for over ten minutes and sat back with his eyes closed. Steve and Jessica could remember a couple of specific locations as they passed, not with fond memories. After his short period of relaxation, Jaime was again active on his mobile making calls to Colon Port Immigration Unit, the camera observer to thank him and inform him the cameras would need watching later in the day and to Paco thanking him for his assistance at the hotels and ensuring that he could stay or if he needed to be replaced. Paco was prepared to stay; he was interested like everyone else on the job. Another call to the Specialist Team commander thanking his team for their efforts which have helped so much. After a short pause whilst making notes in the incident book, he spoke to Juan and Barbra and complimented them on their teamwork and control of the surveillance and suggested that they should change positions at the next stop. He said to them all in the command car, "This is going to be one very interesting debrief, should be fun. Arturo get Headquarters to book" he counted down the list including Paco, camera observer, the specialist team members and Marine Section, "24 rooms at same hotel as last night, hopefully we will get finished this evening, contact everyone, use this list," he gave Arturo his deployment list," let them know, I want them there, to stop tonight, debrief will be tomorrow"

14:25

The coach was entering the outskirts of the city of Colon, the following surveillance team closed on the bus. Jaime asked Alejandro to go ahead to the port security office and liaise with the Immigration Unit who were expecting him to monitor the bus on arrival into the port area, he accelerated away on the Suzuki overtaking the bus and made good headway and distance on the coach. Car 4 a taxi, was told to get ahead and deploy on the harbour on foot. Enrique passed the coach, with Gloria sat in the back of the taxi.

Twenty minutes later the coach entered the port gates and headed towards the cruiser harbour, it was in port,' The Western

Horizon', an impressive looking Cruiser was moored and activity had started. Alejandro was commentating on the progress of the coach as it was directed by the port workers to the harbour and parking area allocated for coaches with passengers for the cruises.

4:1, Gloria was with the Immigration Officer as the coach stopped. They were both smiling at Maria as she opened the coach door and came down the steps to greet them carrying her passenger list. The coach was soon attended by port workers to remove the luggage on to the trailers on to the back of the heavily worked tractive units. Maria handed the immigration officer the passenger sheet on the clipboard, she passed it to Gloria who took her pen out of her newly acquired blazer, which she intended to keep. The passengers started to disembark the coach one at a time and waited until their passport had been examined by the first officer then ticked on the list by Gloria, then stood in the shade from the fierce sun while they waited. When the list was completed Gloria gave Maria the clipboard back but kept the sheet of names and gave consent to unload the luggage, Maria opened the compartment doors on both sides. Gloria watched as only two of the workers went to the driver's side door and waited for the door to be open, Alejandro had zoomed into the two workers and recorded excellent images as they loaded the trailer with ten suitcases, Maria returned to the officer and Gloria and made conversation while the luggage was removed. Alejandro was continuous with precise commentary. The luggage had been removed and the passengers walked towards the boarding ramp, the two officers walked away from Maria as she closed the compartment doors, got back into the coach and started to drive back through the port. She was thinking this is so simple, police are so stupid, without my help anyway.

15:10

Barbara had finished her last entry in the log and signed it over to Juan who confirmed to the crew he was now loggist. They had exchanged seats and Barbra adjusted her sitting position. Jaime asked Juan to communicate with car 4 for Gloria to ring him when she returned to the car. Now for an easy drive or ride back to Panama City, the convoy were in control and the commentary was regular and correct.

Jaime was as usual making entries into his incident log, making phone calls, spoke to Paco, there had been no movement at the penthouse. His mobile rang it was Gloria, "Hola Gloria, what are your close-up impressions of Maria?"

"She is nice, I like her," she gave a laugh "it is hard to imagine what she is, she is very pleasant, beautiful face and skin and all natural."

CHAPTER 35

Sunday 22nd May

Maria was driving the coach faster on the return journey with no passengers, her days spent driving the coaches in Colombia for the family business came back in to her head. They were good times, happy times, learning everything about the business from her family, all of the family and bringing her friend Susanna from the University in to the business. House parties, holidays, outings in the ocean fishing, diving, life was brilliant and exciting. Plenty of work but the rewards were plentiful. Her mobile ring tone stopped her happy thoughts.

"Have you done your work?" it was Emilio.

"Yes, I'm heading back"

"Come straight here"

"In the coach?"

"No, in your car, park at the side of the hotel it is quiet. Ring me ten minutes before you arrive and I will be waiting."

"What?" she exclaimed

"Do it, ring me."

The call was closed.

What the fuck was Maria's first thoughts, he is dead, I'm sure he's dead, he looked dead.

Paco was in the reception office monitoring the CCTV when a call was received from the penthouse suite requesting a hotel wheelchair to be taken to the room. The respected guest had accidently injured himself doing some exercise. Emilio politely explained it was no fault of the hotel it was just a strenuous exercise accident and it needs to be checked by their private consultant; an appointment had been arranged. He just wants privacy and will use a side exit, he would not be going through the reception areas with people looking on.

Jaime mobile was ringing it was the listening office. They slowly repeated the call, which Jaime wrote down as it was told.

He closed the call and was about to talk to the command car when the mobile rang again, it was Paco, who gave him the update from the Hilton which he wrote immediately into his incident book. He deliberately waited in the expectancy of other calls, everyone else in the car was waiting impatiently for the updates. The surveillance commentary was still on the radio but no other distractions.

"First, the listening office, Maria has been told to go back to the hotel in her car and park in a side street. Paco has told me that the minder, possibly this Emilio, has asked for a hotel wheelchair to be taken to the room as the guest has had an accident and is being taken for a check by his consultant."

He held his hand up to stop anyone from talking, he was thinking. He dropped his hand "I believe we cannot go further than the Hilton pick up, that is where I want to co-ordinate the strike, if it is safe, Juan will we pick up communications at the Hilton from the coach unit?"

"Yes, sir."

"Arturo, I want to go there now to make an assessment will the surveillance be ok with your command from there or do you want to be closer?"

"It should be ok but I can get into car 4 in the back with Gloria and you go ahead."

"Yes, call car 4 and arrange a pick up as soon as possible I want to get there well ahead."

Arturo made the pick-up arrangements with Car 4 which parked with hazard warning lights at the side of the road. It only took a minute to reach the car, Juan also got into the taxi with the log book. Jessica took the opportunity of stretching her legs and jumped in to the front passenger seat, Steve took the seat in the middle row next to Jaime.

Barbra now pushed on towards Panama City and the Hilton hotel. They could still hear the commentary but as Steve would say, 'belt and braces', to be sure.

Steve took a call from Newcastle, "Hiya Jimmy it's Sarah, are you busy or can you talk,"

"I'm not but the team is, quickly."

"Josh is back home with Maddison in Alderley Edge, they're both fine and feel safe. Hope you two are ok?"

"That's good news Sarah, I will tell Jessica and we are both ok, speak later"

Steve passed the information on and it was a relief to Jessica. Barbra soon drove passed the coach and continued towards the city.

Jaime had opened a maps page on the table and placed it between himself and Steve. It was zoomed in to the area around the Hilton Panama hotel. The hotel faced onto the Calle Aquilino de la Guardia, a four-lane major road, there was a lane which accessed the reception drop zone and the underground car park, there was only one side road which was a small service road between the hotel and Avenida 5 BS. This was a one-way street running from Calle Aquilino de la Guardia to Calle 48. This could be a good place for a controlled strike, they both agreed.

16:35

Jaime took a call from Paco; the chair had been delivered and took inside by the man known as Emilio. The command car was approaching the Hilton hotel as the coach was driven into Calle Alemania. 7 had taken his covert observation location and was waiting.

Barbra drove down Calle Aquilino de la Guardia and turned right into the service road, it was only 100 metres in length before the junction with Calle 48. There was one narrow pavement on the left side of the road running down the side of the hotel, a small door to the hotel was 40 metres from the turning, two delivery vans were parked at the service gates of the hotel, a further 20 metres down the road blocking half of the width of the road. At this time there were no pedestrians, which was good.

"7 the coach has stopped outside the double gates. Higuita is out of the coach opening the door of the Unit"

Jaime had called the camera observer, they watched as Maria took the red case out of the car and put it into the office, reversed the Rav out of the unit and parked. She moved the coach in to the unit and switched off the engine, leaving the coach with the doors open. She took of her brown blouse and threw it onto an office chair, then took a clean light green Tee shirt from the suitcase and put it on and closed the case. She picked up some keys and carried the case to the rear of the unit and opened the door, she placed the case on the middle rack amongst the others. She left the room and locked the door. She closed the automatic door and left the unit.

16:52

"7 she is in the Rav, making a mobile call"

Jaime had asked Steve and Jessica to go into the hotel reception area as he did not want them involved in the strike, they both had covert radios and could listen to the commentary and assist if they saw anything. Unlike the rest of the officers they would not be armed. Jaime took a call from the listening room, and wrote it down. "Ten minutes down the side of the hotel". He told Steve and Jessica as they got out and walked towards the hotel.

Jaime had contacted the second surveillance unit and had them positioned in an outer cordon, just in case of a break out of the controlled zone. The surveillance was getting closer only six minutes. Jaime spoke to Arturo on the mobile and gave instructions on the approach to the hotel.

The first three vehicles in the convoy to follow Higuita into Calle Aquilino and wait, back three to turn into Calle 48 and wait command for strike, Police caps and weapons ready. They continued towards the strike zone.

Jaime took a call from Paco, "Male believed to be Emilio dark suit and white shirt is out of the room in the passage, he has walked to the service lift and pressed for the lift, it looks as if he is shouting, yes another male white shirt, dark suit pulling a wheel chair backwards through room door, figure in white hotel bathrobe with hood over the head sitting in the chair, now pushing towards the service lift." Jaime now knew that Maria was sat in Rav and was parked outside of the hotel side exit. "Lift door opening, one male pulling the wheelchair and occupant into the lift, Emilio in to lift. The side door is on a spring and will close and lock when they leave."

CCTV camera operator, "Higuita is out of the car and opening the back door behind the driver nearest to the door just two metres, standing at the door."

Paco" Emilio out of the lift walking to the exit only ten metres shouting for the other man"

Jaime" Prepare, Prepare, Prepare,"

The strike team placed on their Police caps and took out their firearms.

Steve and Jessica slowly walked from the reception in the direction of the side exit corridor.

Paco "The wheelchair being pushed towards the door Emilio has opened the door."

CCTV, "Higuita, is standing away from the car the two men are through the door which is closing pulling the figure from the wheelchair."

17:11

Jaime "Strike, strike, strike"

The six cars converged at high acceleration on the Rav and screeched to a halt sideways across and blocking the road, giving a good line of sight, Emilio and the other man stepped into the road and considered pulling out pistols from the holsters concealed under their jackets but quickly realised they were outnumbered and out gunned then raised their hands in the air. Maria used her right foot to stop the exit door slamming shut and jumped into the corridor running towards the lifts and reception, directly towards Steve and Jessica. They saw her running towards them and moved to the side to allow her to pass, as she passed Steve executed a perfect rugby tackle, wrapping his arms around the top of her thighs and knocking her down to the ground with his shoulder, Jessica took hold of her wild throwing arms and restrained them behind her back face down, Maria shouted, "Let me go, they will kill me, I need protection."

Paco was quickly on the scene and used his handcuffs to

fasten her wrists behind her back, Paco told her he was arresting her on suspicion of dealing large quantity of drugs. She told him, "You do not know what you are doing, let me go, they will kill me." Jessica walked to the side door and opened it. Arturo and Gloria came in and took hold of Maria from behind her arms and lifted her off the floor. Maria looked at Gloria and gave a smile, "We have met before."

Gloria, "Yes, just the once."

Maria started to think possibly the police are not so stupid, what do they know, what have they seen, I think I'm fucked.

Three police prisoner carrier vans were waiting in the street, one had Emilio inside, the unknown male was in another and Maria was placed in the third. There was unmarked van where Borja was placed on a gurney, he was not going to be interviewed but he was going to be examined. They left in a convoy to the Police Headquarters detention centre and hospital.

Paco, Steve and Jessica, shook hands and introduced themselves then walked out of the side door and saw Jaime standing, looking not like the usual Jaime but like an angry Superintendent in England might look. They walked over to where he was standing on his own, as if he had cleared the space. He spoke quietly, "I will say this to you here. You fucking idiots what the fuck do you think you are doing? You two have no powers nothing, nothing in this country." Steve made to speak, "Silence, I need to finish. I put you somewhere where you should be safe you chose to ignore that, I understand police instinct but you took Jessica with you" Jessica was going to speak, he looked at her, "I'm not finished, I know your history, but it creates problems. Paco, you are a tourist officer, a very good one, did you have a weapon, no. Yes, she is a woman, she is a killer we know that. And now you Paco, the tourist officer has just arrested a major drug dealing, murderous woman, that all of my team wanted to do". Paco was going to speak but thought better of it. "Ok, that's out," he smiled a charming smile that warmed Jessica's heart, "Thank you, all of you, excellent it was a big help,

Paco I want you in my team if you would like."

"Yes Sir, thank you Sir."

"Jimmy," there was a pause and a smile," I wish you had been born in Panama but I hear there might be an opportunity in the British Embassy, so I have been told, maybe you should apply. Jessica I am sure you could utilise your language and intelligence skills here, have a think. The job is not finished until the paperwork is done, there are some searches now which can progress tonight and a full debrief tomorrow but tonight we party at the hotel and the drinks are on me."

Steve, "Sir"

Jaime, "Please call me Jimmy" and they all laughed.

"The hotel is all inclusive"

"Well that is a cheap round then" they all laughed and walked towards the command vehicle. Barbra jumped out of the driver's seat and hugged Jessica, Steve and Paco, then looked at Jaime, he opened his arms and they hugged. "Barbra take us to the party".

CHAPTER 36

Sunday 22nd May

23:45 England
Rajid received an email from Jaime giving the details of the arrests in Panama City and a breakdown of the intelligence gathered during the course of the day. Further enquiries were continuing and it was anticipated that any interviews of those arrested would take place tomorrow after a full debrief and a strategy had been finalised.

At the same time in Newcastle the phone was ringing on Sarah's desk. She answered, it was Jimmy, "About time, what's going on, wait the boss is here should I get him, "

"It would be a good idea" there was a pause as he could hear Sarah's heels tapping out her steps away from the phone and then back.

"Hi, Jimmy are you ok, both of you?"

"Yes, boss thanks."

"How much can you tell me?"

"I've spoken with Jaime, who I'm sat next to now, he's the Ops commander and I can tell you everything but if I can keep it short."

"The whole team are still here they've been waiting for the result, can I put it on speaker?"

Steve confirmed with Jaime, "Yes boss. I don't know how much you know but here goes. The specialist crime team here are a great team just like you lot, our team. They have done two days surveillance including tracking at sea and the evidence they have gathered is brilliant. I don't know if you are aware but the guy who tried to kill me and Jessica is the father of Maria. Yesterday Maria and Chapman, the Panama liaison officer went to some Islands of the coast from the city and collected quite a bit of cocaine, somewhere. Chapman did not come back and we believe Maria killed him. She has sorted the transport for the drugs and passengers on a cruise to Fort Lauderdale, she was driving the coach and packed the cocaine into false bottom suitcases. One of the team acted as the immigration officer at the port, they were using CCTV everywhere it was available and had put cameras into a couple of properties with covert entries, the images were amazing absolutely cracking work. Now in between this, a guy called Borja who is a top guy in the cartel, has died in his room with Maria, we don't know what's happened there but they were trying to hide or dispose of the body when the boss here, Jaime called the strike outside of the hotel."

Andy spoke up, "Did you see the strike Jimmy".

"Well, not really but what happened was they approached the car from both directions at speed blocked the road with the cars and the firearms were on the guys straight away, they had pistols but put them down on the road. Maria managed to get a door open and ran into the hotel and I dropped her and Jessica pinned her arms down."

The Boss raised his voice and was not happy, "What the fuck are you doing getting involved in the fucking strike you idiot, anything could have happened?"

Everyone could here loud laughing from inside the car where Steve was making the call, "I'm sorry boss, that's Jaime laughing, he only minutes ago said exactly the same thing to me and Jessica, I know but it was instinctive."

Sarah was excited," Did you lock her up Jimmy?"

"No, Paco, the tourist police officer did," they could hear Jaime laughing again and they all joined in. "there is still loads to do, we are debriefing tomorrow and I will be able to tell you more then, Boss, Jaime wants to speak to you in private"

The boss picked up the phone and walked away from the team. Jaime thanked the superintendent for the work that had been done by his team in initiating the investigation which has left him with a great result but some unanswered questions. Steve was praised for his help throughout the enquiry and that they would be in touch regularly as the enquiries progressed.

He requested that Steve be allowed to stay for at least a week until proceedings were commenced against those that will be charged. That was accepted. He explained his team would be having a party tonight but tomorrow the work starts. He finished the call by saying a great win for the toon.

The boss sat with the team and relayed most of what Jaime had said including the final words. It had been a long day, the shift for tomorrow was starting at three, have a good sleep and we can celebrate tomorrow. He asked Andy to contact Walter and make them aware of the plans, they all drifted away. Colin typed an email to the Chief for her morning update, I think she would be happy.

Later that evening, all of those involved were sat around the pool bars, the Latino music was playing loud, they were socialising, playing in the pool, having fun and celebrating together. This one pool area had been allocated for the private party. Sat around a table just a short distance away were, Jaime, Arturo, Jessica and Steve. Jaime still had his mobile where he was getting regular updates from the searches that were being conducted and the forensic examinations, it could all be kept for the debrief. He had a discussion with Arturo, who should conduct the interviews? To interview Maria, it would be Enrique and Gloria. Emilio, would be done by Aaron and Jose, the other teams could be decided tomorrow. Arturo walked through the group while drinking his beer and saw Gloria and Enrique dancing salsa together the way that Latino's do, it was good Arturo thought, joined at the hip, he spoke quietly to them and told them to speak to the boss. They were delighted to be chosen, no reason given, but no more alcohol, of course. It was a good evening, Steve and Jessica joined in the dancing much to the amusement of Jaime who never left the table, his mobile and incident book. He did enjoy a few cold Bilboa beers and some of the large buffet the hotel had provided for the private party, Paco had proved to be a good guy again with his contacts.

CHAPTER 37

Monday 23rd May

11:00

Jaime and Arturo were sat on seats behind a table on a slightly raised platform, there were two large white boards behind them on a wall. All of the operational staff who had taken part in the operation were present unless they were still working but Jaime knew of their latest updates. Steve and Jessica were sat in the rear row of seating. Yesterday this room was used for a wedding reception. The double doors were closed and a uniformed officer stood outside.

Arturo stood and requested that there be silence throughout the debrief, if anyone had something to add to raise their arm. The information was not to be divulged to anyone not in this room. He took his seat and Jaime stood with the open incident book in front of him. He started by welcoming them to the debrief with special mention to the visitors from Newcastle, England, Steve and Jessica. He continued by saying he had enjoyed being with them all last night to celebrate the arrests but it was not the conclusion of the operation it was the start of finding and proving the truth.

He started the sequence of events with the murder of an Englishman on Margarita Island by a woman who has been identified as Gabriella Mariana Higuita, a woman he had met here in Panama on the canal cruise. Steve and Jessica travelled from England to make enquiries and Mario Leonel Higuita, the father of Gabriella, attempted to murder them near to the canal but accidently shot himself in the struggle and died. Higuita had been contacted by the British police liaison officer, Chapman, prior to the attempted murder. It is believed that father and daughter had been acting together on instruction from the MMV cartel in Colombia to organise the drug trafficking from

Panama to USA through Fort Lauderdale. The technical departments have enabled us to establish links with Chapman, Gabriella, Leo Higuita and Borja Sanchez a top figure in the MMV. They have witnessed Gabriella meet up with Chapman and then go on a boat towards the Pearl Islands. The Marine Section were able to track the boat at all times, what is known is that only Gabriella returned, with a substantial amount of what is believed to be Cocaine. I will come back to this, she went to her fathers' home and left with a red suitcase, she later went to the bus unit where the suitcases were loaded with cocaine. She has left there and met up with the guy we know as Emilio who took her to the suite of Borja in the Panama Hilton, something happened there in the penthouse and Borja died. She left there and collected the cases from the unit, drove the coach, picked up passengers and took them to Colon for the cruise and returned to Panama. It was when she met up with Emilio the other guy and the now dead Borja, which was when the arrests were made. Now, searches have been conducted at several locations, the house of Leo Higuita, there was nothing of major significance. In the bus unit the red case was searched and contained Gabriella's clothing, a Ruger automatic hand gun and one point two million dollars. One hundred and forty kilos of cocaine have been found in the two freezer cabinets, also documents and a computer have been recovered which need examining. Other significant items have been found at the hotel and on the boat, which require further investigation. They would all be involved in obtaining evidence which would be allocated from the operation room at headquarters.

There were no questions. Arturo reminded them all of confidentiality and of circumstances if it was not kept.

They all departed the hotel and made their way to their headquarters.

The forensic department had found blood stains on the rear of the boat and the swimming board, they had recovered samples of Chapman's DNA from his apartment and these had been sent for comparison.

Members of the Marine Section were travelling to the location where the boat had stopped overnight, off the coast of Isla del Rey and were to undertake a search of the seabed in that locality.

A search team had recovered a small syringe and a fountain pen type casing on the roof of the reception area which extended beyond the balcony of the penthouse at the Hilton hotel.

Jaime was informed that the autopsy on Borja had shown that he had been poisoned by a lethal injection and a site had been found under his testicles where a needle had been inserted.

The time was approaching for the first interview with Gabriella. This was to be conducted on the offence of drug trafficking, large quantities of cocaine. Jaime had already discussed the tactics with Arturo and out of courtesy allowed Steve and Jessica to be present whilst he briefed Enrique and Gloria. The interview was recorded visually and audibly, the four watched as the officers went into the interview room where Gabriella and her legal representative were sat. After the formalities of introduction, the officers only identified themselves as number 1 and number 2 and then gave the legal requirements, the officers went through the formatted script of not giving her information as to the extent of the evidence they held but asked for some explanations for what they had found. Gabriella was pleasant and smiled at the officers but did not answer one question. The interview lasted forty minutes. There was a break.

Gloria and Enrique had a further briefing with Jaime and Arturo and a short time later the second interview began.

Enrique was asking Gabriella to explain why she was in Panama, where she had been, who she had met, why was she driving a coach, when was the last time she had been to her fathers' house or the business premises. Again, Gabriella was pleasant and remained silent. There was another break and time to prepare for the confrontation.

A further hour had passed before they returned to the interview room. On this occasion Gloria started the questions, "We have met before, I'm sure you will recall the cruise terminal in Colon when we discussed the passengers from the coach leaving for the cruise?"

She smiled but said nothing.

"Do you realise that you have been under surveillance for some time?"

Just a smile.

"Who owns the white Rav motor car you were driving?"

The smile started to wither but no reply.

"What was in the red case you collected from your fathers' house?"

Nothing.

"Why did you go to the unit where the bus was and exchange vehicles?"

Nothing.

"Why did you, take suitcases from a rack and then load them with cocaine from the freezer into the false bottom of the suitcase?"

The smile had disappeared, still nothing.

"What did you print off and attach to the suitcases before loading them onto the coach?"

Gabriella was now staring into the face of Gloria; reality was sinking into her brain and was visible in her face. What else do they know?

"There was one hundred kilos in the cases and another one hundred and fifty or more in the freezers, where was that from?"

A threatening face was now showing on Gabriella, a contempt of Gloria, as she paused between each question and watched her uncomfortable reaction in the confidence of the evidence, and this was just a start.

"Can you explain the automatic pistol and one point two million dollars recovered from the red suitcase?"

She raised her hand in frustration, she was about to speak but stopped herself.

"You and your father have come from Colombia and opened your own cartel distributing cocaine throughout the world from Panama and made millions of dollars, where were you going when you were arrested?"

"Stop, stop asking me questions," she shouted "You don't know anything, stop this now. "

"Do you know your father is dead, you must know. Was it his money you were taking, were you using your father to do your work?"

"Fuck you, fuck all of you. Stop this." She turned to her startled lawyer, "You fuck off, get out, I don't need you, now get out."

The room went silent. The lawyer picked up her papers from the table and her document case and walked to the door which was opened electronically and left the room. "I like you number 2, I like the woman who jumped on me, I don't like men, Sort it and maybe we can talk."

"We have more questions to ask."

"Nothing to say. Sort it."

The interview was ended, it was a time for a full debrief and briefing with Jaime.

Jaime immediately contacted the Police prosecutor's department for advice on allowing a foreign woman, not a police officer into the interview, would it be legal. After several minutes of discussion, it was agreed that it was permissible as long as legal requirements were maintained and there was no danger to the unknown female. It was decided that if Jessica was willing to take part in the process it would be possible and probably beneficial but she should keep her participation in the questioning minimal. Jessica wanted to be involved, it was what she enjoyed most, debriefing soldiers or the enemy in Afghanistan.

After a short rest period, Gloria and Jessica went into the interview room, Gabriella was already sat at the table and smiled as they went in. Gloria introduced Jessica as number 3 and again announced the legal obligations, Gabriella declared that she did not want a legal representation, "I will tell you what you want to know, I'm a dead woman anyway. Where should we start?"

Gloria, "The beginning"

"My father came here when his business crashed in Colombia, he was threatened, we had to leave. He was made an offer; he was told to supply drugs on the cruises to named passengers. Some people would bring the cocaine to him and he would put it into the cases and give it to the passengers."

"What part did you play?"

"None at the start, then I was a passenger and took a suitcase on the cruise."

"How many times did you do that?"

"Just the once about three weeks ago."

"Did you get paid for doing this?"

"Just a few hundred US dollars and a free holiday"

"What happened yesterday, your father didn't do anything you did it all?"

"I got a call from someone, he was menacing, threatening, I was scared. They couldn't contact my father and I was told that I had to do it."

"Where is your father?"

"I don't know, I haven't seen him for a while."

"So, what did you do?"

"I went to the house and got some keys for the unit, I loaded up some suitcases with packages, I think they were drugs. I picked up the passengers and took them to the port in Colon. That's where I saw you."

"You are admitting trafficking cocaine?"

"Yes, but it was under threat, I was scared, I think they may have killed my father and they would kill me. That's the only reason I did it"

"Where did your father get the cocaine in the freezer units, there was a lot of cocaine there?"

"I didn't know how much was there, I have watched my father put it into the suitcases, I didn't know how much was there, I was surprised."

"Who were the men outside the hotel when you stopped the

car and they were arrested?"

"I don't know, I've never seen them before, I got another call telling me to go there."

"Was it the same person who made the call?"

"I think so"

"Who does the car belong to, the white Rav you were driving?"

"I don't know, this man gave me the keys"

"Who was the man, where did he give you the keys?"

"I don't know him, I met him in the city."

"When was that?"

"Early yesterday morning I was told to go to a Park, he knew what I was wearing he gave me the keys and walked off."

"Have you seen him since the park?"

"No. I was busy doing everything I had been told to do. I've told you I was very scared; I just did what I was told."

"Why did you fill the red suitcase in the house and take it with you?"

"I was very scared I was going to fly away somewhere and hide from them they are dangerous; they would kill me."

"Where did all of the money come from?"

"My parents had a successful business and had hid some money in the safe, it is my family money"

"Where is your family now?"

"My mother is dead, my brother is dead, I think my father is dead and I do not know where my sister is."

"What about the handgun?"

"I was stupid, I don't know how to use it but I thought it would help protect me."

"Have you brought any cocaine or other drug into Panama?"

"No, never. I have told you everything I have done and I'm ashamed but I was forced to do it?"

"Have you met anyone else in the distribution or organisation of drug trafficking?"

"No."

"You are not telling the truth, are you?"

"Of course I am, I want to tell you everything."

"Who was the man with you when you boarded the boat 'Pasion del Mar' yesterday?"

Gabriella lost her confidence and started to think hard, she paused for a while.

"You have been busy, I don't know anyway?"

"We have been busy, do you want to tell me more or do I have to go through all of the logs?"

"Ok, where did I meet this man, tell me?"

"You met him in the Uracca Park and had a bottle of cola together."

There was a silence.

"You both got onto the boat and headed for the Pearl Islands, why?"

"He took me fishing and we had a meal on the Island, you can check it out, the restaurant was La Tortuga you can ask the owner?"

"We have, he agrees you did. Then what did you do on the night time, during the night?"

"What would you expect us to do on a boat together in a beautiful location a few drinks, you know what we did."

"I thought you didn't like men?"

"I'm easy, I like beautiful women, like you two, you are my type but I sometimes like a man, that's how life is for me?"

"So why did you motor to a location in the Ocean south of the Pear Islands?"

"We also did some night fishing"

"And caught over 100 kilos of cocaine? That's what you brought back on the boat but no one else"

"He stayed on Isla del Rey"

"Without his wallet? That was found on the boat."

Gabriella started to cry she was really forcing the tears "I'm scared, so scared. Believe me. You have to help me give me police protection away from this place, please help me" She was looking staring at Gloria and Jessica, their faces were straight un-perturbed.

"You have to help yourself, speak the truth?"

"Ok, ok,ok. I don't know who the man is, that is the truth, we never gave our names to each other and were told what to do by a man on a phone." Gabriella paused and looked directly into the face of Gloria, "He was murdered by the Colombians. We had to go to a meeting point in the Ocean, this bigger boat came close, he told me to take the wheel and keep the boat straight, they started loading big parcels onto the boat, he said they should give him money, he was stood at the back of their boat one man shot him in the head and told me to go or I would be killed, so I did, that's why I'm scared can you help me please."

"That man was an English police officer?"

"No, he told me he did fishing trips."

"Why was there blood on the swimming board of the 'Pasion Del Mar'?"

"He fell from the big boat onto the swimming board then rolled into the Ocean?"

"That was where?"

"About an hour South of the islands in the deep Ocean."

"What happened then?"

"I stopped in San Miguel when I knew they were not chasing me and moored in the harbour until the sun started to come up."

"I want to help you but you keep lying."

"No, no I'm telling the truth."

"The police officer was called Chapman, he had your fathers' boat, he had told your father where to go when he was killed. You killed him in a bay on Isle del Rey, when he was on the swimming board and then pushed him overboard."

"No. no. You are wrong. I didn't know that and if I did, I couldn't kill anyone."

"You fired two spears through his chest, the first puncturing his right lung and the second cracking his ribs and going through his heart. You can, and have killed someone."

A smile cracked around the mouth and eyes of Gabriella and yet she looked evil and cold and said nothing.

"His body has been recovered from the bottom of the seabed in the bay. He has not been shot in the head; his body is weighted down with diving weights."

She smiled and said nothing.

Gloria continued, "What can you tell me about Borja Sanchez at the Hilton Hotel?"

Maria sat back in her chair and just looked with contempt at Gloria.

"Why did you go to his room, the penthouse?"

Maria just stared at Gloria and occasionally Jessica.

"Why did you run out of the Penthouse and shout for Emilio, you were in underwear I believe, you don't like men?"

Gabriella was snarling and looking aggressive.

"You killed Borja, didn't you and made it look like a heart attack."

There was silence Maria was in thought, she knew she was facing life in prison if she was lucky. She pointed at Jessica, "Why do you never ask a fucking question are you dumb or stupid?"

Gloria signalled for Jessica to continue, "You killed Borja, very clever."

"She speaks, funny accent. I like you 3, I've gone off you 2." She paused "Yes. I killed Borja, he raped me, buggered me, he killed my friend, he killed my brother, my mother and my father and he wanted to fuck me again! I fucked him alright, I loved it, looking at him so powerful, he thought he had me under control, I played him and he loved it. There I have told you, well done 3, number 2 you were pathetic. " Gabriella had a broad smile on her face, "I don't suppose you would like a threesome" she started laughing and crying.

Gloria and Jessica left the interview room together as Maria was taken to her cell.

CHAPTER 38

Monday 23rd May

21:30

Gabriella Mariana Higuita had been processed and charged with the murder of Martin Chapman and of the murder of Borja Sanchez. She was further charged with illegal trafficking of cocaine into and from the country of Panama. Each of these offences carried a possible jail term of 30 years, a possible total of 120 years, she had been sent to the horrors of La Joya prison to await her trial, whenever that might happen. The murder of Filipe had not been mentioned at this time as it was an investigation into murder by Venezuela, who were considering extradition proceedings but would probably just let it lie on file as there would be no need for any extra sentencing.

Gloria had now picked up a friendship with Jessica, there were a lot of similarities, same age, similar height and physique, confident and attractive to the eye, it helped they both spoke Spanish and English. They sat together at the interview debrief with, Enrique, Jaime, Arturo and Steve. Jaime praised the officers and Jessica for the planning and the execution of the interview which had been exemplary. He explained that the exhibits had been collected and statements from all concerned had been completed. The interviews of Emilio Sanchez Martinez and his associate had revealed nothing in evidential terms of offences committed and they were to be released on bail for firearm offences later that night.

The British Embassy had contacted Jaime and requested that Steve and Jessica be escorted to the Panama Hilton where two rooms had been booked. They would be collected at 10:00 in the morning by the Embassy staff and taken to the Embassy for an informal chat and debrief. The rooms had been reserved for five nights, whilst enquiries pending could be completed and allow some time to de-stress before the flight back to the UK. Jaime was attempting to organise two days leave, which should not be a problem, to show Steve and Jessica the better parts of Panama.

The briefing finished and it was strange for Steve to be kissed on his cheeks and hugged by relative strangers but it did feel good. Jessica appeared to be getting better kisses and longer hugs he thought. They agreed to meet one evening when it was the most opportune as no one knew what to expect. Two uniformed officers arrived with the bags of Steve and Jessica and they were taken to the hotel they now knew fairly well.

They dropped their bags off in the rooms and made their way to the roof terrace bar, it was deserted, a warm night with a slight breeze. A beautiful view over the harbour towards the islands, small boat lights manoeuvring through the channels, a black sky and thousands of stars. They took a seat at a table; the waiter took the order two Balboa beers and they looked out over the city to the ocean. Two minutes later the drinks were placed onto the table, it was Paco. "My friends the hotel told me it was a free night for you, so I came to tell you and I hope you are not offended but I asked a few friends as well."

Paco announced them one by one as Gloria, Enrique, Alejandro, Angel, Balbina, Stefanie, Ramon, Jose, Olga, Aaron, Marisela, Ana, Vincente, Juan, Barbra, Arturo and in England they say, The Boss, we now know him as Jimmy, Jaime. Jaime got a rousing cheer from all, it was clear he was very well respected, a great leader. Each one in turn kissed and hugged Steve and Jessica and the applause grew as more came on to the roof terrace, they hugged and kissed each other, as Steve would say, work as a team, play as a team it's the same the world over. The paperwork was complete the work was done, let justice take its course. The party started and would go on for three more hours, Salsa, Merengue, a night to remember

❖ ❖ ❖

Tuesday 24th May

Steve and Jessica were feeling tired and a bit worse for wear as they sat down to the breakfast in the Hilton and discussed the party.

In the Hacienda Manolo was sat at his large breakfast table and had been served mixed fruit and black coffee, he was in a good mood. The house keeper brought the phone for him and stopped five metres away, she was beckoned forward. He listened and then gave the phone back to the housekeeper and told her to leave the room. He looked at the young woman sat opposite him, he thought she was stunning, long black wavy hair hanging over her shoulders, beautiful unblemished skin, twenty years younger than him and she was good, really good., "I have some news, Borja is dead, that is a shame, your father is dead, it would happen sometime, your sister, Gabriella killed Borja, an English Policeman and was found with 100 kilos of cocaine. Shit happens but I have you, I told you Carmen it would be a good decision to live with me."

"She smiled as she drank her champagne" she was indeed very happy. She didn't want to think of the alternative.

Steve and Jessica had spent four days with the Ambassador extolling the values and benefits in working in Panama, it was well worth considering. They had visited the Pearl Islands and had vowed to return, to fish, dive and relax. Jaime had taken them on a trek into the jungle and they had seen so much wild life, a complete contrast to the ultra-modern city, it was an intriguing country in many ways. Jessica also had several calls from Jaime and not always asking her to stay and work, but just stay, if there was any chance of staying, she wouldn't need to work.

Superintendent Tinkler and Lauren visited the home of the Lopez family. They spoke to Manuel and Angelina and gave them the information that was known and the identity of the person responsible for the murder of their son Filipe. They handed a photograph album that they had bought and filled of the photographs Filipe had taken on his holiday. There were no photographs of the girls included. The likelihood of a trial was highly unlikely in the circumstances. Angelina and Manuel were both in tears and understandably devastated, their son had been in the wrong place at the wrong time and murdered for nothing. Their son had been killed for loving someone, a passion in life. Manuel thanked the Superintendent and Lauren for bringing the news, Angelina and Manuel hugged the officers tightly before they left.

◆ ◆ ◆

Saturday 29th May

They were sat on the plane together waiting to taxi to the runway. They had done so much together and yet they hadn't actually been together, alone, close, very close but. Steve had no doubts about how he felt and longed for Jessica, he was aware that Jaime was showing a lot of interest in Jessica, he thought that much about Jessica he didn't want to complicate any relationship she was thinking of. Jessica was flattered by Jaime, he was a gorgeous man, a gentleman, an excellent leader, compassionate and kind but too far from home. She had found Steve to be an excellent companion, a friend, funny, organised, rugged and just, just bloody lovely. They held hands as the jet was accelerating down the runway, she turned and faced Steve, "We have done everything, every day, full on, working long hours, partying, meetings, boat trips, jungle treks, it's been a blast, we have done everything we could do for everyone. I want us to do something for us. You are stopping at mine Mr. Bond when we get back to Manchester." Then it was lift off.

AFTERWORD

I have at times had to change circumstances to facilitate the story. I know that you cannot get a flight direct from Manchester to Atlanta but it was needed. I have researched Panama and the locations but I have changed a few place names. Margarita Island is a beautiful island but I would not recommend going there at this time.

I have changed intelligence system names but they are realistic.

Steve Bond will return to Newcastle but who knows what crimes may come his way, or will he stay in the Toon?

ABOUT THE AUTHOR

Gabriel Lee

The author was born in the North East of England and worked in the police for over 35 years. He worked locally in Tyneside and Wearside and latterly Nationally.

Having worked on many investigations in differing roles within various squads, he developed an indepth knowledge of their working methods to defeat organised crime and serial offenders.

He has witnessed the pain and suffering of victims of crime, the horrors of murdered mutilated bodies and the anguish of giving the bad news to loved ones. The victims feelings and life changing character are generally overlooked.

He is not alone, many of the thin blue line experience these sights and feelings that are never forgotten.

He has travelled and observed policing in close quarters in different countries and has an admiration for those that do 'The Job' in difficult circumstances.

He is now retired and living in Spain.

Printed in Poland
by Amazon Fulfillment
Poland Sp. z o.o., Wrocław